Praise for
Patricia Loofbourrow

"This author has quickly become one of my all time favorites. Her characters are well developed and interesting. The books are full of plot twists and surprises that will catch even a seasoned reader off guard."

— TESS LA COIL

"The author is an amazing storyteller, all of the characters are well written where you can imagine them as existing in real life, they have flaws and some are more likable than others. These books are fantastic and I can't wait for the next one ..."

— ALEXANDER C. DESTIN

"I'm somewhat envious of those who have yet to discover this author."

— JULIAN W.

"Patricia is a gifted author, creating a rich and imaginative future filled with many complex characters."

— RICHARD BARTON

"Ms. Loofbourrow has created a world that is sinister and intriguing. I can't wait to read more ...!"

— COLLEEN MOONEY

"Lets hope Ms. Loofbourrow NEVER suffers 'writers block'."

— GARY D. GRAYSON

"Any book by this author is superb."

— JACKIE TANSKY

News, clues, backstory, and more at JacqOfSpades.com

FICTION BY PATRICIA LOOFBOURROW

RED DOG CONSPIRACY

Part 1: The Jacq of Spades
Part 2: The Queen of Diamonds
Part 3: The Ace of Clubs
Part 4: The King of Hearts
Part 5: The Ten of Spades
Part 6: The Five of Diamonds
Part 7: The Two of Hearts
Part 8: The Three of Spades
Part 9: The Knave of Hearts

THE PREQUELS

Gutshot: The Catastrophe
The Alcatraz Coup
Brothers
Vulnerable

THE COMPANIONS

Drawing Thin

OTHER FICTION

Weird Worlds: Science Fiction and Fantasy Flash Fiction

Brothers

A Prequel to the Red Dog Conspiracy

Patricia Loofbourrow

To those just trying to make their way.

The time: 1885 years after the Catastrophe.
The place: the Merca Federal Union — a federation of independent
domed city-states in what was once called North America.
Opening the Aperture to peer into the city of Dickens, let us begin.

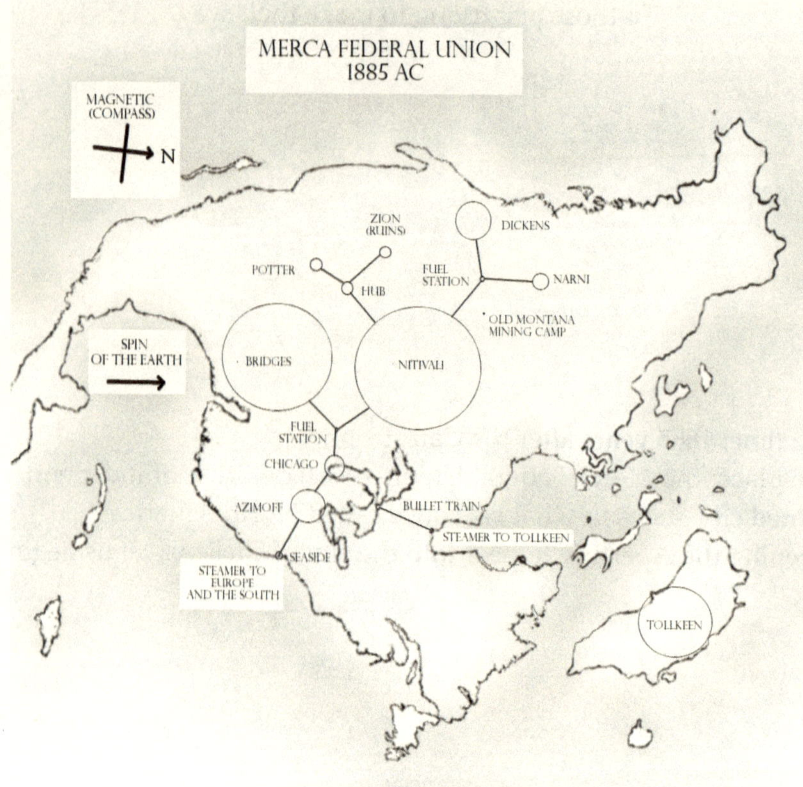

MERCA FEDERAL UNION
1885 AC
MAGNETIC
(COMPASS)
N
SPIN
OF THE EARTH
ZION
(RUINS)
DICKENS
POTTER
FUEL
STATION
NARNI
HUB
OLD MONTANA
MINING CAMP
BRIDGES
NITIVALI
FUEL
STATION
CHICAGO
AZIMOFF
BULLET TRAIN
STEAMER TO TOLLKEEN
SEASIDE
STEAMER TO
EUROPE
AND THE SOUTH
TOLLKEEN

Leaving

"Congratulations. They want you."

"Oh!" Daniel felt so ... surprised ... that he didn't know what else to say.

You went to the viewing the month you turned sixteen. Everyone did. An old, brown-skinned man with round spectacles had come to Daniel's viewing a few months back and talked to him for some time. That had been it.

From what Daniel was told, some were bought at their viewing; a few left that same day. But he'd also been told that it could take a while to find out whether your buyer wanted you, or if they'd changed their mind.

He figured the man had changed his mind.

Daniel peered at Miz Lisbet sitting behind her desk. He was one of the lucky ones. Yet it meant leaving. "What happens now?"

Miz Lisbet smiled like she thought he'd lost half the cards in his hand. "You'll need new clothes for the training in Nitivali. It's a rush order, so you'll leave tonight."

Daniel gaped at her. *Tonight?* "Yes, mum," was all he could muster. He felt stunned, unable to move.

She glanced up at him. "You're dismissed."

Her voice startled him. "Oh! Yes, mum, sorry, mum." He bowed and hurried out, carefully closing the door behind him.

He was supposed to go directly to the big room where the boys lived, but he turned beside her door, hands to his face, and leaned his forehead against the wall.

It's what I always wanted. But it's so soon.

Daniel didn't remember anything before the Home. From the women who ran the place and the men who came to fix things or administer beatings, Daniel learned to be sociable, to be observant, to glean any skill or insight he could.

But the other boys were his real family. They were his brothers.

Daniel had realized long before this that even though he'd never seen it, there was more to this world than inside the Home. Some who never got sold never left: they served here until they died.

He wanted more.

I want to live, he thought. *I want to do something worthwhile.*

Feeling self-conscious, Daniel straightened, wiped his eyes, patted his cheeks, took some deep breaths. He wanted to look like a man who'd pleased his buyers. Someone capable. A man moving up in the world.

I can do this.

When he went round the corner into the huge, door-less room, the other boys swarmed him. "What happened? Why'd she call you? Are you in trouble?"

Daniel forced a smile. "They wanted me. I'm to leave tonight!"

There were sixty boys in there, but the room fell silent. A little one grabbed his legs and began bawling.

He was four, and fairly new. Daniel picked him up, the boy's soft little arms and legs wrapping tight around him. *Lost his parents to fever, now lost me.*

Daniel's eyes stung. But he had to be strong, for them. "It's okay. This is good. I get new clothes to ride on the zeppelin!"

The boy lifted his round, tear-streaked face to him, astonished. "You get to ride the zeppelin?"

Daniel set him down and knelt before him. "Sure do." Feeling moved, he ruffled the boy's straight black hair, kissed his pale little forehead, and stood.

Whoops and cheering. One of them said, "You lucky ..." A flurry of punches and slaps came to Daniel's shoulders and back whilst his hair was ruffled as well. But it was all in good humor.

He had to breathe to keep smiling. *They'll miss me too.*

After a while, the questions died down. He didn't know anything, other than what Miz Lisbet just said. Nitivali must be a city, under a dome like theirs, but he didn't know where.

Soon the others drifted away to their bunks. Some hid their heads under pillows, shoulders shaking, a sob breaking the silence.

Daniel didn't move. He wanted to look at this room he'd spent his life in, fix it in his memory forever.

White walls, painted over every spring. Rusting iron bunks with traces of pale blue. Pillows on coverlets on sleeping pads on boards, each as thick as the other. Windows high in the wall let in the late morning light, but it was a good clean light, and the sky beyond was blue.

After dinner, they'd light the tallow-candle lamps set on the narrow cabinets between each bunk, tell stories, snore. Between that was various work: cleaning, preparing food, taking care of the animals, the gardens. But they always got time off when someone was called to Miz Lisbet.

Jacob stood watching him. Jacob looked like he was twelve, but he'd been chosen last week at his viewing. "I'm leaving today, too. You think we'll ride the same ship?"

"Hope so," Daniel said. "They tell you what you're doing?"

Jacob shook his head. "Kind of worries me."

Daniel chuckled. Everything worried Jacob. "Don't suppose they'd pay all that money unless they plan to keep us a while."

A shriek split the silence.

Miz Albaletta stood in the doorway, brass whistle in hand. She was portly and real old, at least fifty, with a pasty face and round silver-rimmed spectacles. "Luncheon," she bellowed, then disappeared down the corridor.

She didn't mean time to eat — it wasn't yet eleven. She meant time to clean, set the fires, chop, slice, cook, and set the tables.

The oldest ones managed the youngest. So as the middling boys swept the floor, the oldest ones got the little ones' hands washed and dried, which took some time, then had them carry wooden dishes, bowls, and cups to each place, marked with black lines on the narrow wooden tables.

Once that was done, the very youngest were sent to Miz Albaletta. She usually passed them on to one of the monitors, who'd have them do things like gather apples for this meal or wash potatoes for the next. The next older placed the dented metal spoons. The ones old enough to be trusted set the forks and knives.

Babies were in another Home. The ones who survived were brought over once they could use the toilet without help.

When the tables were set, the older ones unstacked the armless wooden chairs for the middlings to put in their places. Sometimes the littler ones helped, other times they played on the floor out of the way or went to Miz Albaletta if she had something for them to do. Usually a couple of middling girls would come running up, breathless, to take them over.

The girls were in another building altogether. The boys didn't do much with them, except sometimes work beside them in the gardens. But that was when all the monitors came out, peering at the boys with suspicion, as if they might steal a carrot or tomato.

Soon enough the little ones were settled. Then most of the boys stood at their places for prayers. They all made the sign of the Board, crossing their arms to grasp their shoulders.

As eldest of the monitors, Miz Albaletta gave the prayer:

"Most Noble Floorman, we give thanks for the bounty You have provided through Lady Luck's Blessing upon our land. Help this food and drink grant us strength to play the Holy Cards the Inerrant Shuffler most generously provided at our birth for the good of all. Praise be to the Blessed Dealer, whose skill gave us bodies and minds dealt true. Oh Holy Cards, teach us your wisdom this day. Amen."

"Amen."

The oldest ones served the youngest, then everyone else, then the cooks (the ones just younger), and then got to eat some.

By this time the youngest were squirming, so it became a race to finish eating before they made a mess. Then it was time to clean up, which took about as long as setting.

Once the youngest ones began scraping the few leftovers into one little wagon and stacking the plates in another, Daniel flopped into a chair, Jacob beside him.

"One more time, then we're done," Jacob said.

Daniel stared at Jacob in surprise. "I never considered it."

"I wonder what they'll have us doing wherever we end up."

A laugh began inside Daniel but never made it out. "Don't get ahead of yourself. I wonder what Nitivali's like."

"What you should be wondering," Miz Albaletta said from behind them, "is whether you'll leave tonight at all." She pointed to the little ones, who had stacked the plates so high they threatened to topple.

Jacob and Daniel leapt from their chairs.

"Hold on there, you!" Daniel shouted. The wagon veered to the right, scattering plates and bits of food across the floor. "Only stack to twenty, understand? Then you bring them to the washers."

One of the little boys began to cry.

Jacob knelt beside him. "It's okay. Let's count them again."

***

Once the room was cleaned, Miz Albaletta brought Daniel and Jacob to a carriage. But before they got in, Miz Albaletta gave each of them a hug, something she'd never done before. She cradled Daniel's face in her chubby hands, then kissed him on the forehead. "Be safe, dear boy."

He smiled, surprised at the emotion in her voice. "I will."

Daniel had never been outside the grounds of the Home before, much less in a carriage, and thought it was great fun. People were everywhere. Other carriages passed by on either side. The buildings were brown and blue and gray.

Jacob lay on the brown leather bench seat, face white, moaning the entire ride.

Once the carriage stopped, they were taken inside, to a room so beautiful it took Daniel's breath away. The walls were made of wood, but this wood was golden brown and ... it shone.

Everything was shiny, metal and glass. The room smelled wonderful, and the most amazing clothes Daniel had ever seen lay atop shelves or hung on forms shaped like men.

"This way," an older man said.

Jacob was already gone. Daniel let the man guide him to a small room with swinging half-doors which hung about the level of Daniel's head and extended past his knees.

The man said, "Let's have these old clothes off you."

Daniel recoiled. "You want me to take off my clothes? What kind of place is this?"

The man seemed unaffected. "Young man, I can't put new clothes on you with your old ones on. If you prefer, I can step into the hall whilst you undress."

Daniel felt foolish. But it all seemed so strange. "Yes, please."

The man sniffed. "Perhaps a bath might first be in order." He moved past, and it was then Daniel noticed another set of doors behind him, just like the ones he went through. The man opened one. "Bath for this one, then call me when he's ready."

The heat rushed to Daniel's face as a young woman came to the doors. "Come on, then," she said, and he didn't know what else to do but follow.

Daniel had heard of baths but never had one: they lined up for a few minutes under the shower once a week in winter, twice a week in summer. The small room with a tub half full of hot water made him hesitate.

"Take everything off and put it in this," the woman said, pointing to a large basket on the floor, then she left, the doors swinging shut behind her.

Towels hung on a golden stand. A chair sat by the wall to his right with underpants, socks, a comb. A full-length mirror on a stand was before that, and Daniel looked himself over.

I don't think I look so bad.

He sniffed himself. He didn't smell anything out of the ordinary. But he didn't know how long he had in there, so he took off everything and got into the water.

Soap sat on a stand beside the tub, and once he figured how not to slide around, the warm water was rather pleasant.

A knock at the door. "You almost done?"

Panic. "Wait!"

A laugh, but it was kind. "Just checking."

Daniel leapt from the tub and dried off as fast as he could, then put on the underpants. The floor was wet, and he didn't want to get the socks wet, so he held them. No other clothes were in the room. "What do I put on?"

"You can wrap in the towel if you want," she said.

It sounded as if she hadn't moved, which made him glad to wrap in a towel. Had she stood there the entire time? The idea intrigued him.

Finally, he took a deep breath, willed himself to relax. He was just one in a long line of orphans to come through there. He pulled the towel tight around himself. "Come in."

Her glance went to the tub, now filled with brown-gray water, and Daniel's cheeks burned.

"Come on." She led him to the room he was in before. The man was there along with several fine suits of clothing which hung on hooks on the wall behind him.

"I hope your bath was pleasant."

The man's tone was so decidedly neutral that Daniel almost laughed. "Very good. Thank you."

The man helped Daniel into a shirt, some trousers, a vest, shoes, and a jacket. Then they moved out of the small room. The man took out a measuring tape and put it around Daniel's head. Then the man moved to a row of caps. "Which do you prefer?"

Daniel's clothes were dark gray, so he picked a cap to match.

The man nodded approvingly. "Do the shoes fit?"

Daniel wiggled his toes. "They seem fine to me."

"I'll have two sets of shoes, four of clothing, and six of undergarments sent to your room."

"My room?"

"At the training. When you arrive. They'll teach you what to do with them there."

Before this, it hadn't seemed real that he was truly going there. But if they were sending his things ...

Daniel touched the fine cloth that now hung on him, soft as the little boy's arms. "What now?"

For the first time, the man smiled. "A haircut and a shave."

New

Everything was new, from the barber chair to a different girl cleaning his fingernails to a new man shining his shoes.

A different man led Daniel back to the carriage and there sat Jacob. Daniel hardly recognized him. "Damn, you look good."

Jacob laughed. "They prettied us up for sure." But then his face sobered. "What kind of place are we going to?"

"We're not gonna dig carrots, that's for sure."

Jacob nodded slowly. "Whoever set this up just spent a hell of a lot of money. What if they don't like us?"

"I'm sure they thought about that before they paid. Besides, what could happen? If they don't like us, they'll send us back."

But no one had ever come back.

Daniel looked at the lengthening shadows outside the carriage window and wondered what the hell he'd just gotten himself into.

"Looking out seems to help," Jacob said.

"Good thing — laying down'd mess that pretty hair of yours."

Jacob's hair was almost as dark as Daniel's, but with a bit of a wave to it. Now it looked shiny too, wet but not wet, slicked back all nice.

"If I didn't know better," Jacob said, "I'd say you were getting sweet on me."

Daniel laughed. "You can like the way things look, can't you?"

Jacob grinned, cheeks reddening, as he stared out of the window. "I suppose so."

There weren't any shops here, just a few homes and some fields. "Hey," Daniel said. "Where are we going? I don't remember this."

"I don't know." Jacob stuck his head out of the window. Then he turned to Daniel, awestruck. "I just saw a zeppelin!"

Terror, excitement, and chagrin filled Daniel all at once. "We're leaving? They didn't let us say goodbye!"

Jacob's face fell. He slumped forward, elbows on his knees, head down. "We're never going to see them again."

Daniel remembered when Miz Albaletta she sent them off. The hug, the emotion in her voice. *She was saying goodbye.*

***

They stopped at a roadside inn to water the horses, to use the toilet, to walk around. A zeppelin rose slowly in the far distance, lit from below by the lights of the city. Daniel never imagined anything could be so big.

It turned out their zeppelin was much bigger.

They went on board and were led up several flights of stairs. Daniel's room was twice the size of the little room he got dressed in. And just as nice: warm polished wood with what the attendant man said was brass, and a round window bigger than a dinner plate by the head of the bed. Daniel got two pillows, a mattress three times as thick as his back home, and his own closet.

He had nothing to put in there except his jacket, which he carefully hung, not wanting anything to happen to it.

Then he sat on the bed, elated. *All this — for me!*

A side door opened and Jacob poked his head in. His jacket was off, too. "My room's just right here!"

"Have you ever seen anything like it?"

Jacob shook his head. "I wonder what we're supposed to do."

A man's voice came from the ceiling, speaking in a language Daniel didn't understand. Then he spoke their language, in an accent Daniel hadn't heard before. "Ladies and gentlemen, welcome aboard Travelers' Federation Flight A26 to Nitivali with continuing service to Bridges. We will launch in five minutes. Please return to your seats and clear the hallways. Signal if you need assistance and a footman will attend you." He continued speaking, this time in a still different language.

Daniel felt overwhelmed. So many ways to speak!

"I better go in here then," Jacob said.

Daniel examined the round window. He moved a latch, and it opened! Daniel peered out at the men far below, tiny figures holding tiny ropes.

The air smelled fresh, clean. Other zeppelins, each with a different shape and size, sat, rose, or descended across the vast field near the giant building off to the right. Only the corner of the building showed in the window: carved stone towers, bluish-gray.

A horn sounded. The men let go: the zeppelin rose.

Daniel grabbed hold of the wall, staring in awe as the ground slowly fell away. He could see the entire city!

The ship turned to the left, the mountains in the distance receding. After some time, they went through an opening so huge that Daniel didn't understand it. His head hurt trying to grasp what had just happened as they moved along.

Daniel had no words for what he was seeing. It was the most amazing thing in his life up to then.

He saw plains and mountains, but they were blurred, as if looking through something not quite clear. Sort of like looking up on a really clear day to see a bird fly way high past the dome.

A knock.

Startled, Daniel closed the window, feeling as if he'd done something wrong. "Yes?"

The door opened. "Your dinner, sir."

No one had ever called Daniel "sir" in his life. "Thank you."

The man brought in a tray with a silver dome on it, and behind him another man held a small table. After the table and tray were set down, the first man removed the dome by its handle — and underneath lay a full dinner!

The food smelled so good. And so much! Daniel gazed up at the man in amazement. "Thank you!"

The man's face was carefully neutral, but underneath he seemed amused. "If you need anything, sir, signal by pulling the cord there." He pointed to a thick white cord hanging between the bed and the window, which had a large red wooden bead on the end. "Someone will come to assist you."

"Does everyone get rooms like this?"

"These are the first class sleeping cabins, sir. If you prefer to sit in the main area, you'll find it to be much like the train."

Daniel had never been on a train, but he nodded anyway. The men bowed and left.

First class cabins for orphans newly sold? Nothing about this made any kind of sense.

Had they made some mistake?

Daniel fully expected to be asked to move, but finally decided that if they were going to give him dinner, he might as well eat it.

After some time, the men returned, taking the tray and small table, directing Daniel to the facilities.

The sky darkened. No one said anything about moving to a different room. So Daniel carefully undressed, hanging up his shirt and trousers. He examined his shoes for any scuffs and laid his socks on the chair which sat at the end of his bed.

But he couldn't sleep.

Jacob opened the door. "You awake?"

"It's too quiet."

Jacob had only his underthings on too, but he still had on his socks. "Can I sleep with you?"

Daniel moved over.

Jacob lay on his back, staring at the ceiling. "If you want me to go away just say it. But me and Skip, we always sleep in the same bed ..." his voice broke then, "and I miss it."

Skip was a couple years younger. "I had no idea."

"When he was little he got scared so I let him climb up and sleep with me. We just got used to it I guess. But I love him, Daniel. I do. More than anything."

Jacob didn't say anything for a few minutes.

They never let us say good-bye.

"I'm never going to see him again, am I?"

Daniel let out a breath. "I don't know. That's the truth." There was something strange going on here. "They're treating us too well. I don't know why. It doesn't make any sense. But maybe we're going somewhere ... I don't know, where we're ... important somehow. Or with important people. I mean, why give first class cabins to someone you just bought? Unless you can't imagine people — even bought people — being anywhere else."

This concept made Daniel's mind feel stretched somehow. Then he laughed. "How did you both fit in one of those beds?"

Jacob laughed then, and sniffled.

Daniel thought Jacob would be okay.

Life

Kick. Kick. Kick.

Daniel sat up.

Kick. Kick. Kick. Kick.

Where was Jacob?

Daniel rushed into his room and turned on the light. Jacob was hanging from his belt, hands at his throat, kicking the wall.

Daniel grabbed him around the waist, lifted him up enough to get the thing off from around his neck, then threw him on his bed. "You damn fool! You want to never see Skip again for real?"

Jacob was sobbing, choking, a dark welt on his neck. "No ..."

"Then you stop this. How can you figure a way to get him to you if you're dead?"

"I ... just ... can't do this, Daniel. I can't."

"Yes, you can. You're sixteen years old. You're smart. You're going somewhere they value you enough to put you in a first class sleeping cabin, dress you like a gentleman, and give you the best dinner ever. Right?"

"Y ... yeah ..."

"Look at me."

Jacob's eyes were full of tears.

"I don't know who wants you, or why, but if they went to all this trouble, then they might listen to you when **another** job opens up. Right?"

Jacob thought about this, hard, as if he hadn't considered the matter before. Then he seemed calmer. "Yeah."

"But if you're dead, you can't help anyone. So why don't you quit trying to die and start figuring out how you're going to **live**?" Daniel let go of him and sat up. "Okay?"

"Okay." Jacob sniffled, coughed. "I'm sorry I'm such a fool."

Daniel turned away to sit on the floor beside him, trying not to laugh and feeling sad at the same time. "It's okay. At least you got someone. Be happy for that."

Daniel brought Jacob back to his room and made him sleep by the wall this time. But they woke up in the same places. Jacob seemed subdued, remorseful.

Good. Maybe he'll think of something.

Jacob went to his room. As Daniel dressed, he listened for Jacob, to make sure he was getting dressed too.

Jacob gave him a wry grin as he opened the door between our rooms. "Don't worry, I'm done with that." He touched his neck, which was now covered by a cravat. "It hurt bad."

A knock at the door, and Jacob ducked back into his room.

"Your breakfast, sir."

Daniel rushed to straighten the bed. At the Home they would have been beaten for leaving it that way. "I'm sorry, I'll make it up at once."

"No need, sir: we'll care for it after we land. Enjoy your meal."

There was so much to eat that Daniel could hardly finish it. After he ate and dressed, he opened the window to peer out just as they passed another monstrously large opening.

Hot, dry air flowed into the room.

Daniel recognized another zeppelin. But there were other things in the air around them that he had no words for. They looked like they were made of metal, and they rose and descended much faster than the zeppelin. Blue fire came from them in places.

Past them, a vast orange-tan city spread below. As they drew closer, he saw that many of the roofs were made of rust-colored curved tiles.

Tan dust flew past in great billows. He hurriedly closed the window, coughing.

After quite some time, the zeppelin landed. Daniel and Jacob followed the crowd through the zeppelin, down a long flight of stairs, and over the dusty packed earth towards a huge brown wooden building.

A giant booming sound to their left startled him. Blue fire came from what looked like four massive squat table legs as one of the metal floating things sitting three hundred yards away rose, turned, moved away in a great cloud of dust.

Daniel gaped at it, astonished. "What the hell **is** that thing?"

"How should I know?" Jacob pulled at Daniel's sleeve. The crowd was far ahead. "Come on, we gotta go."

Once inside the building, a man with white hair came up to them. "Daniel? Jacob?"

"Yes, sir," Jacob said.

"I'm here to escort you."

Daniel and Jacob exchanged a glance, then followed the man to a carriage.

The carriage appeared like the last one, but this place was nothing like home. Strange plants with thorns on them. The sky so blue that it seemed unreal. Buildings were made of wood or brick like home, but raised up with wooden beams. Sidewalks made of wood, set eight inches above the ground.

As they went into the city, the carriage slowed in traffic. The sidewalks and streets were packed with people wearing strange clothes, speaking words Daniel didn't understand. Strangely-shaped carriages — some with horses and some without — went along beside them.

Some carriages didn't even have **wheels**.

How did they stay above the ground?

Brilliantly colored lights. Words and symbols and pictures that **moved**!

Daniel turned to Jacob. "What the hell kind of place is this?"

Jacob shrugged. "I don't know."

Eventually they reached a large brick building. The man who'd met them at the station opened the door. Yellow dust flew past.

"Come now." He pointed to the door of the building. "Go on in. They're expecting you."

The wind kicked up: Daniel grabbed his cap to keep it from flying off. "Thanks." He and Jacob hurried up the steps onto the raised wooden sidewalk and inside. They had to push on the door against the wind to get it to shut.

The room was very fine, yet not as well lit as the clothes store. A woman with straight black hair and a round face stood behind the counter. "You must be the new ones. Names?"

Jacob stepped forward. "Jacob Michaels."

She wrote it down then said, "And you?"

"Daniel."

"Daniel what?"

He felt a twinge of embarrassment. Then he shrugged. If he'd ever been given any other name, he didn't know it. "Just Daniel."

The woman chuckled, her eyes almost disappearing as she smiled. "Welcome. I'm Annabel Lee, and this is the Nitivali House-Servants Academy."

Lessons

Daniel and Jacob followed Miz Annabel past the counter. The next room held long seats they called couches, or sofas, where various men of their age sat waiting. It seemed Jacob and Daniel were the last to arrive.

"This is Daniel, and this is Jacob Michaels," Miz Annabel said. She pointed to a narrow-faced man with wavy black hair and large dark eyes. "This is Righly Hanafuda." She pointed to a stocky man with swarthy skin. "This is Feint Barkis." Next to him sat a man even paler than Jacob, with hair so light as to almost be white. "This is Reuben James." Beside him sat a thin man with red hair and freckles. "Kier Connor."

Daniel felt sure he'd never remember them all, but he nodded politely and tried to put faces to names.

Next was Elias Gin, a very tall dark-skinned fellow. Beside him was Hudson Thomas, who had a round, flat face, narrow, triangular eyes, and thick black hair. Adam Card had green eyes and brown hair; Helix Coil was tanned and thin, with black hair in a long braid going to his waist. Yen Tobias didn't look up when his name was called; he seemed to be focused on his knees, his face hidden by shoulder-length brown hair. Dakota Bledsoe reclined calmly, arm thrown over the end of the sofa, nodding at them. He had the darkest skin Daniel had ever seen, with eyes and stiff-straight thick hair to match.

Each had been called up as manservant to a gentleman of high means. Their teacher, Master Wápái Écarté, was a grizzled old man who seemed to know everything about everything.

Some were younger, some were older. All were orphans, just like him.

Daniel got his own room, like in the zeppelin but bigger. But he spent little time there. From dawn until well into the night, he learned what a manservant was and how to be one.

The group first learned about men's fine clothing. Daniel felt astonished by how many kinds of ways there were for a man to dress, depending on their city. Then they learned how to clean different kinds of fabric. How to press them, how to fold them.

Then they learned how to dress someone by dressing each other.

The idea of dressing another man made Daniel feel unsettled, but Master Écarté assured him that this was most of what the job entailed. "You've been called to a high and honorable profession. Gentlemen have different outfits for each various occasion. You're there to make sure they look their best."

He talked about etiquette, a word Daniel had never heard before. Much of their training was in how to speak to the master. "Servants are never to be acknowledged or praised, only summoned, directed, or punished. You are less than an animal to them, only there to do your duty. Never are you to bring notice to yourself by either word or deed."

Yen Tobias put his face in his hands, and when he looked up, his blue eyes were full of tears.

Master Écarté stopped then. "I don't say this to grieve you, but to make sure you understand. This is the path the gods have called you to, and it will only cause trouble for you to deviate from it."

Some of the others looked troubled. Hudson put a hand on Yen's shoulder.

Yen nodded, hands still upon his face.

Master Écarté said, "Let's move on, then."

They learned how to be a good listener, both understanding and discreet. "You're never to influence the master," Master Écarté said. "You can advise in matters of propriety or guide in matters of dress, but it's not your place to tell him his business."

Miz Annabel and her little girl Gia, who was eight, came to help with the next set of lessons. How to handle interactions with the master's wife, when he might get one. How to assist with the master's children. When to stand and when to sit. When to speak and when not to. How to position one's hands when standing. What to look at and what not to.

Once they'd learned this, they were brought to a large bedroom. Master Écarté and Miz Annabel demonstrated how to clean the master's room, make beds, fluff pillows, remove stains. Daniel had been cleaning all his life, yet he learned many things.

"You'll work with the cleaning staff," Master Écarté said, "but you are the master, shall we say, of your master's rooms and clothing. Each item must be perfectly clean. If you can't get a stain completely out, or the fabric is injured, don't hesitate to have the item replaced at once."

Even meals contained lessons: how to set a proper table, how to wait on someone, the most discreet and efficient way to serve. They practiced serving each other in their rooms. "You may often be called to serve your master in his rooms," Master Écarté said, "and you must know how to do it."

They learned to light a fire in the grate, to set up tea tables and dinner trays, to dry the master's shoes.

One day, twelve men came in, each set upon a chair. That day, they learned how to sharpen a razor, how to shave and trim a man and care for his skin, including the surgical treatment of blemishes and boils.

Another week was spent in learning how to care for the master in sickness, how to communicate with the doctor, if need be, and how to speak with the master's family, both older and younger. "Some of you, like Daniel here, are going to be a young man's first manservant. These boys will be looking to you to show them how to be proper gentlemen."

Daniel had never even seen a real gentleman. Now he had to show some boy how to be one?

Dakota laughed. "Look at his face!"

Master Écarté smiled reassuringly at Daniel. "We won't let you leave here until you've learned everything you need to know."

Every night, Daniel collapsed into bed, falling asleep almost as he hit the pillow. But before then, it was instruction on the care of his own clothing and body.

"You must have no foul odors to offend. So your diet must be healthful and your teeth cared for. You'll rise early to bathe, or if your master prefers an early morning, bathe the night before. You must keep your nails short and smooth, so as not to damage either your master or his clothing. His barber will care for your hair after he visits your master. And your clothing will be as fine as his."

For some reason, this lesson stayed with him the rest of the day.

So this is why they've taken such care of us, Daniel thought as he drifted to sleep. *They're getting us used to the idea of being treated well.*

The thought made him happy.

***

Many things Daniel later took for granted he learned in the Academy. For example, how to work with the butler of the house to arrange the master's schedule. "The master must never be late, so you must manage your time. You must begin dressing the master so he departs on schedule to arrive on schedule, even in inclement weather and travel delay."

This involved figuring, which Feint Barkis had a particularly difficult time with. He'd sigh, and grumble. "I'm going to serve a restaurant man. Why do I need to learn this?"

"Oh, my dear boy," Master Écarté said. "Scheduling is everything in the food business. Perhaps we should look at this in reverse. If your master's event begins at eight, and the event takes three hours to set up, when must he arrive?"

Feint sighed, counting upon his fingers. "Five."

"And then if it takes an hour to travel, when must he leave?"

"Four."

"But you must allow a half-hour for delay. It's much better to arrive early than late. When must he really leave?"

Feint sighed. "Half-past three."

"And if it takes a half-hour to dress him? When do you begin?"

"Three."

This process went on for some time, but eventually, Feint became as good at it as anyone. Daniel marveled at how patient Master Écarté was with each of them.

Once basic scheduling had been mastered, they learned about travel: how to arrange the trip with the butler, how to set the master's schedule, how to judge what clothing to pack for various outings, how to pack a suitcase so the master's clothes and valued items arrived safely. Master Écarté said, "Righly here will be manservant to an Army officer. Miss Annabel has arranged separate lessons on packing military garments and their honors."

For the first time since meeting him, Righly looked surprised.

This made Daniel feel better. So he wasn't the only one who had no idea what lay ahead.

Yuletide came with more lessons, although perhaps the teachers there didn't realize it. The Home never celebrated Yuletide, nor had Daniel ever gotten a present before. He felt so happy for the silver tie-clasp inside — even though it was identical to everyone else's — that he rushed out of the room before anyone might see him weep. That someone, anyone, might think of him, might select something to give to him ... it felt overwhelming.

When he returned to the others with his tie-clasp on, Master Écarté looked up from where he sat, a fond smile on his face.

Winter came with torrential rain, and Daniel understood now why the sidewalks were raised: the dusty streets outside the Academy had turned to flowing mud. On one particularly stormy day, Master Écarté said something startling: "Your primary job is to protect your master."

They learned how to examine food for any tampering, including tasting it themselves before allowing the master to eat from plates brought to his room. How to protect the master with weapons, with fists, with their own bodies if need be. "This man you care for is your life. If he dies from foul play in his chambers, you die. That is the manservant's burden, and his boon, because your master will come to trust you as he would his own."

This affected Daniel so much that he couldn't sleep, though as exhausted as any night. He left his room and walked the hall. Moonlight streamed through large windows. Daniel slumped into a chair, frightened to the bone.

"I thought I'd find someone here," Master Écarté said, but his voice was kind. "That last lesson is a hard one." He pulled up a chair and sat, his face calm.

"I know nothing of this boy I'm sold to," Daniel said. "What if he's cruel? What might he ask of me? Yet I'm to protect him with my life or die?" He put his face in his hands, eyes stinging.

"You didn't ask to be an orphan, nor to be sent to the orphanage, nor to be chosen and sold," Master Écarté finally said. "Yet these are the cards the Shuffler sent, the ones the Blessed Dealer has placed in your care. Mourn your cards if you must, but it's your duty to play them."

Duty.

Daniel once whined about some minor task, and Miz Albaletta took him aside. "Your duty is to these children, just as mine is to you. They need you. We're tasked with bringing them up to be men of worth. If they see you falter, what will become of them?"

He would be responsible for this boy Daniel didn't know. Had never met.

They needed someone.

*They chose **me**.*

Master Écarté watched, eyes solemn.

"I'll do what's required," Daniel finally said. "I only wish I knew what it was."

At that, the old teacher smiled. "That's the way of it, dear boy. We never know what the next round holds." He leaned forward to place his lined hand upon Daniel's. "But the gods gave you a keen mind, a kind heart, and a steady hand. Use them." He leaned back, placing his arms on the rests beside him. "I've taught manservants for sixty years, and not one has failed me." He raised his arms to the roof. "That's why we sit here in comfort."

Daniel stared at him in amazement. How old **was** he?

"I tell you this because you're taking on a task few could. This is not a happy child, nor even a kind one. The boy needs help, and his family has chosen you."

*They **chose** me.*

For some time, Daniel had no thoughts in his mind whatsoever.

He remembered standing at the viewing, being asked to speak with that old brown-skinned man.

*Why would they choose **me**?*

No one ever told Daniel if he was a baby left there, a toddler found, or a small child abandoned. But he remembered the boys whose parents had been killed whilst they watched, the ones taken from parents who'd tried to murder them. The horror in their eyes. The way they screamed at night.

Something had happened to this boy. "How old is he?"

My teacher's face softened, relaxed. "Thirteen." He chuckled. "And already a hellion. But you'll learn more than you want to." He stood up then. "Get yourself to bed, son. You'll need your rest once morning comes."

Bridges

The next day after breakfast, Jacob and Daniel were called to Master Écarté's office. There stood Miz Annabel with two folders. She handed one to each of them.

Master Écarté said, "You're to learn about the city you'll be in. Study well."

Miz Annabel brought them to a small room with walls lined by bookshelves and a large table filling the center. "Sit," she said. "The folders hold what we know about the boy you've been tasked with." She turned to Jacob, surprise in her voice. "Yours is still quite young for a manservant. Only eight!"

Jacob stared blankly at her.

Daniel could tell that Jacob didn't know what to say, but more from fear of saying the wrong thing than from any surprise.

She collected herself. "What you read is not to be shared with anyone, even each other. This is for your eyes alone." Then she stood. "I'll return in an hour."

Jacob took up the folder at once. Daniel let his lay on the table, too frightened to open it.

"It'll be okay," Jacob said.

Daniel took a deep breath, then nodded, feeling a bit foolish. How bad could this boy be?

On the first page, a portrait of a solemn young boy with very dark skin. The name: Jack Roland Diamond III.

At the time, Daniel knew nothing of the Four Families, but something in the boy's eyes drew him. Daniel studied Jack's face, trying to glean why this child was so unhappy.

Nothing in the folder gave him much insight. As Master Écarté had said, Master Jack Diamond — the term Master in Bridges indicating never-married — was thirteen. He had six brothers. Five were older, with an identical twin born moments after. His sister had just turned eleven. His mother was a former Apprentice to the grandfather, an Inventor.

"These people are rich," Daniel murmured in awe.

"As are mine," Jacob said.

"Does it say why they want you so early?"

Jacob reddened. "I don't think I should say."

The warning. "I'm sorry. I shouldn't have asked."

"No, you shouldn't have," Miz Annabel said as she walked in. "But you did well, Jacob." She held out her hand. "I hope you read your folder, Daniel: you won't get another chance."

Daniel handed the folder back, embarrassed and annoyed.

Miz Annabel gestured for them to follow. On the way, they stopped by Master Écarté's office, where she returned the folders, then they went to another book room, much larger this time, with many round tables scattered about. All the others were there, as well as the other helpers. Along one wall lay a large drawing.

Daniel had never seen a drawing like this before, and as Reuben and Keir moved off, Daniel pushed forward. Many circles had been drawn on parchment, and lines connected them. Helix stood beside it, off to the right, as if waiting.

Miz Annabel said to Jacob and Daniel, "This is called a map. It represents Merca, our homeland." She pointed to the center circle, the largest one. "We're here in Nitivali."

Then she pointed to the slightly smaller circle to its left, "and this is where you're going. The city's name is Bridges."

Jacob stirred. "Where'd we come from?"

Miz Annabel pointed to a much smaller circle at the upper right. "Dickens. We have many come from there." She turned away. "Come sit. We have much to discuss."

The class had split into many groups, each at a six foot wide table with a helper speaking to them. Righly and Helix each had a helper all to himself. But whilst Righly and his helper took a table, Helix and his helper stayed over by the parchment, talking.

Daniel pulled Miz Annabel's sleeve. "What kind of manservant will Helix be?"

She smiled. "He'll be manservant to a new zeppelin pilot."

"Oh," Daniel said, surprised.

Jacob and Daniel followed Miz Annabel to the far corner table and sat. A round map lay upon the table top: four thick blue wavy lines met in the center around a circle the size of Daniel's thumbnail. Various buildings were marked, as well as roads, and different areas of the city.

"This is Bridges," Miz Annabel said. "As you can see, it's split into four quadrants, each owned by a Family." The way she said the word "Family" made it feel important somehow. "The Four Families are, shall we say, extremely wealthy criminal enterprises. Each Family owns their quadrant entirely. Most of the quadrant is farmland, but the real power is in what they call the 'city proper,' or the urban center of the city. In each quadrant, the streets closer to the center island are poorer. So in Bridges, the main goal in life is to move to a higher street, or better yet, get into a Family."

Daniel considered what he'd read. "Diamond's one of them?"

"Yes," she said, "along with Spadros —" She pronounced it "SPA-drohss."

Jacob flinched.

"— Clubb — two b's now, never one — and Hart, spelled like the deer: H-A-R-T."

Daniel felt glad she'd spelled it out, because he had no idea what a deer was.

"They're quite particular. Proud, quick to anger, utterly ruthless in their treatment of those who displease them. But generous beyond imagining to those who pledge their loyalty. This is what we must discuss today. Are either of you religious?"

They said prayers daily but ... "I don't understand."

"Bridges is special because it's the home of the old Cathedral. Though that Cathedral was destroyed in the Coup, the people of Bridges still perform many of the old customs and rites even today." She hesitated. "The manner of pledging loyalty to a Family is a highly kept secret, but we do know it involves the Cards. You may be asked to harm or destroy one, or spill your blood, or both, to swear to them —"

Daniel shuddered. Harm one of the Holy Cards? Spill his own blood? Miz Albaletta had said that either one doomed you to the eternal Fire.

"— but you must do whatever they ask, even unto death." Her face turned grim. "They paid for you, and you must obey. We can't come to your aid if you falter."

Jacob's face was deathly pale.

"I want to live," Daniel said, heart pounding. He hoped it would remind Jacob of Skip. "I'll do whatever they want."

Jacob nodded.

Miz Annabel let out a breath. "It's settled then." The bell for luncheon rang. "Return here after your meal, and we'll discuss matters further."

Jacob walked beside Daniel. "What have we gotten into?"

"No idea." Daniel stopped then, remembering what Master Écarté had said. "But it's our duty to play this out, whatever they want from us."

Vision

Daniel presumed that after luncheon they'd discuss matters of great import. But Miz Annabel wished instead to speak of men's fashion in Bridges. "Part of your job is to know the fashion for men of your master's station and age, and to make certain his wardrobe is kept up to date. Also, if your master is uncertain of the proper attire for a situation, your job is to advise him. He must always look his best. Never allow your master to be embarrassed by his attire, or mocked by his peers for it. This is your responsibility."

After that, Daniel listened attentively. The thought of this child under his care being shamed because of something he'd neglected troubled him.

Jacob and Daniel learned about neckties and hats, of frock coats and pocket-watches, and which went with what. Much of it was similar to the attire they'd already learned, but with subtle differences in cut and fabric which gave a different effect. Of course, then they had to learn how to clean, brush, air, and mend these all over again.

After the fourth time he pricked his finger, Jacob muttered, "I hate sewing."

"Suppose you're on a trip and your master's button falls off," Miz Annabel said, "or his trousers rip. Do you want the boy to arrive disheveled?"

"No," Jacob said. "But I still hate sewing."

She chuckled. "You'll improve with practice. Or if you have no talent for it, you can pay your lady's maid to mend for you." She peered at Daniel's work. "Very nice."

Jacob glared at Daniel.

Daniel's cheeks burned. "We get paid?"

"You'll have an allowance for your entertainment and meals on your hours off-duty — when your master is away for the day — personal clothing not part of your uniform, and anything you wish to buy for others." She shrugged. "You're not a slave."

But they could make us do anything for them, even up to death.

Miz Annabel shifted in her chair. "Let's discuss hygiene and body care in Bridges."

As it turned out, they were expected to know — and order — the best body-care products in the city. To learn their master's preferences, or guide him if his standards were low in that regard.

If he complained of health issues — no matter how intimate — they were to know the most up-to-date remedies, how to administer them, and when the doctor needed summoning.

At dinner, Daniel put his elbows on the table, head in his hands. "Is there anything we won't know about our masters?"

Scattered chuckles went around the table.

Master Écarté smacked the table. "Elbows, Daniel!"

The rest laughed, even Elias and Yen.

Their teacher's voice was stern, yet with an underlying tone of amusement. "You are correct, sir. You'll know as much about your master as his wife does." He let out a short laugh. "Perhaps more."

Daniel pondered this. "Might I ask a personal question?"

Master Écarté smiled. "I knew you would be the one to ask. How did I come to be here. Is that your question?"

Daniel stared at him in astonishment. "How did you —?"

He raised a hand. "Because every class wants to know." His face grew sad. "And perhaps you can learn something of it."

The old teacher sat quietly, gazing towards the table. "I was not much older than you, hired by an elderly gentleman here in Nitivali whose manservant had died. I'd been trained by the best, yet once I arrived I realized my training left me woefully unprepared. But my master was generous beyond belief, offering training, guidance, and advice."

Daniel felt moved at the grief which lay in his teacher's eyes.

"He had no heir. In his last testament, he granted me freedom and a small amount to use as I liked. This place was being sold for a pittance, the owner having himself died without heir, so I bought it. I wanted to be like him —"

In that instant, Daniel saw what he wanted: to help this boy Jack as his teacher had helped him, and as his teacher's master had helped him before that. To teach this child to help others as well.

His vision stretched, like a chain, unbroken.

"— and train others as I had so generously been trained." He smiled, peering at Daniel. "And for sixty years, no student has failed me. I pass the charge to you to remain true."

***

That night, Daniel again couldn't sleep, but this night it was in excitement as to the vision he'd had.

And once more he wandered the halls. He only had a few weeks left here. What did he need to learn to truly help this boy? His teacher had called Jack unhappy, unkind. How might he greet the boy? How might he gain his trust?

Daniel knew he couldn't influence the boy directly. But if they chose me, he reasoned, they must feel I can help him.

He rounded a corner, and to his surprise, Master Écarté sat there at the window, gazing out. Daniel expected to be sent back to bed, but the old man only smiled. "Good evening."

Daniel bowed. "Good evening, sir. I didn't mean to interrupt."

"Not at all. Please, sit down."

Daniel sat, wondering why Master Écarté was out here. "Is something wrong?"

His teacher's lips curved up at the ends, but the smile never made it any higher. "Yours will be my last class."

"Why? What's happened?"

Master Écarté did smile then. "I'm old, son. And every year I feel it more." Their eyes met. "Then once in a long while, I find a bright spot in all this, and I regain the energy to go on." He turned back to the window with a sigh. "But it's well past time."

30

Daniel didn't quite understand. "Could you not train someone to help you?"

"I could. But who? Most here lack the interest. Those who do, sadly, are already sold to another."

Daniel shrugged. "Go buy someone, then."

Master Écarté drew back. "I'd never considered that." He hesitated. "I've always hired men and women freely, from their own choice." He sounded dismayed. "To buy a **person** —"

"They bought **me**." Daniel looked around. The place looked rich, in a way he'd never imagined before coming here. "You surely have enough?" Daniel leaned an elbow on the arm of the chair, his chin on his hand. "You may do as you wish, sir, of course. But if you can find no one willing to take over from those you have here, it'd be a shame for all this good you've built to go to waste."

Master Écarté sat quietly looking at Daniel for quite some time. Then finally, he said, "You may be right."

Daniel went to his rooms, thinking about the exchange. Up to then, he'd thought it natural that he should be sold, like the rest. He'd been considered one of the lucky ones.

To hear Master Écarté, a man he trusted and respected, considering buying another as wrong somehow ...

As he lay curled in his bed, clutching his covers, the memories of life at the Home now took on new meaning. To Miz Lisbet, had he and his brothers been only like the chickens in their garden? Kept there to be raised, then sold?

Daniel didn't sleep for some time.

***

The next day, Master Écarté called the group together. "It's time you learned the ways of the world."

They all glanced at each other. Daniel had no idea what his teacher meant.

"There's a world outside your master's chambers. Until you learn of it, you'll be a target for those who mean you and your master harm." He moved to the door. "Follow me."

The group walked the dusty streets of Nitivali. Master Écarté showed them the pickpockets, the addicts, the thugs. He took them to the bank and showed them how to make a deposit, how to speak with a bank official. They walked to the market and learned how to haggle, how to speak with merchants, how to fill out a purchase order. They went to a fine restaurant, where they learned how to read a menu, order a meal, speak with waiters.

Most times, Master Écarté taught by his actions. But they were eager to learn, because their lives might depend on it.

They walked to the train station, bought tickets. They just went to the next stop, but Daniel felt awestruck by the train's power.

Jacob went pale at the motion, like in the carriage, but he peered out of the window and no one was the wiser.

When they left the train, they walked to a building with "Rising Sun" carved in fine golden letters above the door. Men dressed almost as well as they were opened the carved wooden doors for them. The group entered a room as large as Daniel's bunk room back home, carpeted in rich red.

The room was half full, with many round tables. Men were eating, drinking, playing at dice. Waiters passed by with trays. Music and the sounds of talk filled the air. The room smelled of food and tobacco.

Along one entire wall, bottles filled with liquids of various colors stood on shelves.

In front of that, men poured drinks to other men who sat perched on tall stools along a dark wooden counter.

Master Écarté went to the counter — Daniel later learned this was called a "bar" — and spoke to one of the men, who stuck his fingers in his mouth and whistled.

Several men emerged, leading the group to a room at the far end. The doors were like the ones at the clothes shop — mid-thigh to face level — and swung freely.

On the other side of these half-doors lay a room with low tables, food, and beautifully-dressed girls Daniel's age or a bit older seated here and there. There were more girls than boys.

"These are your Companions," Master Écarté said. "Sit wherever you like."

While the rest hurried over, Daniel surveyed the remaining girls. One had straight black hair to her waist, light brown skin, and gentle brown eyes. Daniel felt drawn to her. "Hi." He felt suddenly shy. "May I join you?"

She smiled, and Daniel thought he might not ever breathe again. "Of course."

Her name was Baraja, and she was twenty. Like Daniel, she was an orphan, sold to the Rising Sun when she was sixteen.

A maid passed by, handing each a drink of something called gin. Daniel didn't like the taste; he set it aside.

Baraja said, "You want to go upstairs now?"

Half of the others had already left. Master Écarté sat watching, an amused smile on his face.

Daniel took Baraja's hand. "Certainly."

She wore a loose silken dress which didn't show her skin but implied a great deal. Her hips mesmerized Daniel as she drew him along the polished wooden stairs to her room.

Daniel saw her bed, lit by the setting sun, and his mouth went dry. "This is what you do here."

Suddenly she was in his arms, her firm body pressing against his. "This is what I do here."

He'd never been alone with a naked woman before. In all the days after, he never forgot how beautiful she was, every bit of her.

Some time later, they lay gazing at each other, their bodies drenched in sweat.

Baraja asked, "What's your name?"

"Daniel."

"Do you have other names, Daniel?" She said his name in the old way: Dan-yel.

He pulled her body to his, savoring the feel of her. "Just Daniel. Why do you ask?"

"Because I like you very much." She brushed hair from his face. "I want a child, and they allow us one when we want it. If the gods have given me one tonight I'll not stop it. Because your child will be beautiful." She kissed him. "And if they give me a boy, I'll name him for you."

Daniel never considered such a thing. He felt as overcome as when he learned he'd be coming here. "Thank you." His vision blurred. "You'll treat him well? Care for him?"

She stared at him, mouth open. The she smiled, kissed his forehead. "If the gods give me a child, I will. Girl **or** boy."

He took her face in his hands. "I don't know how long I have here, but if I can I'll return."

She nodded, but her face said she doubted he'd return. "We have until the sun rises." She slid her hand between his legs and he gasped with the sheer intense pleasure of it. "Shall we love again?"

Beauty

Early the next morning, the group returned to the Academy, silent.

Daniel felt overwhelmed with what happened. Would he leave a child here? The thought excited and moved and terrified him.

He won't be an orphan, he told himself. *Baraja will care for him.*

At breakfast, Master Écarté said, "If you wish, you may return to the Rising Sun after dinner. But you must be back by breakfast. You must complete your assignments even if they go past dinnertime, and you must never sully your master's name with drunkenness or unseemly behavior. You belong to him, not to yourselves. Do you understand?"

"Yes, sir," they said.

But all Daniel could think of was her.

***

Daniel and Jacob sat with Miz Annabel, learning to polish boots.

Jacob nudged him. "Daniel."

"Young man," Miz Annabel said, "attend to your work."

"Yes, mum," Daniel said, heart pounding, and set to the boots with vigor.

"Not too hard," she said, "or you may damage the surface."

"Yes, mum." His cheeks burned.

On the way to luncheon, Jacob grabbed Daniel's arm. "What's wrong with you?"

"I don't know —" Daniel peered at him. "Last night. I —" He felt confused. "Didn't you —?"

Jacob snorted. "All I could think of was Skip back home without me." He sighed. "We called for tea. We soaked in the tub together. We cuddled." He grinned. "She said it was lovely to relax."

35

Daniel felt stricken. Was that what Baraja thought?

Jacob said, "I think I got a woman-lover." He laughed. "She almost said as much." Then he patted Daniel's shoulder. "Did it go well for you?"

Daniel thought of the way Baraja pressed herself into his arms. The way she put her hands on him. "I think it went well."

When Baraja saw Daniel, she looked dumbfounded. Then she threw herself into his arms. "You came back." Tears stood in her eyes. "You came back."

He smiled at her fondly. "Of course I came back. I said I would if I could." Daniel took her face in his hands and kissed her. "Did we make a child?"

She laughed. "I don't know! It takes a while to tell. A few weeks at least." She got a sly grin on her face. "But we could make sure."

So they made sure every night for the next three weeks.

But not every moment was spent in play. Baraja loved to read, and she brought him to their library. "Look at this one," she said. "My teacher used to read it to me at night." Her face grew sad. "I miss him sometimes. He was very kind to me, even at first when I felt afraid."

She opened the book and read: "The poet is the sayer, the namer, and represents beauty. He is a king, and stands in the center. For the world is not painted, or clothed, but is from the beginning beautiful; and the gods have not made some beautiful things, but Beauty is the creator of the universe." She leaned over to touch Daniel's face. "You are my Beauty."

He kissed her palm, moved. "As you are mine."

Daniel thought about what he might do for most of the night. The next morning, Daniel went to his teacher. "I would like to stay here. I could help train whoever you end up buying to take over this place."

But the great Master laughed softly, his eyes kind. "A good try, dear boy. But I'm afraid there are other paths for you to take still. Remember, you're not a free man." He sighed. "No, as much you might help, they own you, and they'd not be happy should you fail to arrive on time."

Daniel felt dejected for a short time, then realized he was being stupid. He had things to learn still, and he refused to spend the short time that still remained with Baraja thinking of anything else but her.

His days were filled with training, his nights with exploring Baraja and all the things she had learned.

On their last night together, she said, "I should have started my blood." A hint of fear lay in her eyes. "I never had a child before."

He kissed her forehead. "I want so much to be here. To see our child grow up." Pain pressed at his heart. "But someone's bought me. Once I leave Nitivali, I don't think I can come back."

She glanced down, nodding. "I know. They've been good to me here. They've not made me take anyone else. Because you're with the Academy. But once you go, every night I must take another."

Daniel held her as she sobbed, trying desperately not to cry himself. He wished he could free her, bring her with him!

But what could he do? "I love you, Baraja. I'll never forget you."

"You've been better to me than anyone," she said. "I'll never forget you either."

Traveling

The next day, the sun shone too bright. And he hated it. Why should the sun shine so brightly every time he had to leave the people he loved?

Jacob wasn't traveling with him: he had to stay another week for some further work he wouldn't speak about. Some of the others — Elias, Dakota, and Yen — had left already.

Helix, Righly, Adam, and Keir were also leaving that day, on their way to another city called Hub. Feint, Reuben, Miz Annabel, and Master Écarté came to the station to see Daniel and the others off. Reuben shook Daniel's hand without a word. Miz Annabel gave Daniel a kiss on the cheek. Master Écarté gave him his travel documents. "Your luggage is being sent. Your ticket price covers luncheon on the train and breakfast on the zeppelin. I've included some money for dinner in your packet. Just follow the instructions and you should do well."

"There's a girl at the Rising Sun named Baraja," Daniel said quietly. "She carries my child. Check on her for me, will you?"

Master Écarté smiled. "I will." He put his hand on Daniel's shoulder. "I'm very proud of you."

"Thank you, sir."

He hesitated. "I have advice for you, but I doubt you'll take it." He sighed. "Look upon the experience with this girl as a pleasant time, Daniel, and nothing more. Forget about her and the child. Focus upon your future."

"Yes, sir," said Daniel, who intended to do no such thing. "Thank you, sir."

Master Écarté nodded, glancing away, and put a hand upon Daniel's shoulder. "Go with the gods, my boy."

Daniel smiled to himself. The old man meant well. But if Master Écarté really thought Daniel would abandon his own child, no amount of talk would dissuade him. And they didn't have the time for it in any case.

Feint Barkis stood nearby. Daniel held out a hand, "Don't let anyone fool you: you're as good at all this as anyone."

Feint let out a belly laugh, grasping Daniel's hand in both of his. "Here's hoping."

Jacob hugged Daniel, hard. "You saved me. I'll never forget it."

Daniel smiled. "Tell Skip hello for me."

Jacob hesitated for just an instant, then beamed, eyes reddening. "I will. Someday, I do believe I will."

Nitivali was so big it had three zeppelin stations at intervals around the dome. Bridges was almost the complete opposite direction from Dickens. The zeppelin he'd taken to get here didn't fly today; the flight across the Nitivali dome — in one of those strange metal "ships" — had left at dawn.

So instead of going to the nearby zeppelin station, the carriage took Daniel, Righly, Adam, Helix, and Keir to the train station.

The five went inside the station. "Our train goes the other way," Keir said, "so I guess this is where we say farewell."

Daniel shook their hands, feeling moved. Would he ever see any of them again? "I wish we might have had more time here. To know each other."

At that, Helix gave him a rare smile. "Thank you."

The four walked away, Daniel watching until they were lost in the crowd.

Now he truly felt alone.

Daniel followed the signs to his platform, and studied his travel papers as he waited for his train to arrive.

He'd need to change trains twice. The first train was identical to the one they'd taken before going to the Rising Sun, and its last stop was the Rim.

Mountains ringed Nitivali, and the air grew cooler as the train chugged up and up.

Daniel had never been so close to the Rim of any dome. Its surface shimmered with the faintest hints of gold and pink and blue as his train approached the station.

Once he left the train, he followed signs to another platform. When this second train pulled free of the station to travel along the Rim, the dome arched high over them.

The train went through several tunnels, coming out into forests of pine. An attendant brought luncheon: a bowl of spicy noodles with sweet baked beans, bits of meat, and some green crunchy vegetable mixed in.

After a long tunnel, the train emerged onto a wide view of grassy plains to the right; men riding horses herded vast numbers of large horned animals. Daniel said to the man across from him, "What are those?"

"Those? They're cows. Cattle. They breed them here." He grinned proudly. "Nitivali beef is the best in the world."

Daniel felt impressed.

"Just passing through, then?"

"Yes, sir. On my way to Bridges."

The man nodded. "I see."

"And you?"

"I have business in Chicago, then Azimoff."

Daniel vaguely recalled the names from the map he'd glanced at. "Do you travel much?"

"My work takes me many places." The man fell silent, picking up a newspaper.

It certainly sounded exciting, yet tiring.

The man opened his paper. "Off to a new job, then?"

They'd been warned about such questions. *Your first job is to protect your master. Your second is to protect yourself.* Unscrupulous men had been known to haunt trains and platforms, looking for young, inexperienced servants to draw into their schemes. Or even get them to do something unseemly so as to blackmail them — or their master — later.

He used a response he'd been taught. "Just visiting friends."

"Very good," the man said. He turned a page of his newspaper.

After disembarking several hours later, Daniel took a short train ride to the air station, where he bought dinner from a nearby street vendor. That evening, Daniel boarded the zeppelin to Bridges.

This zeppelin was as big and grand as the one he'd arrived in, yet his darkened room seemed too quiet.

Would he ever see Jacob again? As likely as seeing Baraja.

He missed the boys back at the Home, the commotion before dinner, the shushed chaos at nightfall.

Why had he wanted to leave so badly?

"It's the way of things," Miz Albaletta had once said. She'd been an orphan, too, raised in the Home just like him, yet never sold. "You grow up, and you go."

Did she miss us, too?

***

The old brown-skinned man who spoke to Daniel at his viewing met him at the gate. He held out a lined hand. "Name's Swan, in case you forgot."

A gold band lay on the old man's left ring finger. "A pleasure to see you, Mr. Swan."

The old man let out a laugh. "Just Swan. Let's get your bags."

The station was spectacular — an immense half-cylinder of stained glass set into polished wood. Intricate designs, a riot of color, all lit by the morning sun. Daniel stood in the wide doorway, overwhelmed with astonishment and wonder.

Swan waited for him, an amused look on his face.

After going through the huge hall, they stood with a crowd in front of a wide stone bench. Past the bench was an awning, open to the air and the field beyond.

Soon horses arrived, pulling huge flat carriages piled with luggage, which men unloaded onto the bench. At once, people pressed up to take their items.

When Daniel saw his bags, he moved forward, but Swan stopped him. "Let the footman get them."

Swan gestured to a man standing next to him, who fetched Daniel's bags. Then Daniel and the footman followed Swan to a white and silver carriage pulled by white horses. Inside, the seats were black and fuzzy soft.

Once the carriage went into motion, Swan spoke up. "Tell me what you know of this place."

Daniel told him what little he knew about the city and the Four Families. "I know a lot about men's fashion in Bridges." For a moment, he felt dismayed. "Not a lot about much else."

Swan laughed. "Figures. Well, I don't suppose you need to know much, other than anyone not a Diamond is probably gonna try and kill you."

Daniel peered at him. "Then why choose me?"

Swan leaned back, ankle over his knee, elbow to his chin, and considered this. "We looked a long time," he finally said. "You know we get reports on you every week."

"I had no idea."

"So we know about the whore, and about your bastard. Keep them to yourself."

Daniel felt infuriated, but he said nothing.

"So you can hold your tongue. You'll need to."

Master Écarté reported what Daniel had just told him!

Or had his teacher already known?

"Assume everyone you meet is reporting to someone," Swan said, "and you might just survive."

Daniel took a deep breath. "You never answered my question."

"I picked you because you were the best we found. And we've run out of time to do any more looking. So we sent you to the best trainer, and —" He scrutinized Daniel for a moment. "— you'll have to do."

Daniel laughed. "That's hardly encouraging."

"Well, you got a tough job ahead of you. You know anything about the boy?"

Daniel shrugged. "What you gave them."

"Then you know he could use a firm hand."

Daniel leaned forward, those dark eyes in Jack's portrait haunting him. Swan's eyes were dark too, but a pale haze lay in their depths. "I don't know what your young master's done. But perhaps what he needs more than a firm hand is to know someone cares about him."

Swan gazed at Daniel for several seconds. "I think you'll do well here. If you don't end up getting yourself killed."

Job

They passed miles of green crops, stopping to eat luncheon at a roadside inn. The sun was starting down as they entered the city.

Swan spoke from time to time, saying things which Daniel supposed were meant to be helpful:

"This quadrant is Clubbs. They're known for spying."

"Don't talk about important stuff in a carriage. The driver can hear ya."

"Anything happens upset you, you come to me with it."

Each time, Daniel would nod, hoping he could remember these things on top of what he'd already been taught.

The buildings here in Clubb were of a golden wood, the lampposts brass, the streets laid in tan stone. As Miz Annabel said, the further they went into the city, the poorer the people were.

They reached an area with tall hedges on either side. Exhausted, Daniel leaned back, closed his eyes. When he woke, the carriage had almost finished crossing a bridge over a wide flowing river.

This side had hedges, too. But once past them, the area was different. Streets of gray cobblestone. Buildings of black brick mortared in gray, or with silver-gray wood siding. White lamp posts with huge clear crystals atop them. Where the people in the first area were pale-skinned with brown or golden hair, most of the people in this area had dark skin and hair.

Late in the afternoon, the carriage stopped at a white mansion set back from the street. The footman helped Daniel down to a sidewalk of white stone.

Daniel followed Swan past three guards and a wrought iron gate, then towards the house. White rosebuds climbed thin white wooden trellises covering the walls. White flowers with delicate yellow centers spread over the ground to each side of the door. From the third story window, three very dark-skinned children peered out: two identical-looking boys and a younger girl.

One of the boys peered out with excitement in his eyes. The other fixed Daniel with a cold glare.

That must be Jack. He waits to see if I'll hurt him too.

Instead of climbing the wide white steps, Swan turned right, leading Daniel along a narrow walkway which ran along the long front of the building. Then left around the corner, down a short flight of steps and to a door.

Swan rang the bell. A girl a bit older than Daniel with dark skin and green eyes opened the door. "Is this him?"

"It is," Swan said. "Pray fetch Mr. Neuberg."

The girl curtsied, then opened the door wider. Daniel and Swan went in, closing the door behind them, and waited.

The store-room was clean and well-lit, with whitewashed walls. Soon a middle-aged man arrived. Dark as the rest, this man was tall, dressed in a fine black suit. He offered his hand. "I'm Mr. Neuberg, the butler. A pleasure to meet you."

"And you too, sir," said Daniel.

Mr. Neuberg looked Daniel up and down. "You'll do until we can get you used to our ways." Then he turned and walked off.

Daniel glanced at Swan, who gestured for Daniel to hurry along.

Everything was white: walls, ceiling, floors. Steel pipes ran overhead, with open-bulb lamps at intervals. Portraits of dark-skinned men and women in silver frames lined one wall above linen cabinets.

Baraja would like this. Daniel missed her already.

Daniel and Swan followed Mr. Neuberg past the kitchens, already full of men and women preparing food. White lace lined the windows. At the foot of a set of white wooden steps, Mr. Neuberg stopped, turning to Swan as if looking for direction.

"Let's show him to his rooms," Swan said to Mr. Neuberg, "then we can introduce him to the young master."

"As you wish, sir," Mr. Neuberg said.

Daniel followed Swan up the steps, then along a short hall. Up white carpeted stairs with white railings, then along another hall with a long window at the end of it. To the right, a door led to a room ten feet by twenty, carpeted in black, its walls painted in greenish-gray.

Along the near wall, a small round black wooden tea-table and two matching chairs sat before a window curtained in white lace. A door faced him; to the right of that was a black wooden dresser with mirror, a standalone closet, and a wide bed running along the back wall.

The bed had been made up with a grayish-green coverlet and lay in a cove with black storage cabinets reaching to the ceiling above and the floor below. Behind the bed was a raised flat area painted white; a small basket of flowers sat there.

A set of black cabinets filled the bottom right wall; shaving and minor surgical supplies on the counter sat atop them. A shallow set of cubicles stretched along the wall atop that holding medicinals. Past that and beside the bed was the open door to the white-tiled bath, which looked like it went to the left behind the bed area.

Daniel found the room quite impressive.

"Supplies are all here." Swan pointed to the cabinets. "The footman'll bring your bags. You need anything else, let me know."

"When can I meet Master Jack?"

"This way, sir," Mr. Neuberg said from behind.

Daniel hadn't realized the butler had followed them.

Mr. Neuberg opened the door beyond the tea-table. Ten feet ahead stood a door. To the right stretched thirty feet of what looked like an entire men's clothing store.

Hats, shoes — Daniel stared at the sheer mass of it in fear and awe. He was responsible ... for **this**?

"The young master's closets," Mr. Neuberg said, as if this were obvious. Then he opened the door in front of them.

The two boys stood in the middle of the room, their heads reaching to Daniel's chest. The girl beside them was a head shorter, with a dress that went to her mid-calf. All had skin and eyes almost as dark as Dakota's, with black hair.

Daniel's main focus was on Jack, who still glared at him.

"Master Jack, Master Jonathan, Miss Gardena," Mr. Neuberg said, "may I present the manservant Daniel."

The boys bowed whilst the girl curtsied, her long thick braids falling in front of her shoulders.

Daniel bowed low. "A pleasure."

"Master Jonathan's manservant has been delayed," Mr. Neuberg said, "so for a short time, you'll have the care of them both."

Daniel blinked. *Both?* "I shall do my best, sir."

"Very good," Mr. Neuberg said. He held his hand out to the boy who appeared beside himself with excitement. "Master Jack —"

What?

" — pray show your new manservant your quarters."

The other boy let out an exasperated sigh.

He was jealous!

Daniel felt chagrined. *I had this all wrong.*

Daniel turned to Jack's brother, who returned a sullen glare. "Master Jonathan? I should like to tour your quarters as well, sir. Since I'm to tend to you whilst your manservant is delayed."

The boy's eyes narrowed. "Very well."

"I'll leave you to it then," Mr. Neuberg said. "Miss Gardena, your mother wishes you to attend her."

"Can't I stay — please?"

"You may return if your mother agrees. Now off with you."

The two men left Daniel standing alone with the children. Not knowing what else to do, he toured the two boys' suites.

Each of their bedrooms was at least three times the width of his, carpeted in black, connected by a short hallway with a door dividing it. Each had its own bath running along the back of it, similar to his. Each had a door to a walkway with a black wooden banister and white supports which overlooked the main entry.

As the two boys talked, Daniel began to note the differences between them. Jack's voice was already deeper, his body language more animated. And Jonathan's insolent attitude marked him long before he even opened his mouth.

Jack liked books. He also had an impressive collection of knives.

Jonathan's room was on the corner of the mansion, with windows on two sides. He liked to draw, it seemed. And sports: a racquet, bat, and bow hung on his wall.

Daniel turned to him. "You play?"

They'd given Daniel some simple training in sport, mainly so he might know the rules. He expected the young master to warm to his inquiry.

But Jonathan's eyes filled with tears. "Go **away**!" He threw himself on his bed.

Concern filled Daniel. "What's wrong?"

"He's not allowed to play anymore," Jack said. "He's sick."

Daniel sat heavily at the tea-table, stunned. "No one told me. What kind of sick?"

Jonathan turned towards them and screamed, tears in his eyes, "I'm going to die, okay? Go away and leave me alone!"

Good gods. "If you really want me to go away, I will. But I want to be your friend."

"You can't be our friend," Gardena said from the doorway. "You're a servant. Gentlefolk can't be friends with servants. Mama said it's not allowed."

Daniel realized that he wasn't supposed to sit in the masters' presence, either. "Then I'll help in whatever way I can."

Jonathan pushed his face into his bedsheets and began to sob. "Go away."

"Come, let's go into Jack's room," Daniel said.

Was this why Swan thought the job would be so hard?

Daniel closed the door between the two rooms.

Why didn't anyone tell me?

Hope

The three went into Jack's room. Jack and Gardena jumped onto the bed. Daniel stood as he'd been taught, hands behind his back. "How long has your brother been sick?"

"A year," Jack said. "He got rheumatic fever last summer when it went through the city. I was in the country, so I didn't get it."

"I don't know what that is."

"It made his heart weak," Gardena said. Then her eyes reddened. "He's going to die. That's what the maids said Mama said the doctor said."

"Stop listening at doors," Jack snapped. "It's bad manners."

The whole house probably heard Jonathan shouting. Yet no one had arrived to see what happened. "Well, sir, I must get your clothing ready for dinner. It was nice talking with you."

"Must you go?" Jack said.

Daniel smiled at him. "Yes, sir. Or else your parents won't be happy I came here."

Jack's eyes widened. "Then you better go. I don't want them to send you back."

After the door closed, Daniel chuckled. They were good children. He wondered why Swan called Jack a "hellion" or why he seemed to think he'd have such trouble with him.

Jonathan, however, was another story.

Daniel found suitable clothes for Jack, set them aside. He found his way round to Jonathan's closet, selected Jonathan's clothing, then knocked softly. "May I enter, sir?"

"Yeah."

Daniel brought in Jonathan's clothes, laid them out. "Do you require assistance, sir?"

Jonathan's tone was biting. "I can dress myself."

"Very good, sir."

Jonathan didn't say anything, so Daniel made the same inquiry of Jack.

"Would you?"

Daniel dressed Jack and sent him on his way. Then he straightened both their rooms and unpacked his bags, which sat neatly upon his bed.

Daniel didn't have much compared to Jack and Jonathan, but it was enough. His room had a view of the front garden through the window and everything he needed to do his work.

He pictured Baraja in the library, curled in a chair, a book in her hands. The sweet curve of her cheek, her full lips.

He rested his hand high upon the door-post to lean his head on his arm. *How can I live without her?*

There must be a way to see Baraja again.

Perhaps his master would travel.

But he couldn't depend upon that: he had to make a plan.

He was going to get paid. If she could learn how much they bought her for, perhaps between the two of them, they might save enough for her to be free.

What until then? Would the rest of his life become duty? Caring for these boys, this girl?

These children seemed left behind by their family. How could he teach them how to live in a place he didn't understand himself?

A knock. Daniel swallowed, took a deep breath. "Yes?"

The high-pitched voice of a child. "Your dinner, sir."

Surprised, Daniel opened the door to the hall. Behind it stood a boy of perhaps ten: coiled black hair, dark skin, dark eyes. He held a tray covered with a cloth, which shook slightly from his effort.

Whatever was on the tray smelled wonderful. Daniel took it from him. "Come in."

Daniel walked to his tea-table and placed the tray upon it. But when he turned back, the boy stood in the doorway, his arms at his sides. "Won't you come in?"

"No, sir. It's not allowed. Will there be anything else?"

Daniel went to the door. "What's your name?"

"Flannery Hook. But I'm Diamond-born, on my mother's side."

His words, perhaps meant to reassure Daniel, instead left him perplexed. But he held out his hand. "A pleasure to meet you, Flannery. I'm Daniel."

The boy seemed hesitant, but he shook hands. "And you as well, sir. Will there be anything else? The masters' menservants are the first served after Mr. Neuberg," he let out a weary sigh, "and the rest'll be cross if I'm late."

A wave of compassion swept over him. "Then I won't delay you. When you've eaten, will you call Mr. Swan for me?"

Flannery bowed. "Yes, sir, at once." He hurried down the hall.

They used their own children as servants?

Daniel sat at the table and took the cloth off of the tray. A full bowl sat there, along with utensils, a teacup, and a small pot of tea. The food was excellent — diced roast mutton mixed with cubes of some orange vegetable that he'd never tasted before, spiced sweet and savory. Though he felt ravenous when he began to eat, the food left him feeling completely satisfied.

Perhaps life here might not be so bad after all.

He finished the pot of tea, then poured a glass from the water pitcher on his nightstand. When would he be introduced to the staff? What should he be doing now?

Attend to your duties, Daniel.

His teacher's voice scolded, but kindly.

Daniel went into Jack's closets, examining the items there one by one. All this for one boy?

When Jack returned from dinner, he'd likely want some play clothes, or perhaps his pajamas. But which?

Daniel brushed and laid out sets of both upon Jack's bed, so he might choose, then did the same for his brother Jonathan. It might take time to learn their habits, but he would eventually.

When Daniel returned to his room, Swan stood there as if he'd been waiting for some time. "You need something?"

This threw all Daniel's questions completely out of his mind.

Swan snorted. "You don't even know what to ask, do you?"

"When do I meet the others? What do I do with this tray?" Heat rushed to Daniel's face. "You're right, sir, I don't. Know. And I feel as if I should."

Swan's lined brown face turned amused. "Put the tray outside the door, to the right. The boy'll pick it up. You met your master already, that's all you should concern yourself with."

"Surely Master Jack's parents want to meet the man caring for their son?"

Swan laughed. "Why would they concern themselves with the choosing or oversight of **servants**?"

As if that explained it all. What trust they placed in this man! "When will I meet the others?" Surely this enormous house had dozens to keep it up so well.

"Morning meeting is at ten. I'll have the house-boy bring you down. Now, unless you have some pressing concern, I'll be off."

A door opened in Jack's room.

Swan smirked. "Get to work, boy." Then he left, shutting the hall door behind him.

Daniel hurried to Jack's room. "Let me get you out of those clothes." He took the boy's coat and draped it over a chair. "Master Jonathan," he called out, "I'll be there momentarily."

Jonathan snapped, "I can dress myself. I'm neither an idiot nor a child."

Jack recoiled, eyes reddening.

Daniel went to Jack, loosening his necktie. "I'm sure your brother didn't mean it like that."

"Daddy — Father — said it was our duty to allow you ... here. To care for us." Jack let out a breath. "Jonathan hates everything these days. He hates all of us." Jack pushed Daniel's hands away, and unbuttoned his pale blue shirt himself, flinging it off. His white cotton undershirt was damp with sweat. "I don't think he wants to live anymore."

Daniel whispered, "**What?**"

Matters were worse than he thought.

Jack moved his pajamas over to sit on his bed, head drooping. "They told him he would die. It's all he talks about." Jack's lower lip trembled. "I think he wants it over with."

Daniel didn't know what to say. He didn't know what to do. He wasn't even Jonathan's real servant: soon his manservant would arrive. "What would help?"

Jack shrugged, head down.

"Well, then, let's get you dressed. Pajamas or regular clothes?"

"Mama said to go to bed."

After Daniel left Jack sitting up in bed with a book, he went to Jonathan's room. The boy lay facing the wall, a dim lamp lit atop his dresser. His dinner clothes were strewn across the room, his play clothes still lying on the covers where Daniel had left them.

Daniel could tell Jonathan wasn't asleep. But he picked up the boy's clothes and put them away.

He stood there gazing at the boy's shoulder for some time, grieved at what Jack had told him. Grieved that the boy felt so helpless, so alone, so in turmoil. Daniel didn't know how to help or what to do.

"Are you just going to stare at me all night?"

"I'm sorry to bother you, sir. Master Jack told me about — how sad you've been lately, and —"

"And you want to help." He made that sound as if Daniel wanted to humiliate or hurt him. "No one can help. And I don't need to become some servant's project."

You must never forget your place. They don't see you as their equal, so be very careful in all your dealings.

"Yes, sir. I'm sorry to intrude." What should he say next? His mind raced. "There's no bell from your room to mine. But I can sit at your door, in case you should need anything. On the other side, if you prefer."

"I do prefer."

"Goodnight then, sir."

The lights in Jack's room were off, save for a small lamp on his dresser. Daniel took a chair from Jack's tea-table and sat slumped in the darkened hallway between the two rooms.

Ever since he left the Home, he'd felt helpless, lost, lonely.

Baraja made him feel less lonely. But that night in the hallway, he truly felt how unprepared he was.

We won't let you leave until we've taught you everything you need to know. What had they taught him that pertained in any way to a dying boy who'd given up hope?

Jonathan didn't want him here. He didn't want his help. And it was only a matter of time until his manservant arrived, and Daniel would have no reason to speak with him.

The boy needed a friend. Yet the one thing Daniel was forbidden to do was become familiar with his masters.

Daniel put his head in his hands. At that moment, Baraja probably lay with some other man, even whilst carrying Daniel's child. It was her job. And there was little chance of ever seeing her again. But the fact that she lived, that she loved him — he felt stronger, more able. He felt hope.

Jonathan needed hope. Perhaps Daniel could figure out a way to help the boy find some.

White

Daniel jolted awake, disoriented in the silent half-darkness, until he realized where he was.

The sky outside Jack's window had just begun to pale. Daniel replaced Jack's chair by its tea-table, gathered his bedding from the hall floor, and went to his room.

The tooth powder can had been opened, and the entire room was white.

His suits were covered in it, his tools, his furniture.

Well, Daniel thought. He set his armful of bedding on the clean floor behind him. *I can imagine who did this.*

Jonathan hadn't been sleeping when Daniel left him.

Giggles came from across the room, behind the door to the hall. But when Daniel crossed the room and opened the door, it was Jack who stood there.

When Jack saw the room, he began to laugh.

Daniel stood watching him. Now he knew what his teacher had meant: *Thirteen and already a hellion.*

But he still had a card to play. Once Jack settled, Daniel said, "I'm sorry my service has displeased you, sir. It was an honor to have known you."

Jack looked shocked. "What?"

Daniel gestured to the room. "I have nothing to wear. When I'm presented to your father dressed as I am, I'll be beaten." Daniel paused for effect. "And if I survive, sent back." He shrugged. "I presume that's what you wanted."

Jack's shock turned to horror as he stared at the mess. "No! No! I just thought to have a bit of fun, that's all." Jack grabbed Daniel's arm. "Oh, gods, please, no. I don't want you to leave!"

"What's all this commotion?" Mr. Neuberg's deep voice echoed down the hall as he strode up, already dressed. He looked inside. "Dear me."

Jack turned to the butler, terrified. "I'm sorry, I'm sorry, oh, gods, can you help? I made the mess, not him." The boy's voice broke. "Please? I don't want Daniel sent away!"

A tinge of amusement crossed the man's eyes. "Very well, sir." He turned to Daniel. "Come down when you're done here. I may have something in your size." When he looked at Jack again, his face grew stern. "And you will clean this room. I'll not have my maids waste their time on your folly."

Jack's face fell, but Daniel thought he felt relieved. "Yes, Neuberg. I'm sorry."

The butler glanced at Daniel. "I'll have the suction cleaner sent up for the floors."

"Thank you, sir," Daniel said.

As the butler walked away, Daniel turned to Jack. "We'll do the highest points whilst we wait for the cleaner."

The sky lightened as they shook out and brushed suits, whisked off furniture, wiped down tools. After a time, their clothes were well-powdered. Daniel surveyed Jack and grinned. "You look good in white."

The boy beamed.

The green-eyed woman who'd met them at the door the day earlier wheeled in the suction cleaner, a large mechanism of brass and leather. Its electrical cord's cotton wrapping was gray with age and a few dents and scratches marred the surface, yet the machine gleamed as if new.

Daniel had learned to use one like it at the Academy. After instructing Jack in the machine's use, Daniel followed the woman, whose name was Cora, to a door across from his. They went two floors down a winding ironwork back stair, then down a hall to what could only be Mr. Neuberg's private quarters.

Portraits of some age, mementos, and a well-kept hunting rifle were mounted on the wall. But the room was spare, immaculate.

"He'll be with you shortly, sir," Cora said. She curtsied and left.

"Here you are." Mr. Neuberg's deep voice came forth from the other room. "Come in, my boy, you've not had chance to bathe since your trip."

Daniel hesitated.

"Come on, now. Your young master is having his first tray as we speak, and you'll soon need to be ready to draw his bath."

Daniel hurried in. A suit was laid out, and another door lay open, a bath drawn and hot. He felt humbled. "Thank you, sir."

"Don't mention it." Mr. Neuberg gestured to the tub. "Go on, now. I'll leave you to your duty." He left, closing the door.

Daniel rushed to bathe — which felt wonderful after the long trip and the events following — dress, and return to his rooms.

The suction cleaner stood in the midst of a half-swept room. Daniel went to Jack's room, where the boy sat eating toast.

Jack's face brightened. "I'm glad you're not going to be beaten."

That made Daniel chuckle. "As am I, sir."

Daniel laid out Jack's house clothes, finished suction-sweeping the floor, made the bed, and drew Jack's bath. Then he went round through Jonathan's closets to his room. Jonathan sat morosely in front of uneaten toast.

"Good morning, sir," Daniel said, laying the boy's clothes out. "I hope you had a restful evening. I'll draw your bath now."

The boy grunted in reply.

But Jonathan did let Daniel comb out his hair and shave the bit of fuzz on his chin once he emerged from the tub.

Jack stood in the doorway between their rooms, watching intently. "How did you learn to do all this?"

Daniel wiped down Jonathan's face and turned to Jack. "There's an Academy for house-servants, sir. In Nitivali."

Jonathan gave Daniel a startled glance. "Like school?"

Daniel considered his time there. "I suppose. I've never been to school, sir, so I couldn't say."

"But you stayed there," Jack said. "At the school. Academy."

"Oh, yes, sir. Many months." Daniel whisked a few stray hairs off of Jonathan's collar. "There you are, sir, ready for breakfast."

Neuberg opened the door to the hall. "Breakfast is served."

Jonathan gave a resigned shrug, then he and Jack went off to their meal.

Daniel cleaned up, shoving Jonathan's untouched toast into his mouth as he went.

When Daniel finished straightening both boys' rooms, a tray sat on his tea-table. The bowl of scrambled eggs were cold, as was the tea, but nothing ever tasted so good.

Yet he felt weary. How could he care for two masters at once?

Daniel hoped the new manservant would arrive soon. With the tooth powder debacle, he'd just barely gotten them both ready for breakfast, and he had a pile of clothes to clean. Daniel glanced at the clock. He'd missed morning prayers entirely.

A knock at the door: this time, little Flannery stood there. "Morning meeting, sir. I'll take your tray down."

Daniel felt a great fondness for this little boy. He handed over the tray, following the boy down the back stairs. "How long have you been here?"

"From birth, sir," Flannery said. "My mother is lady's maid to Mrs. Rachel. My father is manservant to Mr. Julius. Mr. Neuberg says if I study well I could be butler one day!"

As they approached another hallway, a commotion of voices came from down it. "Go that way," Flannery said. "I'll bring this to the kitchen and join you."

It took a moment for Daniel to realize he was in the passage he'd first gone through when he arrived. A group of dark-skinned men and women lined up to file into a door. Daniel followed them into a large room with two long tables. It seemed the men sat at one and the women at another, so he moved to follow their lead.

Mr. Neuberg, who stood close by, laid a hand on Daniel's arm. "You'll be there." He pointed to a row of chairs near a raised area across from the men's table.

Another set of chairs sat on the other side, across from the women's table. There sat a woman who could only be Flannery's mother: the boy looked just like her.

Only one man stood near the chairs Neuberg pointed to, so Daniel approached him, holding out his hand. "I'm Daniel."

The man, perhaps forty, didn't offer his hand. "Brelan Hook. You from Cuebid?"

Daniel had no idea what, where, or who Cuebid might be. "I'm originally from Dickens, sir. But then I went to the house-servants' Academy in Nitivali."

Mr. Hook's eyes widened. "Master Écarté?"

"Why, yes."

At that, he gave a broad smile and shook Daniel's hand. "Glad to know you. One of my good friends was his student, oh, twenty years or so back. When I saw your suit, I thought you were one of those Cuebids. Insufferable chaps."

Daniel chuckled, still not sure what the man referred to. "I borrowed this from Mr. Neuberg. My clothing suffered mishap."

He nodded, his face guarded. "I see."

A bell rang, and the room instantly quieted, everyone hurrying to find a seat. Daniel looked to Mr. Hook for an explanation.

Mr. Hook rolled his eyes. "Our betters deign to descend."

Yet he didn't sit, so Daniel didn't either.

Everyone rose as two men and one woman, all dark-skinned, handsome, and well-dressed, strode into the room. One of the men was much older than the other. Father and son?

The woman took the arm of the younger man, who was in his late thirties. The three went up two small steps to the raised area.

The older man said, "We will be at home until tea, which will be at the home of the Jotepas. We shall return forthwith and have guests for dinner."

Mr. Neuberg said, "Very good, sir. Any requests?"

"No fish. Anything else will do."

A stout graying woman sat at the far end of the women's table taking notes.

"Yes, sir," Mr. Neuberg said. "Will there be anything else?"

The woman upon the raised area spoke. "The manservant."

Mr. Neuberg peered at Daniel.

Fear struck. *Have I done something wrong?*

"Would you care to speak with him, mum?"

"I would."

"Daniel," Mr. Neuberg said, "please come forward."

Daniel's mind raced. What could he have possibly done differently? But he went forward and stood facing them, his back to the room, then dropped to one knee and bowed low.

"I hear my son caused harm to your belongings."

Daniel stood, yet didn't dare look any of them in the eye. "No permanent harm done, mum."

"I also hear," she said, "that he cleaned your room himself. And that you left him operating a suction cleaner."

Murmurs from behind.

Daniel stared straight ahead, cheeks burning. Manual labor was the one thing a gentleman **never** did. *Why did I allow him to do it?* He felt everyone staring at his back. "Yes, mum."

The woman gazed at Daniel a long moment, then broke into a smile. "Good. The boy needs to learn responsibility."

"Thank you, mum."

Mr. Neuberg said, "You may return to your place."

Daniel bowed, then stood next to Mr. Hook.

Mr. Neuberg then began to read from a page: garden duties, the menu for the day, merchants who were scheduled to make deliveries, and so on.

Mr. Hook chuckled softly.

"What's so funny?" Daniel whispered, more than a bit annoyed.

"You turn remarkably pale when scared out of your wits."

It was then Daniel realized that although he was in no way as pale as Jacob, he was by far the lightest-colored person in the room. He smiled to himself. He couldn't help that any more than being an orphan — or being sold here, for that matter.

Finally, the uppers swept out of the room, and everyone relaxed into their seats. Mr. Neuberg continued to stand. "We have a newcomer," he pointed to me, "as you are all aware: Daniel here is manservant to the twin masters, until Master Jonathan's servant arrives next week."

A whole week of this?

"He's not a Diamond, nor even of Bridges. But he comes highly recommended. Picked by Swan himself."

Many regarded Daniel with new respect. Some whispered to others, then glanced at Daniel warily, shaking their heads.

Mr. Neuberg turned to Daniel. "Speak to Mrs. Whist," he pointed at the stout graying woman, "if your room lacks anything." He then spoke to them all. "Dismissed."

The others rose. Some filed out, some stood talking.

Mr. Hook said, "What'd the little scamp do this time?"

Your job is to protect your master at all times. "This time?"

Mr. Hook laughed. "You know he was expelled from school for stabbing a boy."

Avoid even the appearance of gossip. Daniel felt shocked by the news, but managed to keep his face and voice still. "No, I didn't."

"He's a terror, that one. The other children call him 'Black Jack'. They say he frightens them. Not at all like his brother."

A wave of sadness came over him. "I fear for Master Jonathan."

"Indeed. A pity. The boy showed such promise."

Daniel recalled the sports equipment. "Is he really that ill?"

"Dreadfully. He was in the midst of sport and suffered a faint. Nearly trampled. They brought him home from school, and he hasn't been back since." He stood, and Daniel rose as well. "Good thing Mr. Julius has seven sons — that one'll be lucky to make it another year."

No wonder the boy was angry. This must all seem so unfair. "I fear the poor lad's end will be melancholy."

Mr. Hook gave Daniel a startled glance. "Go on."

Daniel shrugged. "He and his brother have said as much." This man had the ear of Jonathan's father. "He needs cheering." Should he dare say anything? The boy was only thirteen. "In Nitivali, there were these women —"

At first, the man gave Daniel a confused frown. Then light dawned in Mr. Hook's eyes. "Why, I'd never considered it. Yes! I suppose he's old enough. I know just the place." He clapped a hand on Daniel's shoulder. "I can see why Swan picked you out. Good lad. Smart."

He gave Mr. Hook a slight bow. "Thank you, sir."

Daniel went to Mrs. Whist — the housekeeper — to get the boys' schedules. The rest of the day was spent with their clothing: cleaning, brushing, pressing, hanging. After finding trousers in Jack's closet with a stain on the leg, Daniel decided to go over everything to make sure each piece was fit to wear.

Never slack in your work, no matter how great the temptation. The one time you do will be the time that you need the item you should have prepared. Master Écarté had laughed at that as if he'd been caught at it himself.

So even though Daniel felt ready to drop, he made himself examine each item in Jack's closet. He resolved to go through Jonathan's closet the next day.

Jack stood at the door to his closets, wearing his pajamas. "Aren't you going to bed?"

"I'm almost done."

"I don't want you to get sick too."

Daniel draped the shirt he'd been pressing over the ironing board. "What do you mean?"

"The doctor said overwork can make a man sick."

"Very well." Daniel moved the iron aside to cool. "Now take your own advice, sir."

Sick

After another night on the floor in the hallway, Daniel ached all over. *Just a few more days.*

No mess greeted him when he went to his rooms, thank the gods, so he bathed and dressed, drank his tea and opened the curtains in the boys' rooms, just like he'd been taught.

He followed the boys to morning prayers, which was held in a room so beautiful it took his breath away. Perfectly white, with a ceiling which drew up to a point high above, like they stood inside some giant crystal.

On one wall, a window of stained glass depicted the Blessed Dealer. Her skin dark brown, her hair a stormcloud, surrounded by a rainbow sky. Aces from the Holy Cards and flowers of every color danced round her.

It was one of the most beautiful things he'd ever seen in his life.

After prayers, which were much like those at the Home, the uppers stood chatting. The entire household was there — except the five older sons.

This mystery was answered easily enough: boarding school.

"The youngest master's been so ill," Mrs. Whist said in hushed tones, "and I'm sure you know what happened with the other."

The little girl began to pester Jack and Jonathan, until Jonathan snapped at her.

"What about the girl? Gardena, is it not?"

She gasped. "A high-born girl ... in **school**? By the Shuffler! We have a governess from the Dealers to instruct her! And her mother and I are here to teach the little miss anything else a woman of standing might need know." She shook her head. "What kind of place do they **bring** these servants from!"

Daniel chuckled to himself as the housekeeper went off fanning herself and mumbling. This seemed just as strange a place to him.

Since the boys went right to breakfast from prayers, Daniel returned to his room to have his. Then back down to morning meeting, then back up for more work whilst Jack met with his tutor, a solid, no-nonsense man named Master Toran.

That day, Daniel went over Jonathan's closets, leaving the door open. The boy sat at his tea-table glumly gazing out of the window.

Everyone spoke of how ill Jonathan was. Yet his face wasn't flushed. He never coughed. Every few hours he took a draught from his nurse, a frail-looking middle-aged woman named Miss Kaluki, drinking the clear liquid with a resigned air.

The boy wrote furiously — schoolwork, Daniel imagined — yet seemed distracted, melancholy. Occasionally he'd turn away to hide his face in his hands for a long spell.

He never spoke, and Daniel didn't dare speak to him. Yet he felt perhaps Jonathan welcomed the company as well as the silence.

That evening after dinner, Jack said, "Would you read to me?"

"Certainly, sir." Daniel selected a book from Jack's shelf and opened it, then stood near the end of his bed.

"Won't you sit?"

"I'm not allowed to sit, sir."

"Even if I command it?"

Daniel never considered such a thing. "I don't know."

"You never can sit? Even when you eat? That doesn't seem fair."

Daniel smiled to himself. "Of course I sit when I eat. When I'm here with you, though — no. You're my master. It's not right for me to sit in your presence."

Jack pondered that. "Neuberg never sits either."

"Shall I read now?"

Jack beamed, pulling the covers up under his chin. "You may."

***

During the rest of the week, the days were much the same. Perhaps Jack might go on an outing, or Jonathan might wish to sit upon the veranda at the back of the mansion and need a jacket. But Daniel's time was spent cleaning and mending, ironing and brushing, sweeping and polishing.

Since Jonathan did little but write, Daniel spent more time in Jack's room. Jack was an active boy, and returned with scuffed shoes, trousers with grass-stained knees, or a torn jacket. When not otherwise engaged, Jack would sit in his closets as Daniel worked, or Daniel would bring his ironing board into Jack's room.

But as the days passed, Jonathan began to leave the door to his room open. Jack seemed to want to know everything about Daniel; Jonathan seldom spoke. And little Gardena apparently had no playmates besides her brothers, because she was in their rooms almost as often as they were.

Swan had warned Daniel not to speak of Baraja or their child, so he kept his answers vague. Yes, he had friends back home, and at the Academy. He missed them, but he was glad to be here.

Then he'd turn the questions to them. Jack and Gardena loved telling of their day.

At night, he stood reading to Jack. Sometimes the boy would speak of his thoughts, his worries.

Daniel wished it were Jonathan confiding in him. But the boy's manservant would arrive soon. Perhaps Jonathan realized that, and guarded himself against yet another loss, small as it was.

Daniel lay awake in the hallway thinking of Baraja until exhaustion overtook him. It'd been less than a week since he saw her, but to him, it seemed an eternity.

***

Near the end of that first week, Swan came to visit as Daniel ate breakfast. "Sit," Swan said as Daniel rose. "Finish your meal."

"Some tea, sir?"

"Sure." He sat, taking a cup. "You've managed a good report."

This took Daniel aback. "Just doing my job, sir."

"And another's, plus handling three children." Swan let out a short laugh. "Would drive me mad."

Daniel had been handling children since he was old enough to remember. "How may I help you, sir?"

"Just came to see if you needed anything."

Daniel considered this. "Am I allowed to send mail?"

"Sure. Did you get your packet yet?"

Daniel shook his head, not sure what Swan meant.

"You should get an envelope at morning meeting. It's your pay for the month. The uppers generally go out on paydays to let us do our shopping. You can buy pen and paper from the housekeeper. Post the mail with Neuberg, he'll send it for you."

Daniel wanted to send money to Baraja in case she needed anything. But he wanted to send and receive mail first, to make sure the money would get there safely.

Swan had been peering at him. "First thing you need is some regular clothes. You can't go out on the town wearing house-servant clothing, that's for certain."

As Swan had said, at the end of morning meeting, Flannery came by with a small envelope for each of them.

In Daniel's packet lay a single dollar.

Most of the others had change only, so Daniel thought it best not to complain. But it turned out things cost much less here than they had in Nitivali.

Daniel wrote a short letter to Baraja to let her know he arrived safely. To send it all the way to Nitivali cost twenty-five cents.

"Standard Merca inter-city fee," Mrs. Whist said.

Then Swan brought him to a shop to purchase clothing for the street, for play with the boys should they wish it, and for outings of his own.

Daniel honestly didn't know when he might have time for such things. But Swan offered to pay, so Daniel let him buy.

After Daniel changed, Swan had the rest of the clothes sent to his rooms. Then Swan took him out for a drink. "It's your birthday, or had you forgotten?"

Daniel felt touched. "Thank you, sir."

Swan grinned, leaning back in his chair. "You get as old as me, you start being grateful to be around another year."

Daniel was just seventeen. But a tankard was set in front of him as if he were a man full grown.

"Mr. Hector don't abide with drink," Swan said. "But out here on Market Center we can do what we want." He chuckled. "And what he don't know won't hurt him."

Daniel didn't care for the taste of ale, but he sipped it anyway, and took a bite of the pork pie set before him. "How long will the uppers be gone?"

"The weekend. At times, I think they're as weary of us as we are of them." He let out a short laugh. "I wager they'll be in good spirits when they return."

It turned out the Diamond Family had another, much larger home in "the countryside," as well as several other smaller homes elsewhere. But Daniel felt alarmed. "Should I not have packed the boys' suitcases, traveled with them?"

"If the boys were older, I'd say yes. But I told the master —"

By this, Daniel gathered Swan meant the boys' father.

"— the situation and he agreed they'd be fine for a day or two without you. Their nurse will accompany them to the Country House this time."

The house was quiet when they returned, too quiet. But Daniel got to lie in his bed for the first time ever. It felt wonderful.

"Happy birthday, Daniel," he whispered. He hugged his coverlet, thinking back to the day he learned he'd been bought, and wondered why he'd been so afraid.

Friends

The next day after morning meeting, Daniel returned to his rooms to find workmen installing two bells in his bedroom.

Swan came by later to explain. "The first should have been installed before you arrived. Master Jack tells me you've been sleeping in the hallway." He frowned, shaking his head. "That's no way for a manservant to live."

Daniel felt overwhelmed by the fuss being made over him. "But won't you need to tear this out when Master Jonathan's manservant arrives?"

Swan shook his head, glancing away. "There's been an incident. And we can't get another for quite some time." He pursed his lips at that, and put a hand on Daniel's shoulder. "Looks like you'll have them both for a while yet."

When Flannery brought Daniel's lunch, he was all too eager to share the news. "Master Jonathan's manservant got run over by a carriage, dead!" The boy's eyes were wide. "Why didn't he get out of the way?"

"Good question," Daniel said, as he took the tray. "What do you do here, when the masters are out?"

Flannery considered it. "I like to play ball with the dogs."

"What are dogs?"

Flannery's little mouth made an O. "You've never seen **dogs**?"

Daniel shook his head.

A woman's voice, from downstairs. "Boy! Where are you?"

"Coming," Flannery called out. Then he turned to Daniel and said, "I gotta go."

Daniel ate his luncheon, staring out of the window at the passing traffic. Dark-skinned men in black suits and dark spectacles stood casually in twos on either side of the white wrought-iron fence, watching outward. People crossed the street rather than approach the men.

What did it mean?

When Flannery came back for the tray, he said, "You want to play now?"

Daniel considered this. All his work was done. And they'd told him that he could wear his "regular" clothing whilst the masters were out on their holiday. "I would!"

Flannery led him through the door across the hall and down two flights of the winding ironwork stair. "We go this way so the masters' fine guests don't have to see us," he said, as if this was both normal and desired.

When they reached street level, Flannery went downstairs to replace the tray in the kitchens. Then the two of them went through a side door, past a long set of stables, and around to the back gardens. "They let me play here when the uppers are gone!"

Flannery stuck two fingers in his mouth and whistled. Four large white four-legged animals with bushy tails bounded up from far off in the trees.

At first, Daniel felt afraid, but the animals seemed so happy to see them that his fear disappeared.

"Hold out the back of your hand so they can smell you," Flannery said. "Then they'll know you're a friend."

Daniel felt amazed. "Their hair is so soft."

Flannery began pointing at each one. "This one is Leo. He sniffs for bombs. These are Cash, Gem, and Pocket. They help herd the sheep." He stared at Daniel. "You really never saw dogs before?"

"No." They never had anything like this at the Home.

"How about cats?"

"I know cats," Daniel said. "They eat mice."

Flannery nodded sagely. "They do. They eat birds too. You know about birds?"

Daniel smiled to himself. "I do. And bugs, and bats."

"What are bats?"

"They're like birds only they have fur, not feathers. You see them in Dickens at twilight. They eat bugs."

"Ohhh," Flannery said.

The two walked as the dogs raced back and forth around them. Flannery tossed a ball, or a stick, and the four dogs would tussle amongst themselves as to which would bring it back. After a bit, they sat on the grass, the dogs lying beside them.

"Out past here is the shooting range," Flannery said. "That's just for the uppers who are grown-up men. But sometimes they let me help with tea-time when they spend the day out there. They let me carry the tablecloths." He rubbed his nose. "I don't like shooting, though. It's too loud."

"Ask for ear-plugs," Daniel said. "It's still loud, but it's better."

Flannery seemed astonished. "You know how to shoot?"

They'd taught him at the Academy. "I do. How else might I protect Master Jack?"

Flannery nodded, his face thoughtful.

The day was bright and the flowers glowed with color. *Baraja would like this so much.* "What do you know about the masters?" For an instant, he felt confused, hoping he got the title right.

Flannery shrugged. "The Old Master, he's real nice — he gave me a sweet once. He's a real live Inventor! I remember when the Old Mistress turned in her cards — everyone was sad." His face turned sad for a moment. "The Young Master is their son, Mr. Julius. The maids say he'll take over someday — when the Old Master folds. But I hope he never folds."

Daniel smiled fondly at the real love in the boy's voice.

"The Young Mistress is his wife. She talked to you in morning meeting the other day."

Daniel nodded at the memory. The Young Mistress seemed pretty old, at least thirty!

"Then there's the Heirs. Seven there are." Flannery rolled over to lay on his stomach. "The maids say they're matchmaking the oldest one."

"What does that mean?"

"Getting him a wife." Flannery shrugged. "A wife is a girl." He seemed disgruntled at the notion. "Not sure what you need with girls anyway. The Little Mistress is a girl, and she sticks her tongue at me."

Daniel chuckled at the image of Gardena in her frills and bows, sticking her tongue out. Then he thought of Baraja. "Not all girls stick their tongue at you. Some girls are nice. You'll see."

Flannery didn't seem convinced.

"Aren't there any other girls here? Little, like you?"

"No, I'm the little one. I have three brothers. One helps with the horses, and the other two go round fixing things. The maids are all big." He settled his chin on his hands. "Ma said that if no more boys come along they might buy us a hall boy when I get big enough to move up."

Daniel nodded. The goal in life here was to move up.

From the gossip and what he'd gathered at the Academy, his position as manservant was in some ways as high a rank as butler. Which for a servant was as high as you might possibly go.

In matters involving the entire household, Mr. Neuberg ranked over them all. But when it came to the young Masters, Daniel answered to Mr. Swan.

It seemed confusing at times. "What about my two little Heirs?"

Flannery laughed. "They're big!" But then he sobered. "They used to be nice to me." For a time, he seemed discouraged, but then he shrugged. "Pa says uppers get that way when they grow up. That's why you can't be their friend."

One of the dogs whined, putting his head on the boy's back.

Daniel patted Flannery's shoulder. "I'll be your friend."

Messages

That day, tea was served in the staff room, where they had morning meeting, and Daniel finally got to meet everyone.

Miz Johnson was the Cook, and seemed to be in a perpetual bad temper, pounding the table to make her point. Kindra, Laura, and Ellie-Mae were the kitchen maids who helped her. The "sculleries" were Malena, Nancy, and Lilah. Despite what Flannery had said, they weren't much older than Gardena. They blushed and curtsied, hands behind their backs, when introduced.

Mr. Wheeler was First Footman, which seemed important — at least he seemed to think so. Garrett, Oscar, and Anton were also footmen, but much younger. Mr. Lucas was manservant to Mr. Hector, the man Flannery had called the Old Master.

The house maid Cora he'd already met, but there were others, who were much older: Pippa, Eliza, and Penny.

Of course, Mr. Hook and the rest were there, too.

This time, the men and women sat where they liked. Eliza, Penny, and Ellie-Mae frowned at him and whispered to each other when they thought he wasn't looking.

Mr. Hook came up to speak with him. "Thank you for your kindness to my son."

"It's no trouble at all," Daniel said. "He's a good boy."

Mr. Neuberg came in last. Everyone stood then, and he sat at the end of a table. Flannery's parents sat next to Mr. Neuberg, one on each side.

Cora, Kindra, Laura, and Lilah gave Daniel secret glances as they ate. Which at the time, made no sense. There seemed to be no end of men here — why the interest in him?

Then with a sudden surge of melancholy, Daniel remembered Baraja, so far off without him.

The lady's maid, Mrs. Hook, peered down the table at him. "Is all well, Daniel?"

He gave a quick nod. "Just thinking of home."

Some of the rest looked down, or glanced away.

Those are the orphans, Daniel thought.

Mr. Neuberg's tone was kind. "This is your home now."

***

After tea, Mr. Neuberg showed Daniel around "more properly." They went all round the house downstairs. Daniel learned where things were kept, and Mr. Neuberg brought him to the housekeeper's office, a tiny alcove taken up by a small desk. "If you need to buy anything, and we don't have it already, Mrs. Whist here can order it for you"

"Are there any books?"

Mrs. Whist and Mr. Neuberg exchanged a glance. Mr. Neuberg seemed hesitant. "There's the master's library ... But you can buy books for yourself if you like. Or I have some you might borrow. What sort of books do you mean?"

At that, Daniel had no words. What sort of book had Baraja shown him? "I don't know the sort. About life, I suppose."

At that, Mr. Neuberg gave him an amused smile. "Let me show you what I have."

But Mr. Neuberg didn't have the book Baraja had shown him.

If she gets my letter, and writes back, Daniel thought, *I'll ask her the name of it.*

He wanted the book she read to him — something he could hold in his hands to remember her by.

After returning to his rooms, Daniel felt unsure what to do next. The boys' rooms were clean, their clothes pressed and ready, his own items taken care of. He sat listening to the rise and fall of voices in the hallway.

He missed his home. He missed Baraja. He even missed Jacob.

I'll write to him. Then he won't worry.

But when he went to Mr. Neuberg to post the letter, the butler pursed his lips, shaking his head. "You don't want to be doing this, my boy."

Fear struck: he couldn't write to Jacob? "Jacob is my friend. We were at the Home together in Dickens." A sudden rush of emotion came over him. "On the way here, he —"

Mr. Neuberg closed the door and gestured for Daniel to sit. "You don't understand. It's bad enough, you being an outsider. You don't know us. You don't have our connections. Yes, you're manservant to the young masters. But you can't send messages to the Spadros Family. Not now, not ever."

"But, sir —"

"But nothing." He grabbed a hand mirror, held it up so it faced Daniel. "Look at yourself."

Daniel stared at his reflection: straight black hair, light brown skin, brown eyes. "What about me?"

"I'm trying to keep you alive, son. They get the idea that you're a Spadros spy, and —" The butler peered at Daniel for a long moment, then his face changed, as if coming to some realization. "Have you ever **seen** a Spadros?"

Daniel shook his head.

Mr. Neuberg turned aside, setting the mirror down. "Let's just say you wouldn't be out of place on any street in their quadrant." He sat quietly for a moment. "Give me your letter. I know someone who can get it to your friend. But you must never send another."

Daniel opened his letter, adding:

> I'm not allowed to write you anymore. The butler says it's not safe for me to do so. But I want you to know I'm with you always. I'm right here, just across the river, and as long as I live I won't forget you. We're brothers. Don't forget me. Don't lose heart.

***

Late that night, Daniel couldn't sleep. He rose in darkness, went to the window and sat peering out. Why would they think he was a spy just because of how he looked?

He hoped his letter made it to Jacob. Alone, with so much to do and not knowing anyone ... Daniel worried about him.

He couldn't just abandon him. But he didn't know what to do.

Men walked past the white spiraling wrought iron in the glow of the street lamps. But something else lay there along the fence: a faint glow of palest blue.

He asked Swan about it the next day. "Security," Swan said. His voice dropped to a whisper. "Illegal tech from Azimoff, it is, but better. It's been modified by the Inventor to work on our electric. You need a special code to get through."

"Oh!" Daniel felt astonished. "But people can see it right there."

Swan snorted. "The streets are well-guarded, my boy, day and night. At night, no one's allowed within six blocks of here that's not one of our own, not even to visit. Our guest rooms are in the back of the house, where they can't see the fencing. And neither zeppelin nor balloon may fly over us," he let out a laugh, "or we'll shoot it down."

Daniel felt impressed. "That sounds good." Then he remembered that Helix Coil was going to serve a zeppelin pilot.

"Even better at the Country House," Swan said. "And at the school where the young Masters are. One of them's gonna run this Family someday. We gotta let them grow up enough to do it."

"Do the other young Masters ever see their parents?"

"Sure, when they go to the countryside." Swan clapped Daniel on the shoulder. "They're almost grown; they don't need Mommy and Daddy watching their every move."

"I thought they weren't much older than our young Masters."

Swan nodded. "When you put it that way, yeah, the youngest is just a year older. Our Heir, Master Cesare, is six years older." Then Swan's face brightened. "They just found him a good match."

"Oh?" Daniel had as yet not seen this Master Cesare, but he played along. "How do you know if it's a good match?"

Swan's eyes widened. Then he let out a short laugh. "Guess it would be different where you're from. This gal's smart, real smart. And beautiful. Got good hips for bearing sons. Tough, too. Knows how to play the game." He nodded approvingly. "A fine partner for the man who'll lead the quadrant one day."

Daniel thought of Baraja. Swan had called her a whore.

"Don't matter to you none, I imagine," Swan said. "But we're all happy for it."

You belong to them now. "Then I'm happy for it too."

Behavior

When the family returned home, Daniel got many days' worth of distraction from the children's questions out of asking about their trip. But the goodwill Jonathan had towards him before he left seemed to have vanished. Each day went about the same way:

"We have animals there," Gardena said. "Cows, and —"

"— sheep." Jack pushed her aside. "And goats, dogs, and —"

Jonathan scowled. "Who the fuck cares?" He got up, stomping into his room.

Jack and Gardena just sat there, chagrined.

But that day, little Gardena's eyes filled with tears. "Why does he **hate** us so much?"

Jack sounded disgruntled. "We didn't do anything to him."

"Your brother doesn't hate you," Daniel said. "And you did nothing wrong. Let him be for now."

Gardena said, "It's not **our** fault he's sick." Then she scowled. "I hate him. He's mean."

"Don't say that," Daniel said. "You don't hate him." He bent over to look in her eyes. "Do you really?"

Her lower lip stuck out. "N-no." Tears rolled down her cheeks. "But why is he so **mean** all the time?"

Daniel squatted in front of her. "I don't know. I think he's scared. None of the regular things seem important any more. They seem stupid when you're going to die." Daniel shrugged. "That's the only thing I can think of." He stood. "Do you want to tell me more about the animals?"

Jack shook his head.

"We should get Jonathan a better doctor," Gardena said, "so he won't die."

"They took him to lots of them," Jack said. "Besides, doctors don't keep you from dying. Nana had lots of doctors and she still died. They — they just make you feel not so sick."

Daniel didn't know. He'd never actually seen a doctor. At the Home, you either got better or you didn't.

And he had no idea what to do.

Mr. Neuberg knocked on the door. "Luncheon is served." He opened the door, glanced around. "And Master Jonathan is —?"

"In his room," Jack said.

"Very good, sir." Mr. Neuberg closed the door.

As the children went to luncheon, a knock came at Daniel's door: Flannery, carrying Daniel's lunch tray as usual.

Daniel said, "Is Mr. Swan around?"

"I'll go find him," Flannery said. "Once I get the trays done."

All the while he ate, Daniel thought about what was going on, what he might do to help. At the Home, Miz Albaletta or Miz Lisbet took care of problems like this. But he'd never seen what they did. He could only hope that Swan would know what to do.

He finished eating and set his tray out in the hall, then straightened the rooms. The boys already had their play clothes on, so there was no need for laying anything out yet. He swept the floors, then retrieved a coat for Jonathan at Mr. Neuberg's request.

When Daniel returned to his room, his tray was gone from outside the door. Yet Swan was nowhere to be seen.

So Daniel got out his pile of mending. He'd replaced three buttons and mended two seams by the time Swan arrived.

Swan looked as if he'd been conducting business: instead of his usual attire, he had nicely shined shoes and fine clothing. "What's going on?"

Daniel told him about Jonathan's behavior. "It's causing trouble between the children. Miss Gardena is particularly upset by it. I don't know what to do."

"I'll talk to Mr. Julius," Swan said. "It's not your responsibility."

Daniel spoke sharply. "That's what I thought."

Swan snorted. "You do speak your mind."

"Why did they even have these children if they didn't want to care for them? Do they ever see them? I —"

Swan held up a hand, his voice kind. "I've seen this before." He rested his hand on Daniel's shoulder. "You're a servant. Nothing else." He shook his head. "Don't let yourself get twisted up in their lives. It'll bring you nothing but grief."

His teacher had told him this many a time. "I never realized how hard this would be." Then he remembered his discussion with Jack a few nights earlier. "Must I do whatever they command?"

Swan blinked. "What do they want you to do?"

"Master Jack likes me to read to him at night. He's asked many a time if I might sit with him. I know I'm not supposed to sit in their presence, but —"

Swan gave a bemused smile. "They're children." He thought about this for a moment. "I don't see how sitting beside him when you read will hurt anything." Then his tone became serious, concerned. "But be careful, my boy. Be very careful."

Impulse

Later that day, after Jack went out to play, Daniel went into Jonathan's room. "Sir, might I speak with you?"

"What do you want?"

"I'm sorry to intrude, sir, but I simply wondered if your trip went well."

Jonathan shrugged. "What business is it of yours?"

"It's only that you've seemed upset since you returned."

Daniel thought for an instant that the boy might speak with him. Then Jonathan scowled. "It's none of your affair."

Daniel bowed. "Forgive me: I'll speak no more of it."

Jonathan didn't speak to Daniel the entire next day, even when spoken to, and refused to come in to sit with Jack and Gardena.

The next night, Jack asked if Daniel might sit with him.

"If you command me to, sir."

"I do."

So Daniel sat on the edge of the bed reading.

Jack sat leaning on his headboard, arms around his knees as Daniel read, listening with an intensity Daniel found disturbing.

Daniel came to the end of the chapter, then set the book down. "May I ask something?"

"Anything you wish," Jack said.

"Did anything bad happen on your trip? Something that made your brother unhappy?"

"I don't think so."

Daniel sighed. "I just wish I knew why he's so upset."

Jack shrugged. Daniel went back to reading the book. When Daniel finished, Jack said, "Thank you for sitting with me."

Daniel smiled at the boy, covered him up. "You're welcome." On impulse, he kissed Jack's forehead, as he'd done with the little boys back home whilst tucking them into bed. "Rest well."

Returning to his room, Daniel felt a surge of pity for these children. Their father never visited them; their mother never came to their rooms. Night and day, they seemed cast adrift, alone. He recalled the questions, the feelings he'd had at that age. While he didn't have parents, he did have the other boys older than he, like older brothers, who he could talk to.

Maybe I can be that to them. If they'll let me.

The next morning, a letter from Baraja sat on his breakfast tray:

My Beauty —

I am well, and the healer says our child is also. Thank you for writing to me. I have never had another man do so, which tells me I chose well.

I think of you often. It pleases me that they've been kind to you.

May today bring much happiness.

Baraja

Daniel used the last of the month's pay packet to write back, sending a nickel and asking about the book she'd read to him at his visit. Then he stretched upon his bed for just a moment, hands behind his head, staring at the ceiling.

For the first time, everything felt real. *I'm to be a father. I'm to be a father!* That made him feel as if he'd moved up somehow. As Master Écarté was to him, so he would be to these boys, even if he could never be one to the child waiting to be dealt in.

Yet even this last thought didn't make Daniel sad. He felt excited. Even if he must stay in Bridges, some small part of him was there, with Baraja.

It was one of those secret thoughts, never to be shared, because saying so would sound foolish. But knowing his child lay within Baraja made him feel comforted: she wouldn't be alone.

A small noise reminded him that the boys would return to their rooms soon. He had work to do.

Questions

As the days passed, Jack asked more and more about Daniel's life. It became harder and harder to avoid Jack's questions. Daniel had to remind himself never to volunteer a scrap of information.

"Where did you live before here?"

"I went to the Academy in Nitivali."

"You told me that already. Before that."

"Dickens."

"What's Dickens like?"

"Cold, most times. But the days are nice in the summer. Even when it's cold out, the sky is blue much of the year."

"But what's it like?"

Daniel put the iron aside. "What do you mean?"

"You speak differently."

Daniel shrugged, turned over the pair of dark gray trousers he was ironing.

"What do people do there for fun?"

What did we do for fun? Daniel didn't know. Most of his days had been filled with work. "Played games." He pictured the other boys in their bunks at night, faces lit by the candles on their small chest of drawers. Guessing games, memory games, telling stories ... "Much the same as you do, I suppose."

Jack fell quiet. Then he said, "Are there horses there?"

"Oh, yes, lots. And carriages too."

"What color?"

Daniel shrugged. "Brown, mostly."

"Did you ride much?"

"I never have."

Jack sat up, eyes wide. "You never rode a horse before?"

"Never." Daniel put the iron aside, and slid the trousers over a hanger to add to Jack's collection.

"Then I must teach you! It's fun."

Daniel felt uneasy. "Is that allowed?"

"If I command it, it's allowed. Right?"

"I suppose," Daniel said. "I'd be glad to learn to ride."

"Hurray!" Jack ran to Jonathan's room. "Guess what? I'm going to teach Daniel to ride a horse!"

A thump, and the door shut.

Jack returned crestfallen. "Jon threw a water glass at me!"

"Did it hit you?"

Jack shook his head.

"Did it break?"

"I don't think so."

Daniel patted Jack's shoulder. "I'll go see." He went to Jonathan door and knocked.

"What do you want now?"

Daniel didn't open the door. "Master Jonathan, if there's broken glass, I should call for the suction cleaner. You don't want glass in your foot."

Silence for a moment, then: "It didn't break."

"Very good, sir. Can I get you anything?"

"No."

"I'll leave you to your work, then, sir."

"You do that."

Disheartened at Jonathan's sarcasm, Daniel returned to the ironing board and chose a shirt from the pile. Jonathan seemed so unhappy. It was hard watching him push everyone away.

Jack was watching him. "Do you like me?"

"Of course, sir."

"Why do you call me sir, then?"

Daniel hesitated. "It's a term of respect. Others would think it disrespectful for me not to."

"Would you not call me that, though? When it's just us."

Be very careful. "What would you prefer me to call you?"

He gave a shy smile. "Jack."

"Master Jack it shall be, then —"

"No. Just Jack."

Daniel took a deep breath to keep his voice from shaking. *You must do whatever they command.* Yet he had the boy's father to consider. "Very well. When it's just the two of us. But if I think someone may be listening, I may call you sir. Or Master Jack. And you mustn't correct me." Daniel searched for how to make the boy understand how serious this was. "I don't wish to be beaten for disrespecting you."

Jack's eyes widened. "Of course! But who would do that?" Then realization spread over his face. "My father. Oh."

Daniel felt shaky. "He only wants the best for you." If Julius Diamond thought he was turning his son against him ... "He loves you. He wants people to respect you. It's what you deserve. You're a Diamond Heir."

Jack fell quiet. Finally, he said, "What if I don't want to be a Diamond Heir? I don't even know what that means."

"I don't know either," Daniel said. "But I'm sure your father and brothers will tell you, if you ask them."

"They hate me," Jack said bitterly.

Daniel went back to his ironing. *Don't become inquisitive,* Master Écarté had warned them. *There are things it may put you into danger to know, and others which they will hate you for after they've told them to you. When in doubt, hold your tongue.*

"I suppose they told you what I did," Jack said.

Daniel focused on ironing the collar. "Not really."

"It was this kid in my History class. He made fun of Jonathan falling. It made me so angry!" His eyes fell. "I didn't like the blood, though. It made me feel sick."

Daniel recalled when he got so angry he kicked the door to the bunk room. He was Jack's age, and big as he was now. The door's hinges broke. When he left three years later, they still hadn't replaced it.

Remorse flooded through him. That whole room of boys had suffered cold and lack of privacy because of his anger. He couldn't remember what he'd been so angry about. "Remember that feeling, the next time you get angry."

Jack nodded in all seriousness, eyes wide.

Daniel placed the shirt on its hanger, hung it upon a hook, and began to button it. "The way I see it, whatever you do affects other people. Whether the effect is for good or for ill is up to you."

Companion

When Daniel had finished his work each day, Jack would bring Daniel out to the stables. Jack loved horses, riding fearlessly with saddle or without. Over time, Daniel learned to ride with a saddle, but never quite felt safe about it.

In the evenings, Daniel would read. Soon it felt right and normal to sit with Jack as they read. Jack sat a bit closer each night, eventually sitting directly beside Daniel as they read the books together, discussing various details of each.

Baraja sent word that she'd received the money. On his next payday, Daniel found the book she'd read to him at a bookstore in the merchants' area.

Each night, alone in bed, he read from Baraja's book, remembering the way she looked as she read it to him. When the book ended, he felt such loss, such longing for her, that he lay hugging the book and wept.

The young Masters turned fourteen, with a grand party to celebrate. Jonathan let Daniel dress him that time.

Of course, the servants weren't invited. Daniel spent the time helping the kitchen staff move pans about and fix platters of food to go upstairs. He had to be cautious: Garrett always tried to trip him. He'd never say why, even when Daniel asked.

The Cook was cross the whole time, hitting the kitchen maids with a wooden spoon when they annoyed her. The whole affair was hot and noisy, and by the end of it, Daniel felt exhausted. But afterward, there was leftover cake and tea in the staff room, with bright ribbons adorning the chairs.

The next evening, after dinner, a knock came to Jonathan's door.

Daniel, who sat reading to Jack, jumped up and went towards the door between the boys' rooms, book in hand.

"I want to take you out somewhere," a deep voice said.

Daniel thought it might be the boys' father, so he stood still.

"Okay," Jonathan said.

Daniel knocked. "Do you need me to dress you, sir?"

Footsteps came towards Daniel, and the door suddenly opened. Alarmed, Daniel took a step back.

Julius Diamond snapped, "Why are you in here?"

Daniel raised the book."Reading to Master Jack, sir."

Mr. Julius glared at it. "Very well." He glanced back at Jonathan, who had his trousers on and was putting on his shoes. "You won't be needed."

Daniel bowed and returned to stand at the end of Jack's bed. He opened the book. "Let me find the place, sir."

Julius Diamond still stood in the doorway, but at Daniel's glance, closed the door with a click.

Jack said, "Where do you think they're going?"

Daniel shrugged. "Your father didn't say."

"Would you sit with me again?"

Daniel glanced at the door, fearful of Mr. Julius returning. "Not tonight, sir."

The next morning, Jonathan seemed subdued, quiet.

"I hope your evening was pleasant, sir," Daniel said.

Jonathan looked up from where he sat. "I don't feel like a man."

Daniel blinked, unsure what Jonathan meant. "Your cards hold a manly form."

Jonathan let out a laugh. "That's not what I meant. My father said this would make a man of me. What I did." He peered at his toast. "I don't feel any different."

Daniel laid Jonathan's jacket on the bed. "What did you do?"

Jonathan blushed. "Um —"

So Mr. Hook had passed the message along. Why did it take so long for them to act? "They found you a Companion, didn't they?"

Jonathan nodded.

Daniel recalled his first night with Baraja. "Do you love her?"

The boy shrugged. "I don't know what to feel." Then he looked up at Daniel, face full of alarm. "What if I gave her the fever? I don't want anyone to have the sickness I have."

"I don't know, sir." Daniel hadn't even considered such things. "I don't think your father would have brought you there if you could spread contagion!"

The boy seemed relieved.

Daniel felt grateful the boy had softened towards him. "Come, Master Jonathan, it's time for your bath."

***

That night, Daniel went to Master Jack's room, laid out the boy's clothes. He never needed to ask anymore: Jack always allowed himself to be dressed. He undid the boy's buttons, took off his shirt and undershirt.

Normally — well, as far as his teacher said, anyway — men undid their own trousers. Jack, on the other hand, never raised a finger, just stood there, eyes shut, until time to step out of them. His belt was often so tight it took a while to get it undone.

It was clear the boy imagined other things.

This at first disturbed Daniel, then he remembered what he was like at that age. *Some girl he's enamored with.* As he held the pajama bottoms for the boy to step into, the thought amused him. Flannel shirt on, then buttoned, and a tuck into bed.

Daniel asked, "Which book tonight, sir?"

"Would you sit with me?" Jack pushed off the covers, sat on the edge of the bed.

Daniel sat beside the boy. "Does something trouble you?"

Jack shrugged, glancing away.

"Whatever troubles you, I'd be glad to help."

The boy's eyes were huge. "Have you ever loved someone?"

Daniel nodded, picturing Baraja.

"Did they love you in return?"

Daniel considered this: what she'd said, what she'd written, the fact that she chose to carry their child. "I think so."

Jack let out a breath. "I love someone."

Daniel smiled to himself. "Does that trouble you?"

"Only if they don't love me in return."

Daniel remembered never being allowed near the girls. Sometimes it felt excruciating. "Is it someone you know well?"

Jack shrugged. "Well enough."

Could he advise a gentleman in this regard? "You are the gentleman, so you must make the first move in this matter." Daniel turned away, feeling unsure of himself. "Perhaps your father could arrange an introduction?"

He turned towards Jack, who kissed him full on the lips.

Daniel felt complete surprise. Then everything which had happened since he arrived fell into place. Jack Diamond was enamored with him!

Jack's hands caressed Daniel's face, his head, his shoulders.

What could he do? This was his master. Jack could command him to do anything, even throw himself from the roof, and he'd be obliged to do so.

Jack pulled away softly, gazed into Daniel's eyes, and smiled at him with such tenderness that Daniel didn't know what to say.

Daniel's heart raced. What should he do? He took a deep breath, then held the boy's hands in his, hoping some course of action would come to him.

"Do you love me, Daniel?"

A great fondness and pity came over him for this child. It seemed the boy had no one. And he decided to speak the words. For in one way, they were true. "I do."

To Daniel's utter surprise, Jack pulled him atop him. At first he laughed, thinking the boy meant to wrestle. But then Jack held him tightly, his back arching, his hands pressing on the small of Daniel's back. The boy's body was rigid — had no one taught him what to do?

Daniel froze, mind racing. If he pulled away, it could ruin his chances here forever. These people didn't fully trust him as it was;

he needed Jack's favor. To strike Jack, push him away ... it could mean death.

Maybe he could make the boy see reason. "Jack —"

Jack only pulled him closer, eyes closed.

To Daniel's horror, his own body began to respond to the pressure. "Please, Jack —"

But Jack seemed to pay him no mind.

Daniel tried to pull away. "Jack, please, we need to —"

Jack pulled Daniel so furiously hard that the jolt of physical pleasure pushed the air out of him.

Daniel lay atop Jack, gasping for breath as the boy held him tight, pushing, pushing up onto him.

Then Jack became more urgent, his hands on Daniel's buttocks pressing, pressing Daniel's hips onto his, until with a cry, the inevitable happened. "Oh, gods, I love you," Jack panted, his face covered with sweat.

Daniel felt sick, angry, and his eyes stung. *What do I do?*

Daniel gritted his teeth. He must not react. *This is a child. He has no one to guide him. He deserves not my anger, but my pity.*

Bit by bit, he got his emotions under control, calmed his rage and humiliation.

The pressure in his groin felt unbearable. It had been so long since Baraja; his body desperately wanted more.

He raised himself on one elbow, avoiding even the touch of clothing upon his skin, trying to keep his voice from shaking too badly. "Do you feel better now?"

Jack smiled up at him in the moonlight. "Ever so much."

You must do your duty. Daniel turned away and stood. "I must get you into some clean clothes now."

Jack collapsed into the pillows, eyes closed, panting. "I don't think I have the strength for it."

"Just rest; I'll be back." Daniel went into Jack's closets, heart pounding, and leaned his head back against a wall.

Did Jack think they were lovers? How could he possibly retreat from this without hurting the boy, or worse, drawing his ire — or that of his family?

Oh, gods. Daniel went weak. *His family.*

They'd be horrified! This was their Heir. A younger Heir, to be sure, but if they thought he'd turned their child into a man-lover ...

Hands shaking so badly he could hardly grasp the clothing, he retrieved a new set of pajamas, helped the exhausted boy into them. Then he covered Jack and kissed his forehead.

The boy had a smile on his face as Daniel went to his bed.

Daniel bathed, changed into his nightclothes, lay in his room.

But he didn't sleep. He'd never been so frightened in his life.

Trouble

The next day, Daniel searched out Swan. Once they were far in the gardens, where no one might hear, he told Swan what happened.

"You wouldn't be the first manservant who's ended up as a bed maid. Did he hurt you?"

Daniel shook his head. Then he shrugged.

Swan stood quiet for a moment. "Was it agreeable, at any rate?"

Daniel re-lived the night's events. What could he possibly say? "I prefer women."

"Don't worry; all will be well," Swan said. Then he chuckled. "We might be able to use this." His manner became more animated. "The boy's just lonely. Tell him whatever he wants to hear. I'll suggest his father start taking him along on his business trips. This time next year, he'll be besotted with some girl. If you play your cards right, you'll become his most trusted adviser."

Daniel hesitated. "It just seems so dishonest."

"Well, you gotta do what you gotta do. Most of this job is helping the uppers feel good about themselves." He grinned, clapped Daniel on the shoulder. "You did the right thing."

But it didn't feel that way.

As Swan hurried off, Daniel stood in the garden, his hand on a tree, and watched little Flannery far off past the gardens, playing fetch with the dogs.

Was this what Baraja had to endure? Even now, she lay with some man she didn't love. The thought felt crushing.

That night, Daniel told Jack, "We have to be careful. If someone hears, I'll be whipped, or perhaps killed."

Jack gaped at Daniel, horrified.

"So we must be very, very quiet. It would be better to only do what we did when Jonathan's away."

The next time Mr. Diamond's men took Jonathan on their nighttime outing, Daniel had an idea. "Even though we can't lie together every night, I can show you what to do to help yourself in the meantime."

That turned out to be a mistake: Jack insisted Daniel demonstrate on him, and Jack insisted on reciprocating.

Daniel had fooled around with the other boys at night once or twice when he was younger than Jack — they all did. And he recalled a time where a boy played pranks on the others, his hand under their covers as they slept to see them react. The man who came to beat that boy sat them all down afterward. "Don't let this fret you none. Anyone's gonna stand up if touched enough."

But it all seemed so serious to Jack, as if the boy was starved for attention, willing to do anything to feel loved.

Soon Daniel began to dread the nights Jonathan was away. Each time, he tried to get the whole thing over with as soon as possible. And it seemed to work: Jack was much too focused on his own pleasure to notice once his needs were satisfied.

After getting Jack into bed, he'd think of Baraja, her beautiful body, how it felt to be inside her. Soon he was able to sleep as well.

***

As time passed, Daniel began learning the names of the other servants, the ones who weren't often inside. The head driver there for Diamond Manor was an older man, a Mr. Talon Tolo Stock.

He liked being called Tolo, but Mr. Hook insisted on calling the man Mr. Stock. "I don't hold to that African nonsense," Mr. Hook said. "Have a dozen names and all. Too much bother for my taste."

He snorted in derision, but then spoke to Daniel as one man of substance might to another. "All about the past, these Diamonds are. My wife's the same way."

Daniel didn't know what to say, so he merely nodded.

"I say it's best look to the future, don't you?"

It seemed Mr. Hook had decided opinions about everyone there, with no qualms about sharing them. Master Écarté had warned them not to get into any of the many factions that tended to form in large households. So Daniel was intentionally noncommittal about most of what the man said.

Siziba tended the Manor's dozen horses. He'd sit out in the garden smoking a pipe the days the uppers were away, smiling at Daniel and Flannery as they played ball with the dogs.

Apparently, he did so in secret, because after the first time, he came up and said to Daniel, "Now, the Old Master don't go with smoking or drinking. So let's keep this between us, eh?"

Daniel shrugged. It seemed no concern of his what the man did on his day off. "Of course."

After that, Siziba was all smiles.

Shortly after, Siziba and Tolo took Daniel to The Twenty-Eight, a tavern upon Market Center. Daniel didn't like any of the drinks, but he really enjoyed the food there. "We should come here again."

At that, Tolo laughed. "Sure, if you're paying."

They all laughed. And as the days passed, Daniel began to feel as if he had actual friends there.

But try as he might, there were several who would hardly speak to him. Whenever he saw Daniel outside, the old groundsman, Mr. Vukay, would glare at him, spitting on the ground. Daniel had to take care when getting into a carriage, as the young footman, Garrett, would try to trip him, or close the door on his hand. And a few of the older maids cast suspicious glances his way whenever he passed by.

After one such instance, he sat out with Siziba watching Flannery throw a ball to the dogs.

"Something troubling you, lad?"

Daniel shrugged. "There's people here that don't like me. I don't understand why: I've never done a thing to them."

Siziba chuckled, leaning back, and tapped his pipe on the arm of his chair. "You'll never be anywhere that **everyone** likes you."

"But Mr. Neuberg says people might think I'm a Spadros spy, I guess from how I look. But I've never even been to Spadros."

He felt discouraged. How might he prove to these people that he was trustworthy?

"Heh," Siziba said. "I know the ones you mean. Some of them hate anyone who's an outsider. Could be the Blessed Floorman in the flesh and they'd hate him, if he wasn't from here. Older folks especially. They've seen too many captured by the Spadros Family over the years and never seen again, I suppose. The others, well, they're just jealous you got put in over them."

"Oh." Now it made more sense, especially for Garrett, who might actually have been in line for the position.

"Just go about your work, my boy. They'll get over it."

***

As summer progressed, Mr. Julius began taking Jack out during the day on trips of his own. The minute Jack returned, he'd rush in — wherever Daniel might be — and tell him everything. Bit by bit, Daniel began to learn about the city.

"The streets in Hart quadrant are red!"

Daniel couldn't picture it. "What sort of red?"

"Made of bricks."

"Oh." That day, he'd been shining Jack's brown wingtips. "Do they use mortar, or —?"

"No, the bricks are laid right next to each other. Very smooth, too — it's rather impressive."

"Must have taken a lot of work."

"Indeed. And all the buildings are brick, or white stone. They use white siding, but it's a painted white. And silver everywhere!"

"Silver wood? Like here?"

"No, metal. It looks like polished steel, most places, although there's some chromium-plating on the older buildings near the Pot. A pity the CCC doesn't allow it anymore."

"Did your grandfather go with you this time?"

"Yes! However did you know?"

Daniel smiled to himself. "Just a guess. What's the CCC?"

"The stupid Cultural Correctness Committee. Everything here has to pass their inspection."

Daniel nodded, not understanding. He wiped down the shoe he'd been buffing and picked up the other. "Why'd Mr. Hector go with you this time?"

Jack shrugged. "Negotiations of some kind. I don't know. It was boring. All the men went into this one room and left me in the hallway. There was nothing to do and just this little girl there. She was five or six." He leaned back. "Her nurse was there too, of course. Tedious old woman."

"What did you play?"

"I didn't play anything. The girl had dolls with her." He rolled his eyes. "I don't know why Father made me go along."

"How come Master Jonathan didn't go too?"

"I don't know." Jack fell silent, and whatever his thoughts were, they seemed to dishearten him. "I can't remember the last time my father even spoke to him."

Whatever was going on between Mr. Julius and his son, Jonathan was taken for an evening outing by his men twice weekly like clockwork.

Yet instead of this encouraging the boy, Jonathan seemed only more withdrawn. He stopped writing, and lay on his bed or sat at his desk, staring out of the window.

Living and working in such proximity, Daniel heard much. Jonathan's tutor, Mr. Clay, scolded the boy for not completing his schoolwork. His nurse Miss Kaluki left the room in tears after Jonathan slapped the glass with his tonic from her hand.

His father called for him then; Jonathan sat gingerly afterward. The other servants whispered that Jonathan had been caned.

"Not right to beat a boy who's dying." The old housekeeper Mrs. Whist shook her head. "Not right at all."

Daniel had begun laying a towel on Jack's bed the nights Jonathan left. He stopped dressing Jack for bed unless asked, which saved washing two sets of bedclothes.

Every night he got to sleep well after midnight and had to get up before the sun.

Late one night, a knock came at the door. Bleary-eyed, Daniel stumbled into some trousers and answered it.

Swan stood there. "Get dressed."

"Is something wrong?"

"Master Jonathan's not in his room."

Gone

The sky was barely beginning to pale. "How do you know?"

"Anton patrols the halls at night to guard the Little Masters. Said he felt uneasy, so he checked the room."

Daniel began putting on his shirt, his belt, his shoes. "I thought you took Master Jonathan out last night."

"No," Swan said. "He's gone out on his own. And he's not at the brothel. I've called for more men to search for him."

Daniel grabbed his cap from its hook on the wall. They still had a few hours before Jack woke.

Swan seemed to be thinking along the same lines. "If we can get him back before breakfast, we might be able to keep his parents from knowing." He let out a breath. "I had to help drag young Hector out of a situation or two back in the day."

The Inventor? The man was near seventy.

How old **was** Swan?

He certainly seemed spry enough — Daniel had trouble keeping up with him.

The blue glow was gone from the fencing and the air felt chill. They hurried to one of several waiting carriages, not a footman to be seen, and set off.

The carriage was full of men Daniel didn't know. He glanced out of the window. "Where are we going?"

"Diamond Pot," Swan said.

He had no idea what that meant.

"Didn't they tell you anything before you came here?"

Daniel's cheeks burned. "That the city's split between the Four Families ..."

The other men in the carriage glanced at each other.

"Well," Swan said, "it didn't use to be. You know the four rivers, right? So there are the four quadrants, and the island in the center. The city used to just cover the tips of each quadrant. Then there was a big war, way before I was born," he let out an amused chuckle, "and all that got ruined. They call it the Pot now."

"Why do they call it that?"

"Hell if I know," Swan said. "Anyway, that's where the brothels are. If the little Master's run off, we'll likely find him there."

"Seems like you do everything here," Daniel said.

The other men exchanged amused glances.

Swan grinned. "Not me. But I make sure it all gets done."

For a while, Daniel considered that. Swan seemed a powerful man. But he was a servant, too. "How'd you get to do all this?"

"Thinking ahead, are we? Sorry to say, you're no Diamond-born. But if you serve well, you might get sworn in."

Daniel had no idea what that meant.

"Ah," Swan said, "don't worry about that — you'll likely find out sooner or later. To answer the question, my Grandpa was first cousin to Mr. Hector's Grandpa. But since my Grandpa was born 'under the table,' as you might say, we don't get the benefits."

Daniel struggled to understand. "You were an orphan?"

"Naw, nothing like that. But it was pretty rough and tumble back then. Only way to survive was for the clans to stick together."

"The clans?"

"The Diamond clans, boy! What you think I'm talking about?"

All Daniel could do was stare at the man, mouth open.

Swan leaned forward, elbows on his knees. "Forty-two clans come here from the diamond mines in southern Africa back in the 1500s. You know where Africa is?"

Daniel shook his head.

"Don't matter. What matters is that if you ain't born into one of them forty-two clans, you ain't Diamond-born, I don't care what you look like or where you live."

"Born? So what if you marry in?"

"If you're a man, you can be sworn in. Diamond men don't tend to marry out. Not that it never happens — Mrs. Rachel's grandfather was one of those —"

The man sitting next to Daniel nodded.

"— but it don't happen often. Then their kids are born Diamonds. Like the little house-boy."

Flannery. No wonder he'd mentioned it, back when they first met. "Do I need to learn these clans?"

"Naw, don't matter, really," Swan said.

Daniel looked at the other men, who merely shrugged.

There was so much he didn't know.

We've taught you everything you need to know.

Maybe he didn't need to know the history of the city, or the names of the Diamond clans, or the things he didn't even know enough to ask Swan about. But he wanted to.

Maybe he could ask Jack about it! For a moment this excited him, but then his teacher's words came to him:

Don't be inquisitive. Servants are not to bring notice to themselves, either by word or deed.

If he asked Jack, then the boy would become fixated on finding the answers. His tutor Master Toran would surely want to know why, and that would bring attention back to ... him.

Daniel leaned on the door. He never imagined this job would be so difficult.

After some time, Swan gestured at the window. "That there's the Pot."

Daniel was appalled by what he saw. Thin, dirty children asleep in stairwells, living in the worst filth. Tired girls his age hanging laundry in the early dawn with hollow eyes. Old men in tattered clothing standing around burning piles of trash. Women — some heavy with child — giving him looks which made his cheeks burn.

What kind of place was this?

"Don't fret about them," Swan said. "These folk'll kill you for your clothes." He clapped Daniel on the arm. "Keep your wits about you. We gotta hope Master Jonathan's still living."

Daniel gaped at Swan. "They'd kill a boy for his **clothing**?"

Swan snorted. "Hardly a boy if he's running off to brothels, now, is he?" He gestured with his chin as the carriage came to a stop. "Let's see if he's at this one."

They found him at the fifth place they visited, lying in a clump of three women and two men, a bowl of white powder and several empty liquor bottles beside them.

Daniel stood horrified at the scene. But Swan strode forward, leaning down to grab Jonathan's arm. "Come now, young Master, we needs be getting home."

Jonathan's eyes were bloodshot, dazed. "What?"

"Oh, Master Jonathan," Daniel said. "What have you done?"

"Grab his feet," Swan said. "Let's get him into the carriage."

After they bundled the boy inside, Daniel said, "What was that stuff? That powder?"

Swan scoffed. "Party Time." He shook his head. "It's a drug. We make some to sell, but mostly because all the other Families do. But most of our cash we make other ways." He gave Jonathan a dismissive gesture. "Nothing good's gonna come of this."

By the time they returned, the sun peeked above the trees. Daniel and Swan got Jonathan into pajamas and in bed. They turned to find Jack standing in the doorway. "What's wrong?"

"Your brother's sick," Daniel said, going to Jack's side. He put an arm around the boy's shoulders. "But all will be well. Did they bring your tray yet?"

Jack shook his head as they went into his room. Then he yawned. "Too early."

Daniel lifted Jack's covers; Jack slid into bed. "Just rest, then."

Jack got up at his usual time. Jonathan slept much of the day, then he lay there moaning.

Daniel called for Swan. "What's wrong with him?"

"Hung over, most likely," Swan said.

Daniel had no idea what Swan meant.

"Alcohol addles your brain, makes you sick the day after. You never been drunk before?"

Daniel shook his head.

"Don't bother: it's not worth it." Swan let out a laugh. "Specially if you're in charge of men." He tapped his right temple. "Gotta keep your mind sharp. Drugs is even worse." He shook his head. "You there, young Master, let this be a lesson."

Jonathan moaned, covering his head with his pillow.

For a few days, Jonathan seemed as he had when Daniel first arrived, withdrawn, scribbling in his notebooks, speaking little. And his father's men continued to take him out as always.

But soon there was another rap on the door in the middle of the night: Jonathan had disappeared.

Daniel felt astonished. "How'd he get out? Is there no guard?"

"Most of the trellises on the front there are wood. They can barely hold the weight of the roses. They talked me into putting in steel underneath the trellises to their windows, though, in case of fire." Swan looked abashed. "Probably climbed out."

"Good gods." Daniel felt more than a bit annoyed. "Very well, I'm coming."

They found Jonathan in yet another brothel, with much the same scene as before. Swan grabbed a pitcher of stale beer and threw it in Jonathan's face. The men and women who lay around him shrieked when the cold wetness hit them. "Get up," Swan said to Jonathan. "I'll not carry you again."

Jonathan sat up, eyes bloodshot, wet and cursing, and let them lead him to the carriage.

"Get the horse blanket," Swan said.

The men wrapped Jonathan in it and set him shivering upon the bench seat, the stench of stale beer filling the carriage. But Swan wasn't done yet. "You're going to pay these men for getting from their beds in the midst of night to find you. And you'll pay to have this carriage and that blanket cleaned as well."

Outrage filled Jonathan's face. "**You** threw the beer at me!"

"Had to get you up somehow — I'm getting too old to carry men about."

"No one asked you to come get me."

Swan leaned forward and pointed at him. "If you think I'd let your father suffer the shame of going into the Pot, you have another thing coming."

Jonathan recoiled. "Why did you bring me there, then? You treat me as if I'm nothing!"

Daniel and Swan exchanged a glance. "Your father thought only to ease your burden," Daniel said. "The place he brought you to was well-chosen. These others," without meaning to, he grimaced, "they sicken me."

"Well, I like them. They don't care who I am. No one treats me like some invalid child."

"You wanna be treated as a man," Swan said, "act like one."

Jonathan apparently had nothing to say to that: he lay curled up on the bench seat, eyes closed.

That afternoon, Jonathan's manservant arrived, an elderly olive-skinned man named Mr. Escoba Bastra. Daniel and Swan met with the man in his rooms as Jonathan lay sleeping.

Mr. Bastra shook Daniel's hand as one gentleman would to another. "Very nice to meet you, sir."

He still wore all-black mourning garb, having come from service to one of Mr. Hector's cousins, who'd recently died. And he'd known of Master Écarté. "Reputation only, of course," he said. "But very well thought-of indeed. You're a lucky young man."

"Mr. Bastra here is Diamond-sworn," Swan said. "So you can speak about any concerns you may have with his young master."

Despite his age, Mr. Bastra seemed agile and spry, climbing the polished dark wooden ladder to examine Jonathan's caps without hesitation. Once they toured Jonathan's closets, Daniel and Swan apprised Mr. Bastra of the situation.

"I've seen this before," Mr. Bastra said. "Perhaps if we find him some new entertainment?"

But Jonathan refused to speak to the man, and eventually became abusive. "I already have a manservant!"

So the matter turned into a group affair: Swan, Daniel, and Mr. Bastra all stood round the boy.

"Master Jonathan," Daniel said, "whilst I deeply appreciate your loyalty, you do me no service by it. You well know that the situation was only temporary. I shall always be ready to serve, sir, but Mr. Bastra is your manservant now. He's a fine servant, far more experienced and capable than I."

Jonathan pouted, refusing to allow Mr. Bastra to dress him. But at least he stopped throwing things at the man.

Yet the next few months were a nightmare. They locked the window; Jonathan snuck out past Jack, or Mr. Bastra, or even Daniel, as they lay sleeping. They put guards on all the doors; Jonathan broke the window and went out. They changed the codes for the security field; Jonathan managed to trick the code from a stable-hand and escape yet again.

The only good thing in all this turmoil was a letter from Baraja: she'd given birth to their daughter. "I have named her Hermosa," she wrote, "because she is beautiful, like you."

An oval portrait which fit in his palm lay there with the letter: Baraja, holding a baby. Daniel's vision blurred when he saw them.

A noise from Jack's room. Startled, Daniel hid the letter and portrait behind one of his books.

I'm a father, Daniel thought. *I'm a father!* He wanted to shout it to the world. Yet no one could know.

He wished so desperately that he could be with Baraja and his little girl. How cruel it was to be sold away from those you loved!

The next time he was paid, Daniel spent his whole packet to buy a glassed-in frame for the little portrait. And at night, before he slept, he held it in the candlelight, kissed Baraja's face.

You are my Beauty, he'd whisper, then hide it away safe, to dream of being with her and their child. And he could almost hear her say in reply: *As you are mine.*

Changes

Strangely enough, it wasn't until the tenth time they'd had to fetch Jonathan from a brothel — and that in broad daylight — that the boy's father noticed. Jonathan was brought to his father and grandfather, still drunk. When he returned, he seemed chastened.

"This is no good," Daniel said to Swan. "If so much alcohol addles your brain, what does it do to the rest? I fear for his health."

"I've seen this before: he's past caring." Swan patted Daniel's shoulder. "The little Master's dying, son. Focus on your work. Let him have his pleasures as he can."

Jack and Gardena seemed frightened by the changes in their brother. Gardena, now twelve, drew Jonathan pictures every day, bringing him flowers from the garden until he threw them at her, vase and all.

He then locked the doors and refused to let her into his room. So she slid the pictures under the door, where they lay until Mr. Bastra came in with his key. The pictures sat, untouched, in a large basket by the door.

Jack, on the other hand, hardly left Daniel's side. At any time in the day or night he might appear, asking to be held, or would slide into Daniel's bed at night.

After one such time, Daniel took it upon himself to lie. "Please, Jack. You mustn't come in here. The servants suspect!"

Jack drew back in alarm.

"Please. I beg you. Stay in your rooms. You know I'll come to you when it's safe."

"I'm sorry," Jack said. "I — I just don't know what to do."

"Yes, you do."

"I don't mean that. Jon's trying to die. I don't want him to."

Daniel sat up. "Have you told him that?"

Jack shook his head, dejected. "He won't talk to me anyway."

Daniel recalled all the writing Master Jonathan used to do. "Perhaps write him a letter. Tell him everything."

"So he can stick it in a basket?"

"You're his brother. His older brother —"

Jack snorted. "By a few minutes."

"Yes. But you're his brother. You have obligation to him." Daniel grabbed Jack's arms. "You love him. You know he loves you. Surely if he'd listen to anyone, it'd be you!"

Jack's face changed, as if he'd come to some realization. Then he stood. "You're right."

Daniel sat on the edge of his bed, alone in the moonlight. He'd given hope to Jack, but he felt trapped, hopeless. He might have given himself a reprieve, for tonight, but he desperately hoped Jack would become enamored with someone else soon. He wasn't sure how much more of this he could take.

Baraja, my love ... what do I do?

***

A few days later, Daniel stood in Jack's closets, dazed, wearily brushing Jack's trousers. He'd gotten little sleep the night prior: Jonathan had been out carousing again.

Daniel didn't know what to do or say to Jonathan anymore. Was the boy determined to die?

He'd spoken to Mr. Bastra. "Master Jonathan never speaks to me unless he must," the old man said. "And that rudely. I've tried to offer advice, but he will not take it."

The day before, the doctor had been to examine Jonathan, then asked to see his father. They were to have a meeting today between the three of them, and Jack had asked to be there.

Daniel had no idea what the meeting was to be about. Jack refused to speak of it, and had been withdrawn most of the day. Which was good, in that it allowed Daniel to finally get caught up in his work.

He felt ready to drop. If he had anywhere else to go, he would. But he didn't, and besides, they owned him. Daniel had no idea how much they'd paid for him, but it certainly was more than what he got each month in his packet.

He chuckled at that. It was enough to send letters to Baraja, and with them, money for her to care for their child. To save enough that their daughter one day might be free. And to go out with the other servants from time to time. That was all he cared about.

Raised voices came from Jonathan's room.

What could possibly be going on now? Daniel put down his brush and hurried into Jack's room.

The door to Jonathan's room stood open. A partially full bottle lay uncapped on the floor, liquor spilling from it. Mr. Bastra, Swan, Mr. Neuberg, and Jack pulled on Jonathan, who struggled fiercely, flinging Mr. Bastra onto the bed.

Daniel snapped, "Stop this, right now!"

Jonathan's eyes were red, his face flushed. He stared at Daniel, mouth open.

"How can you behave so? This is your brother! These men are sworn to your life!" Daniel pointed at Mr. Bastra. "Look how you treat your servant. This is wrong! Now stop this foolishness," he pointed at the door, "and go with them at once."

The other men gaped at Daniel.

Tears filled Jonathan's eyes. "I'm sorry." Shame crossed his face. "I'm sorry."

"Go with them then."

Jonathan went peacefully, Swan and Mr. Neuberg following.

Mr. Bastra, still lying on the bed, shook his head, face astonished. "Whatever got into you, boy, it was the right spirit."

Daniel picked up the bottle and set it on the table. "I'm sick of his behavior, the way his father ignores his children, and how we all suffer for it."

"You're tired," Mr. Bastra said quickly. "Let me see about Master Jack's clothing. You lie down."

Daniel stalked into his room, locked the doors, and slumped onto his bed, face in his hands. For some time, he shook with anger. When that passed, he felt exhausted, fighting tears of despair.

He couldn't go on like this any longer.

A hard knock at the door to the hall. "Daniel?" It was Swan.

"Yeah?"

"Mr. Julius wants to see you."

"What does **he** want?"

"I didn't ask. You want me to go ask?"

Daniel sighed. This wasn't Swan's fault. "No. I'm coming."

Swan and Daniel went down to the veranda outside the back of the mansion. When he stepped onto the veranda, the air was cold, and Daniel wished he'd brought his coat.

Around the table sat Jack, Jonathan, and the doctor. Mr. Julius stood looking at his sons. Mr. Neuberg stood facing away.

On the table lay a revolver.

Daniel gaped at the scene in horror. What had just happened?

Mr. Julius glanced at Daniel. "Ah, good, you're here. Jonathan, you may have your say."

Jonathan looked up at Daniel. "I'm sorry." His face fell, and he wiped his eyes with the back of his hand. "I've caused you all manner of trouble, and I'm sorry."

Daniel nodded, never taking his eyes from Jonathan's. "May I speak plainly, sir?"

Jonathan nodded.

He would get one chance. "I know the doctors told you that you would die." Daniel leaned forward, putting one hand on the back of Jonathan's chair, the other on the table. "But we all die! Suppose you died tonight. Is this really how you want to be remembered? Is this how you wish to meet the Shuffler? Your cards covered with shame and disgrace?"

Jonathan looked down, shaking his head.

"I am nothing. I was born an orphan and will die a servant. But the only reason I'm here today is that I want to live. Look at me, Master Jonathan."

Jonathan raised red eyes, full of tears.

"Do you want to live?"

Tears rolled down his cheeks. "I d-do. I w-want to l-live." He folded his arms on the table and rested his forehead on them, sobbing.

Jack enfolded his brother in a tender hug, resting his head upon Jonathan's back. "It'll be okay, Jonny. We're here to help you. We love you."

It was only then that Daniel dared look at Mr. Julius. The man gazed at his sons, his hands in his pockets, and from his expression, it wasn't clear whether he approved of the scene or not.

He glanced at Daniel and nodded. "The doctor will tell you what needs doing." With that, Julius Diamond strode into the house and was gone.

Familiar

The doctor stood. "You're in a bad way, Master Jonathan. To be so heavily into drink and Party Time at such a young age — well, it may take a while to clear you of it." He leaned forward. "But you must never drink again."

Jonathan drew back, his face alarmed. "How can you say that?"

"I've seen this before — if you should drink, or use Party Time even once, it could cause a relapse. And you're already so ill. If you truly do want to live, your body must have every advantage."

Jonathan nodded, face sober and concerned. "I want to live. I never thought I would before." He looked up at the doctor. "How long do you think I have?"

The man shrugged. "Never heard of anyone living **this** long. Most of those who had the fever as bad as you did are dead now." He patted Jonathan on the shoulder, his eyes moist. "The gods have given you a gift, my boy. Take it."

Jonathan's face changed, his gaze turning inward. "I shall, sir."

Jonathan was put to bed. Jack, Mr. Bastra, Jonathan's nurse Miss Kaluki, and Daniel took turns watching for epileptic fits as they weaned him from the alcohol.

Jack sat with his brother from four in the afternoon until ten at night. Miss Kaluki sat with Jon from ten at night until four in the morning. Mr. Bastra sat with Jon from four to ten. Daniel stayed with Jonathan from ten in the morning until Jack arrived at four.

Since Jonathan and his father gave permission for Daniel to sit during this time, he'd often bring his mending, or a pair of shoes to polish, and work sitting beside him.

The doctor took up a guest room, staying there a week. He'd come in every few hours to listen to the boy's heart, feel his pulse, listen to him breathe.

Along with his usual medications, Jonathan received tonics to help him rest and to clear the damage he'd done to himself. He took these stoically, with resignation.

At first, Jonathan said nothing to Daniel, lying with his face to the wall. As time passed, the need for sleep seemed to leave the boy, and he'd lie on his back, gazing at the ceiling. One day, after many hours of silence, Jonathan said, "What do you think a man should do with his life?"

Daniel felt perplexed by the question. "I'm not sure it's my place to say, sir."

Jonathan laughed, rolling over to face him. He slid his arm under his pillow where his head lay. "I didn't ask if it was your place. I want to know what you think."

"Well, then," Daniel said, feeling uneasy, "I think it depends on where a man finds himself."

"You mean like the hand he's dealt?"

"Yes," Daniel said, now feeling on surer ground. "You're a Diamond Heir. I'm your brother's manservant." He struggled to work through what he wanted to say. "The Dealer gave us such different cards that we don't even sit at the same table." He thought about his life back at the Home. "But we've both been children. And when you go from a child to a man, things change. What you do, what you're allowed to do, it changes. One day, you're in a safe routine, the next day, you might be in a new situation. Where you don't know what to do, what you even should do." He hesitated, not sure of the right words. "You must decide what kind of man you'll be. Before that. What you want from life. Once you do, then your choices become easier."

Jonathan nodded slowly.

"Every day the gods give you knowledge and training." Daniel put down his mending, turned to Jonathan. "Learn all you can, from everyone you can. There's nothing too small but you might be able to use it to play your part."

"What **is** my part, though?"

Daniel chuckled. "I'm sure your father can tell you more of that than I."

"I mean, I'm going to die." Jonathan seemed to stare into nothingness. "I don't know what it means. I don't know what I should do."

Daniel shrugged. "Are you dead today?"

A giggle burst from the boy. "No."

"So what if you **don't** die today? What can you do to make your life better today? To make life better for people you love, today?"

Jonathan sat up in bed, swinging his legs over the side, and stared at Daniel, mouth open. "A noble thought!" His face fell. "Oh, Daniel, I've been such a fool."

"Master Jonathan, as long as you have life in you, you can change things."

Jonathan nodded. Then he turned to the rope to the call bell beside his bed and pulled it. "Fetch that basket of Gardena's."

Daniel brought the basket over. It was a large basket, overflowing with drawings from more than a year.

Jonathan sat looking at it, eyes red. A knock came at the door: Penny, one of the older maids. She gave Daniel a suspicious glance, then said to Jonathan, "You need something, sir?"

"Ask my sister to attend me."

The maid disappeared behind the door.

Jonathan knelt beside the basket, taking the drawing out one by one. He put them into piles on his bed, arranging them by subject. The drawings became simpler and more heartfelt in their sentiments the farther back he went: *I love you, Jonnie. Please don't die. I want you to be happy.*

By the time he reached the bottom, tears streamed down his face. He put his head on the edge of the bed, whispering, "I've been such a fool."

Another knock, and Daniel offered Jonathan his handkerchief.

Jonathan quickly wiped his face, cleared his throat. "Come in."

Gardena came in hesitantly, closing the door behind her and leaning on it. "You want to see me?" She glanced at the bed, full with piles of her drawings, then at the empty basket.

Jonathan opened his arms. "Come here."

Gardena ran to him and began to cry, a big, sobbing cry as her arms went round her brother's neck.

Jonathan turned his face towards Daniel, mouthing: *thank you.*

After a while, Gardena stopped crying. Daniel found one of Jonathan's handkerchiefs and handed it to him.

Jonathan pushed aside the piles of drawings, set her on his bed, and sat beside her. "Here," he said, wiping the girl's face. "Now blow your nose properly."

Gardena giggled and did so.

"You've gotten good at drawing," Jonathan said, taking up one of the piles of paper. "And your writing is much improved."

Gardena shrugged, and sniffled a bit.

"It's true." He turned to Daniel. "Don't you think so?"

"Most definitely."

Gardena smiled at Daniel, blushing. "Thank you."

Jonathan turned to her. "I'm sorry for being so mean to you." He glanced aside, bit his lip for a moment. "I don't know why I was like that. I just felt angry at everything." He looked at her then. "But not you, not really. You didn't do anything wrong. It wasn't your fault." He spoke bitterly. "I was just being mean and stupid." His face fell, his shoulders drooped. "I'm sorry."

Gardena put her little hand in his. "It's okay, Jon. I just want you to get better."

Jonathan nodded. "I'll try to. I want to get better. I really do."

She hugged him around his waist, her face lying on his chest, and after an instant, Jonathan's arms went round her too.

Daniel sat quietly, just watching them.

"Hey, Dena," Jonathan said, "want to make a book of your pictures? We can bind these like a real book!"

Gardena's face went "oh." She clapped her hands. "Could we?"

"We can," Jonathan said. "If you'll sit by me, Daniel can fetch what we need. Or we can send for the maid."

Gardena glanced at Daniel. "Send for the maid."

So they did.

The next few weeks were filled with discussion on how to arrange the pictures, then in binding. They filled twelve books altogether, arranged by topic, from early to later drawings. Some they bound in bark (for tree pictures), others bound in thin-sliced wood and cloth, others in wood covered in cast-off bits of leather.

Daniel made sure to clean their mess before Jack arrived, so as not to leave it for Miss Kaluki to do. After a few days, Gardena asked to help, and so Jonathan did as well.

One day as Daniel, Jonathan, and Gardena scrabbled on the floor for bits of bark, Daniel thought: *What would their parents think of this?*

"What are you doing?" Jack stood in the doorway.

"Cleaning the floor," Gardena said.

"We should get the suction cleaner," Jack said. "For the tiny bits. It's faster." He dashed out, then back. "I called for a maid."

Cora came in. "Yes, sirs? Little miss?"

"The suction cleaner, if you please," Jack said.

"I'll do the floor," Daniel hastened to add. "But if you might bring the device?"

Cora glanced at the floor, then Daniel, then at Jack, then curtsied. "At once, sir."

Jack sat on the bed beside Gardena and told the entire story of the tooth powder incident as Daniel cleaned the floor. "Daniel likes me in white," Jack said, "he said so."

Daniel smiled to himself. "It's true." He turned off the device and moved it off to one side. "I'll bring this down."

Jack and Gardena said at the same time, "Must you go?"

"Well," Daniel said, "yes, I must. I have work to do."

Jonathan grinned at them. "Let him do his work. But if you wouldn't tussle about so, Jack, he'd have less work to do." He pointed at the scuffs on Jack's shoes. "Look at that!"

Jack looked chagrined. "I never considered it."

"Well," Jonathan said, "you should. You should think about others and not just yourself."

Daniel felt surprised at this. "Please don't argue on my account." He picked up the suction cleaner.

Jack said, "Can I help bring it down?"

"You must watch over your brother," Daniel said. "But thank you for the offer."

"Can I help?" Gardena's face shone in anticipation.

"Well, Miss Gardena, if you like," Daniel said. "Come on then. You can gather the cord."

"Awwww," Jack whined.

Jonathan laughed. "What, am I no longer of interest? You'd rather clomp down the back stair with a dirty cord in your hand than sit with me?"

"It's not that —"

Daniel and Gardena went out into the hall, shutting the door behind them as the two chattered on. They brought the cleaner down the hall outside Jack's room then turned right, going down the hall past his room to the back stair. Daniel pushed the button to alert the staff that an upper was coming downstairs, and opened the door. "You sure you want to come down with me?"

"Oh, yes," Gardena said. "I've never gone down this way."

It was dimly lit, and a bit grimy, but Gardena didn't seem to mind. "I love how the stair goes round and round! This is the door to the ground floor?"

"It is," Daniel said. "But we must go down one more yet."

When they reached the bottom, Daniel opened the door for the girl and let her go first. One of the maids, Eliza, took the suction cleaner. "Thank you for bringing it down, sir," she said.

"Now that's done," Daniel said. "Would you like to go back up this way, or the other?"

Cora came rushing up. "There you are, little Miss! Your mother's sent for you."

Gardena turned to Daniel. "Thanks for showing me the stair!"

Daniel grinned at her. "My pleasure."

The girl gave him a shy smile, and Daniel chuckled.

Mr. Neuberg stood nearby. "You have a winning way about you, Daniel. But you must take care not to become familiar."

Daniel blinked. "Whatever do you mean?"

"That girl is not for you. More to the point, you're not for her. Whatever your intentions are, a high-born woman falling in love with a servant is a recipe for disaster."

"But she's a child!" Daniel felt perplexed. "Have I done something wrong?"

"You're Master Jack's manservant. That's all. You're not to be a young girl's nanny, nurse, or companion, and for good reason. Keep a proper distance, and all should go well. I trust we need say no more on the matter?"

Daniel felt chagrined. "Yes, sir."

Then he recalled how he was at twelve, the time he fancied one of the young women who monitored the girls at garden time. She barely noticed him, but any glance, any smile ... he'd felt heartbroken when she left to marry. "I understand now, sir."

"Very good."

So thereafter, Daniel spoke to Gardena as little as possible. It hurt him, as he felt sure she blamed herself somehow for his coolness towards her. But perhaps she'd been reprimanded as well.

Daniel still sat watch over Jon. But when Gardena arrived, he'd simply watch as Jonathan and Gardena made their books, and refused to let them help clean anymore.

Yuletide came. In Bridges, the holiday was celebrated for twenty-one days, each day with a party of some sort. And Jack had to be dressed properly for each one.

And as Yuletide came and went, Gardena's smiles and blushes towards him subsided, and the easy camaraderie between himself and Jonathan faded.

Jonathan never asked why Daniel had withdrawn, and Daniel never mentioned it. Once the making of books ended, they again sat silent.

"I recall you said to learn whatever I might," Jonathan said. "What might you teach me?"

"Me?" Daniel didn't know what to say. "I don't really know much. Other than," a laugh burst from him, "a lot about men's fashion in Bridges."

Jonathan nodded, and they sat silent.

"I do recall my teacher at the Academy," Daniel said. "Once one of the other students — Adam, I think it was — asked how he'd gathered his wealth. The Academy wasn't nearly as fine as this place in some ways, but —"

Jonathan nodded. "I recall my father speaking to one of his men, back when they were looking for someone to tend to Jack. They said it was the best."

For an instant, emotion filled Daniel at the mention of his school, the people there. He took a deep breath. "But what my teacher said was that he took what money he had and used it to buy property he might rent out. In order to gather more."

Daniel thought about this for a moment. He should ask Baraja to use the money he sent to do this same thing. Or if she wasn't allowed to, to do it in their child's name.

"That sounds wise," Jonathan said, nodding. "Thank you."

He wished he knew how much they'd paid for him. How much it would take before Baraja was free. But it'd draw attention to himself to inquire on the matter.

"You used to read to Jack every night," Jonathan said.

"He's here with you in the evenings now," Daniel said, not sure why Jonathan brought this up.

"But I hear you talking after that."

Daniel resolved to warn Jack of this. If Miss Kaluki should become curious and enter ... "I'm sorry to have disturbed you."

"No, it's not that. I don't mean to pry. I was just wondering about it."

Daniel smiled to himself. "He likes talking with me, I suppose."

Jonathan snorted. "Jack's a bully. The guy he stabbed used to be his friend. They were in this big group who'd go round tormenting people." Jonathan seemed downcast. "The real reason he stabbed the guy was that he was talking about **me** instead of someone else."

Daniel didn't know what to say, so he said nothing.

Jonathan sighed. "The worst part of this is that no one really wants to **talk** to me. I know you're only here because the doctor said so. Mr. Bastra won't talk to me about anything important. Gardena's little, and Jack — well, all he wants to talk about is you. Or about things I can't do anymore."

"I'm sorry to hear that, sir. But I'll talk to you. What would you like to talk about?"

For an instant, Daniel thought Jonathan would speak.

But then Jonathan said, "Nothing," in a dejected tone, turning his face away.

"Begging your pardon sir, but what you said isn't true. I've wanted to talk with you from the first day I arrived. Remember?"

Jonathan seemed to ponder this, then nodded. "I remember. I didn't like you being here."

Daniel nodded. "I understand."

"What did you read to Jack?"

"All sorts of things. He has lots of books, you know."

Jonathan nodded. "Perhaps he'll let me borrow some."

Should he offer? "I have one you might read." He glanced at the clock. "Jack should be here soon. Let me get it for you."

Daniel went through Jack's room into his own. To his horror, Jack stood there, the portrait of Baraja and Hermosa in his hand. "What are you doing in here?"

Jack seemed taken aback. "Don't be angry with me! I just wanted to see your room."

You are a servant. He owns you. "Well, it's not polite to go through someone's things without asking."

"Are you angry with me?"

Daniel took a deep breath. "No, of course not. What did you want to know?"

"Who's this?"

Remembering Swan's warning, Daniel said, "It's my sister. And her baby."

"Oh," Jack said. He put the portrait back where it stood by Daniel's bed. "How old is your sister?"

Daniel had to think a minute. "Twenty-one." He went for his book. "We need to get back to your brother: we mustn't leave him alone for long. I'm loaning him this book so he has something new to read."

Jack blinked. "I thought that was our book, to read together."

"I'm not going to read it to him. I thought it might help him. And it's my sister's book." Daniel smiled at him. "We can read it again once your brother's done with it. Or we can find more by the same man."

Jack nodded. "Let's go, then."

Once he gave the book to Jonathan and got Jack settled in, Daniel wrote to Baraja. *If anyone ever asks, tell them I'm your brother.*

Daniel never wanted to lie to Jack. But he trusted Swan. And though he didn't know why Swan told him these things, it seemed right: the less anyone knew about the people he loved, the better.

Purchase

The months passed. Some event Daniel had never heard of called Queen's Night meant the servants had to stay up all night making decorations for a grand dinner in honor of Miz Rachel. Other than that, their lives and duties stayed much the same.

Daniel turned eighteen, the boys, fifteen. To the dismay of the other servants, Jack insisted Daniel be at his birthday party. Gardena still kept coming to her brothers' rooms, but seemed shyer, less talkative.

"She likes you," Jack said one day.

Daniel smiled to himself. "Is that so?"

"Everyone likes you."

Daniel shrugged. Many of the maids seemed to like him, particularly Cora. Nowadays, she seemed to be the one who came upstairs anytime a summons came from the boys' rooms.

But from what he could tell, the group of servants who seemed suspicious towards him when he arrived hadn't changed their views much. He was an outsider, and they considered him a threat.

A few of the men still glared at him, refused to shake his hand. Were they that jealous that he'd been picked over them to take care of the boys?

Then he got a surprising thought: *or does one of them fancy a maid who has eyes for me?*

Daniel wasn't sure what he might do about that, other than tell them all about Baraja. And that was the one thing Swan told him never to do.

Once a month, Baraja would send news of Hermosa: she'd cut a tooth, or learned a word, or was crawling. And Daniel would hold the portrait Baraja had sent of them as he read the letter, never wanting to forget what they looked like.

Daniel would count to the penny how much he must spend that month and send the rest to them. One day, the woman he loved and his little girl would be free. *Tell her every day I love her*, he'd write, the words blurring. *As much as I love you.*

It was times like this that he thought of Jacob. Was he alive? Was he happy? Did the people he'd been sold to treat him well?

Sometimes he wept in fear for him, remembering the horror of him hanging by his belt there in the zeppelin. *Please, Jacob*, Daniel would whisper. *Stay alive. I'm right here. Don't lose heart.*

***

The summer passed, the days grew cooler. One day, Mr. Julius told them he was taking Jonathan on an outing, and that he wouldn't return until late.

Jack took the opportunity to invite Daniel to his bed.

While they lay there afterward, once Jack had been cleaned and dressed, Daniel said, "What do you think that outing is about?"

"I'm sure Jonathan will tell us," Jack said. "But I think they found him a bed maid."

"Really?"

"Yes, really. My father must have heard the servants talking. Maybe he thinks Jonathan's unfit to be wed."

"Oh," Daniel said. "And you?"

"I'm sure he'll arrange a marriage for me someday." He got up on one elbow. "But you'll always be with me, for as long as we live. Everyone will believe you stay by my side simply as my loyal manservant. Of course —" He beamed at Daniel in the moonlight. "We know better."

Daniel kissed him on the cheek, hoping that would be enough.

"But I think it's good to find him a bed maid," Jack said. "Jonathan's a man, just as I am, with a man's desires. If my father thinks no woman would have him in marriage — with his heart injured as it is — then he deserves a bed maid." Jack's upper lip curled in disdain. "Keep him out of those filthy places. I don't know why he liked brothels in the first place."

Daniel recalled the scenes: Jonathan lying on the floor, men and women and bottles and that strange white powder in bowls around them. Without thinking, Daniel said, "They say you can purchase anything you want in the Pot."

Jack shrugged. "I suppose. But people?"

Daniel didn't know what to say.

"What's wrong?"

Daniel sat up, put his feet over the side of the bed. *That was a mistake.* "Nothing."

"No, it wasn't. Please don't hide from me."

Staring at the floor, Daniel said, "Your father bought me to be your manservant. Swan came to where I lived and bought me. At my viewing. You stand for your viewing when you're sixteen." He looked behind him at Jack. "If you're an orphan."

"Sixteen?" Jack gaped at Daniel in horror.

Daniel turned to face him. "You didn't know?"

Jack got up on one elbow. "Not at all! How much did they pay?"

Daniel laughed at the absurdity. "I have no idea. I stood there, and the ones who wanted me went to one side and talked."

"Who got the money? After Swan bought you."

Daniel never considered this. Who owned the Home? Was it Miz Lisbet? Or someone even above her? "I don't know."

"And this was in Dickens?"

"Uh-huh."

Jack sat up. "This is wrong."

Suddenly weary, Daniel lay down, rolled onto his back, and gazed up at the ceiling. "It's just the way things are."

Noises came from Jonathan's room: the sound of his door to the hall opening, shutting.

Daniel sat up. "I better go," he whispered. "They mustn't find me here."

"But —"

"What if your brother wants to talk?"

Jack's face grew alarmed. "Okay. Go."

Daniel hurried out and got ready for bed. But he didn't sleep, not right away.

Jack was too smart for his own good. Eventually, he'd put two and two together. What would happen then?

In the morning, Daniel asked for Swan, but the man didn't stop by until after tea. "What've you gotten yourself into this time?"

Daniel told Swan of his fears.

"What possessed you to say you were sold in the first place?"

"I don't know! We were talking about the Pot. It just came out." Daniel let out a sigh. "I've made a right mess of things, haven't I?"

"Well, not yet," Swan said. "I have an idea. Wait here."

Swan returned an hour later. "Took me a while to find this." He handed over a silver ring with a clear stone. "This was my grandfather's," he said. "Almost forgot I had it. Give it to him."

This was too great a gift. "But —"

"Here, take it."

Daniel felt humbled. "I'm sorry to be such a bother."

"Not at all, my boy. Diamonds always protect their own, even from themselves."

When Daniel knelt and presented the ring to Jack that night, he thought the boy might faint. "T-this ... is for **me**?"

"A token of my deepest regard," Daniel said, as Swan had told him to. "It's all I have to offer."

Jack took it, eyes moist, and slipped it over the small finger of his left hand. "I — I have no words."

Daniel, still kneeling, took Jack's hand and kissed the ring, just as Swan told him to.

Then he looked into the boy's eyes, determined to only speak the truth. "I would die for you, Jack. I'm yours. For as long as we both live."

Fixation

The way Daniel understood it, Jack told Jonathan about the ring. Gardena, who'd been listening at the door, told her mother, who of course told their father.

So three days later, Daniel stood before Jack's parents.

Apparently Swan had explained about the ring, because Mr. Julius didn't seem to care one bit about it. Instead he asked something which completely threw Daniel off-balance: "What claim do you put upon this Family?"

"I don't understand."

"What do you want? The truth, now."

What **did** he want?

He almost told them about Baraja, and his dream of being reunited with her and seeing their daughter one day. But that dream would never come true, and deep down, he knew it.

So he instead told them of Miz Albaletta, and of Master Écarté, and the gentleman who helped his old teacher long ago. Then he told them about his vision of helping Jack — and Jonathan — become men of worth, so that one day they might help others the way he'd been helped.

After Daniel finished speaking, Jack's parents glanced at each other, then back at him.

"You're well-spoken for a servant," Miz Rachel said.

Daniel bowed. "Thank you, mum. You're very kind."

Mr. Julius frowned. "Do you mean to tell me, then, that you wish only to serve my son? That this — alliance — you've made with him carries no obligation?"

"I don't understand."

"You don't intend to take my son's money, or claim position, or make demands for your silence?"

Daniel gaped at him, appalled. "Why would I do that?"

Miz Rachel's face turned amused. "You'd be surprised."

Mr. Julius said, "Well? I want a straight answer."

Daniel struggled to understand. Then when he did, he struggled to find an answer. "I am your son's manservant, and as such, have tried to serve him as commanded."

Miz Rachel gave Daniel a sharp glance. "I don't like the sound of this."

Daniel bowed. "Forgive me." Then he straightened. "May I speak plainly, sir?"

The man's eyes narrowed, then flickered to his wife. "If you also speak delicately."

"Yes, sir. Your son is young. I don't wish him harm. He's done nothing ... unlawful, or injurious." Daniel took a deep breath, let it out. "Swan hopes — as I do — that your son might someday have a productive marriage."

Miz Rachel said, "As do we all."

"Yet I have observed he tends towards fixation. The business with Master Jonathan has helped Master Jack turn his attention to aid of his brother."

"And away from you," Mr. Julius said.

"The last few months, yes, sir. Perhaps this trend will continue."

"That's certainly to be hoped," Miz Rachel said. "So you suggest we say nothing?"

"It's beyond my place to advise you in any way on the care of your son," Daniel said. "But so far Swan's advice to me has been good. And so he advised me."

Mr. Julius said, "Who knows of this?"

Daniel blinked. "Besides those mentioned so far, no one — that I know of."

"Let's see if we can't keep it that way." Mr. Julius shifted in his chair. "But if he asks anything 'unlawful or injurious' of you, you are to refuse it and inform me at once. Is that clear?"

His manner was so fierce that Daniel took a step back in sudden fear. "Y — yes, sir."

"I'm not gonna hurt you, boy. But I won't let my son hurt you either." He let out a laugh. "You cost me way too much for that."

***

Fall came, and Gardena turned thirteen, with great fanfare. Yet for quite some time, he never got so much as a glimpse of the girl: she stopped coming to her brothers' rooms when he was in them.

Mr. Julius began taking Jack and Jonathan to his meetings, sometimes during the day, at other times in the evening. According to Jack, their father always left them in a hallway or antechamber with one child or another. Apparently, after the third time of this, there was an argument. Daniel heard about it in the staff room during tea-time.

They'd mostly finished tea. Tolo and Daniel sat near the foot of the table. Everyone was talking at once, each in their own conversations. "They was sure a-yelling," Tolo said. "Could hear the whole thing plain as day. It was about you."

Daniel blinked, taken aback. "Me?"

"Young Master Jack insisted! He say if they's to be brought to these dangers, that you be made his guard as well as his manservant. Well, Mr. Julius got into a fury! Never heard him so fierce in all my days, and I've known him since he was a boy. Said it's not fair to ya! Definite he was, that." The old man shook his head. "I tend to agree. I seen the way they's a-working ya." He rubbed his nose. "Then young Master Jon got all riled up, asking why they all cares so 'bouts a manservant." He chuckled. "Salty, that one." He threw his arms up in the air. "Ohhh, that got the three of them set to yelling so I bet the whole world heard 'bout it."

Mr. Neuberg looked down the table. "What's this about?"

The room fell silent.

Tolo got a furtive look to him. "Not that I overheard, really. The bell's only good when one person's talking. And I was trying to drive. Far as I could tell it was just yelling."

Daniel said, "So what did they decide?"

Tolo shrugged. "They were fuming when they left my sight, they were."

Mr. Neuberg frowned. "Since when do we discuss the Masters at table?"

"Begging your pardon, sir," Tolo said, ducking his head. "Meant no harm by it."

"Don't let it happen again," Mr. Neuberg said. "I'll not have my staff room turned into a gossip hall."

Tolo rose and turned to Daniel. "I better go. Let me know what all happens."

Daniel chuckled. "I'm sure you'll learn soon enough."

***

From what Daniel might gather, much discussion went on even before he was called down once more. This time, instead of just meeting with Mr. Julius, Mr. Bastra, Mr. Neuberg and Swan were there as well. Mr. Hector presided over them.

Mr. Hector was an elderly man, yet hale, with graying hair and clear brown eyes. He sat, hand to his chin, gazing back."Daniel, my grandson Jack has requested you accompany him as not only manservant, but bodyguard as well. What do you say to this?"

Daniel bowed. "I serve at your command, sir."

Mr. Hector said, "I'm not commanding you. I'm asking. You care for his rooms and belongings. Will you be able to do that and go to these meetings?"

So that was why Mr. Bastra was there. "I don't know, sir. How much time do you plan on being away with him?"

Julius growled, "The whole point of this was to separate him from you so he'd 'fixate' upon someone else."

Mr. Hector snorted.

Mr. Bastra looked entirely surprised.

Swan sat very still.

Heat rushed to Daniel's cheeks. So Mr. Hector knew what he and Jack were doing as well.

Mr. Hector said, "What would you do if someone tried to harm the boy, anyway?"

"Protect him, sir, of course. Defend him."

Mr. Hector leaned forward. "And how would you do that, hmm? Your fists?"

Daniel shrugged.

Mr. Hector said, "Have you ever actually been in a fight?"

Daniel chuckled. "A few times." Back at the Home, with the other boys.

Mr. Julius said, "Ever killed a man?"

The idea had never crossed his mind. "No."

"You any good with a gun?"

Daniel wasn't sure how to answer. "I know how to shoot, sir. But I've never shot anyone."

Mr. Julius leaned back, crossing his arms. "Figured. Okay, what else can you do?"

Daniel shrugged. "I suppose I'd use what I had." Did they doubt his ability, or his loyalty? "I'd let no one harm him, if by my life I might stop it. Master Jonathan, either." Then he came to an idea. "Whether you choose me or not, sir, someone should stand guard for them. A nursemaid and a child would do nothing against any real attack."

Mr. Julius and Mr. Hector exchanged a glance. From Mr. Hector's startle and the sheepish demeanor of Mr. Julius, Daniel doubted that Mr. Hector had known of the circumstances the boys had been left in until then.

Mr. Hector said, "Daniel, Mr. Bastra, Swan: leave us."

So they did.

Once in the hall, Swan chuckled, patting Daniel on the shoulder as they moved towards the back stair. "You did well, son." Then he said, "You really were in a fistfight?"

Daniel said, "Is it so hard to believe?"

Mr. Bastra smiled to himself.

"Sometimes," Swan said. "You don't much look the brawler." They reached the stair. "You all go on up; I got stuff to do."

Daniel said, "When do you think they'll decide?"

Swan snorted. "Them two? They'll spend the next hour arguing. A few days is my guess. Get caught up on your work now, boy, because you'll want to get ahead of this." He clapped Daniel on the shoulder and moved off down the hall.

Mr. Bastra opened the door for Daniel. "If you need help, don't hesitate to call on me."

"Thank you, sir."

They started up the winding metal stair. "This job is big enough for anyone," Mr. Bastra said, "without getting hired on for grunt work besides."

"Is it usual to be asked to do such things?" Master Écarté had never spoken of anything like it.

"Sometimes. Usually a footman or an enforcer is a better choice, as they're usually more proficient at arms. But I stood guard once or twice in my youth."

Daniel clomped up the stair. He needed to be more proficient at arms, then.

At the top of the stair, Daniel held the door for Mr. Bastra, who'd slowed his pace just a tad. "Thank you for your counsel, sir. I promise I won't be a burden to you."

Mr. Bastra gave Daniel a fond smile. "I never once thought it. Come on, my boy, let's see what work those scamps have made for us since we've been away."

***

Daniel stood in Jack's closets for a good hour trying to decide where to begin. His work had been in order up to then, since he did a great deal during the hours that Jack was busy with his schoolwork, off tending to Jonathan, or traveling with his father.

But with this added responsibility, he needed a better plan.

He'd start with an inventory.

Daniel went to his room for a pad and pencil. Jack's voice came from behind. "There you are!"

Daniel turned around, surveyed the boy. "Look at you. You're tall as me now."

Jack tilted his head with a shy smile, face glowing. Then he said, "When do you want to ride?"

Daniel sighed, moved past him into his room. "Not today; I need to be ready in case your father allows me to go with you on your trips."

"What can I do?"

Then Daniel had an idea. "Try on your clothes. Any that don't fit and can't be let out, we'll get rid of." He grinned. "That'll make less work."

Jack's face fell. "I'm sorry I make so much work for you."

"Not at all." Daniel felt chagrined. "I didn't mean it that way. Truly, I didn't. I'm happy to be here for you."

Mollified, Jack looked down at himself. "I wish they'd get me some white clothing, instead of all this stupid gray."

Jack had never forgotten that offhand comment the day of the tooth powder debacle two years before. He only would wear white shirts now, and linen suits in summer.

Mr. Hector — the Diamond Inventor — had his white coat for the laboratory. But only an upper-card bride on her marriage-day wore entirely white. For a man to do so — at least in Bridges — was unheard of. "Well, when you're grown, you may wear whatever you wish."

Jack stood, twirling around the room. "I cannot wait to be grown!" Ducking under the upper cabinets, he flopped back onto Daniel's bed. "Oh, to do whatever I wish!"

Daniel didn't feel he could make any judgment on the matter. "Why not ask your parents?"

"Can't you just order what I want? You're **my** manservant."

"Yes, but your parents pay. I can't go against their wishes."

"I'll ask them now." Jack dashed out.

With a sigh, Daniel went to Jack's closets. He'd set up an area in the back for clothing he meant to discard. Several of the boy's trousers had been set there as much too short to even think of letting out; others had been set aside as too small around the waist. There were too-short shirts and jackets, and ones Jack never wanted to wear anymore. Shoes which were too small, and those which needed more repair than he had the tools to do. Those all went into a pile for Swan to handle.

Daniel didn't know where the extra clothing went, and it didn't much matter. He arranged what was left along the long closet space, making notes as to what needed purchasing. The floor needed sweeping, and Jack's room needed dusting. He was wiping down Jack's bookcases when the boy bounded in. "Woo hoo! They'll let me wear what I want!"

"Well," Daniel said. "Good for you!"

"I want you to buy me all white, every bit."

Daniel blinked. "Even your shoes?"

"Especially my shoes. White everything, even the soles of them." Jack came to him, cradled Daniel's face in his hands. "I want to look my best for you."

Daniel felt flustered. "I don't know what to say."

"And anything I have that fits you is yours. Since we're the same height now, there's probably something."

"I'm honored," Daniel said, and meant it. He wasn't sure if that was allowed, but surely Swan would know. "I'll look to see who makes clothes like that. But it might take time for them to get here."

"It doesn't matter: just knowing they're on their way is enough." Jack flung his arms in the air. "I'm free to do what I want!"

A twinge of envy, which Daniel pushed aside. "I'll put in an order for white shirts and socks today, whilst I see who can do the rest on special."

Jack flung himself into Daniel's arms, hugging him tightly. "I love you so much."

A wave of fondness for the boy came over him, and he held him close. "I love you, too."

Threat

It took several weeks for all of Jack's new clothing to arrive. In the meantime, they went to meetings. Sometimes these took place in Diamond quadrant, other times upon a place across the bridge past the hedges called Market Center.

The meetings seemed much the same: a quick introduction of the twin brothers, and perhaps the uppers would share a meal. Then the men would disappear into a back room, leaving them all to sit — or in Daniel's case, stand — with little to do.

During the meetings upon Market Center, sometimes another much younger boy or two arrived, along with an older woman who had to be some sort of nurse.

Generally, the children began by ignoring each other, then usually Jack would try to start some conversation, which would fizzle into silence.

The idle time felt frustrating. He had so much to do! And yet he stood here doing nothing.

Then his teacher's words came clear: *You must do whatever they ask of you. They own you.*

He'd also been told: *we won't let you leave until you've learned what you need to know.*

What did he know about guarding?

This room had two doors. One they'd come through, and the way to the exit was clear. The other, the men had gone through. That way might contain threat, but any real danger was most likely come from outside, from the way they'd come. He positioned himself so he had a natural view of both doors, keeping himself between the children and the outer one.

Gradually, over several encounters, Daniel got to know the boys. Lance was thin, blond and painfully shy. But Jack managed to get the boy talking when he mentioned boats, which Lance seemed to know much about.

Anthony was a dark-haired fearful boy who never said anything and kept his eyes flickering between each of them as he pretended to read his poetry books.

A boy several years older — who already towered over them all — would always accompany him. This boy stayed within reach of Anthony, but seldom spoke, and never gave his name.

Whoever brought these two boys never entered with them; Anthony always arrived after the men had left to speak privately.

From the start of this, Daniel had the feeling something bad would happen. It happened shortly before Yuletide.

Daniel stood there as he always did, hands behind his back. The door opened and a man came out.

The man was about as tall as Daniel. Heavy set, but moving as a well-muscled man did, not a fat one. His hair was black, his eyes a pale blue. He gestured at Daniel with his chin and came over. "Don't think we've met."

Anthony froze, face terrified. The older boy with Anthony became wary. From the noises inside the room beyond, the other men still conversed, unaware of what went on.

"I'm Master Jack's manservant, sir," Daniel said, wondering why the man — clearly a gentleman — even spoke to him.

"So I've heard. You're from Dickens."

Daniel nodded slowly, feeling wary yet not sure why.

The man's face turned amused, and he held out a thick hand. "Roy Spadros."

Daniel gaped for just an instant, both at the name and the offer, before shaking the man's hand. "I'm honored, sir." Then he bowed low. "Was there something you required?"

At that, the man's face soured. "What, am I not good enough for you to speak with?"

Everything about this man spoke of imminent violence. "Not at all, sir. Forgive me, sir. I — I've never had a gentleman offer his hand before. That's all. I — I'm sorry to offend you, sir."

Roy Spadros peered at Daniel a moment, then began to laugh. "I'm not gonna hurt you, boy."

Relief swept over Daniel. "Thank you, sir."

"Your — friend — is manservant to my son Anthony."

It took a moment to put the pieces together. Instead of being glad to see his father, the boy looked ready to bolt from the room. Daniel nodded. "Yes, sir."

"Michaels, is it not?"

"Yes, sir, Jacob Michaels."

The man's manner seemed easy, but underneath Daniel still felt terrible menace. "You know what they say — if anything should happen to the master ... "

"Sir?"

His voice grew quiet enough so only Daniel might hear. "Well, for example, if something were to happen to me. Everyone in my house would fall under suspicion. Not only that, but these," he let out a disgusted breath, "people would become suspects as well. For almost a hundred years, we've been at war. And now, you and your Jacob being so close and all." He smirked. "Like brothers?"

He'd read the letter Daniel had sent to Jacob!

"Well, then of course Jacob might be seen as a traitor. And you know what we do to traitors."

Daniel didn't know, until Roy Spadros drew a finger across his own throat.

Daniel glanced at Jonathan and Jack. They both stared at him, faces frightened. "I understand, sir."

Roy Spadros gave a satisfied smile. "Very good, then. A pleasure to meet you." He gestured to Anthony as one might a dog. "Come." They left, going around the corner.

Jack ran up to Daniel. "What did he say to you?"

Daniel shook his head. "He was trying to scare me." But why?

Jonathan had come up to them, voice shaking. "Father says that's the most evil hand the gods ever dealt."

***

A few hours after they'd returned home, Flannery knocked. The boy's eyes were wide. "The master wants to see you!"

Daniel blinked. "Master Jack?"

"No, sir. The Old Master. At once."

Fear stabbed at him.

Servants are never to be acknowledged, only summoned, directed, or punished. You are less than an animal to them, only there to do your duty. Never are you to bring notice to yourself, by either word or deed.

So the thought of this meeting left Daniel with a sense of dread. Why would Mr. Hector wish to see him? What had he done?

Daniel followed Flannery to a part of the house he'd never been to. The boy knocked on the right side of a double-wide white door. "They'll open it when they want you," Flannery said, and left.

Daniel stood for at least ten minutes as men's voices rose and fell behind the door. Then the door opened, and Swan said, "They'll see you now."

Inside the room was a large desk and two overstuffed leather chairs. Mr Hector sat behind the desk. Mr. Julius sat in one chair, the other chair was empty. Swan moved to it and sat.

Jack and Jonathan stood beside their grandfather, with their hands behind their backs, much as Daniel did.

Never speak unless spoken to.

Daniel stood before them motionless, staring ahead, frightened as he'd never been before.

"I'm not going to hurt you, boy," Mr. Hector said, yet his voice was so different from that of Roy Spadros that Daniel almost laughed. "Here, look at me."

Daniel felt too frightened to speak.

"You're safe here," Mr. Hector said. "You're part of my Family. My grandsons are happy with your work in my home."

At that, Daniel found his voice. "Thank you, sir."

"They're concerned about something which happened today. Mr. Roy Spadros spoke to you."

The room fell silent, so Daniel said, "Yes, sir."

"Can you tell us what happened?"

"I was with the Little Masters in the anteroom. They sat upon the bench there, whilst I stood aside by the wall, where I could see the doors. Mr. Spadros came to me."

"What did he say?"

"He wished to shake my hand, sir. I didn't know why, and when I said so he took offense."

Swan and Mr. Julius laughed.

Mr. Julius said, "Sounds about right."

Mr. Hector said, "Go on."

"I became afraid, but he said he wouldn't hurt me. He mentioned my friend from Dickens, who is manservant to his son." At that, Daniel pondered what was said. "He said if anything should happen to him — Mr. Spadros, I mean — that they would think Jacob was a traitor."

Mr. Hector nodded. "He wants you to spy for him."

"But sir," Daniel said, "I don't even know how."

Mr. Hector leaned back, and a calculating look came over his face. "You do look the part."

"Sir?"

"We'd have to do something about that accent, but you look like a good Spadros boy, to be sure."

Daniel didn't know what to say, so he said nothing.

"Well, that's all for now," Mr. Hector said. He gestured at his grandsons. "All of you, off you go."

Daniel bowed low before following the boys back to their rooms. But the entire way, he felt dirty.

They want me to be a spy, he thought. *They want me to lie.*

Family

Yuletide came and went, most of it spent getting Jack ready for one event or another. A few weeks later, Daniel was up late ironing Jack's trousers when Swan appeared beside him. "Put that away," he said. "We got work to do."

"What kind of work?"

"Best you don't know."

Puzzled, Daniel put the iron aside to cool, got his cap and coat, and followed Swan.

Swan led him down the curling flight of metal stairs. They went past the first door, past the second door, then down to a third door Daniel had never seen before. Swan unlocked the door, which opened onto a long hallway of gun-metal gray. Doors of the same color alternated on either side, lit by bulbs overhead.

An unpleasant smell permeated the air, musky and damp; Daniel hesitated before following Swan further.

The hallway was quiet, with a small rustling here, a soft moan there. Surely they didn't keep animals in this horrible place?

A man sat on a stool at the end of the hallway, tipping his cap as Swan and Daniel approached. They turned left, where a second long hallway stretched.

Daniel tried to imagine where they might be. As time passed and they continued on, he realized they'd gone beyond the house itself. "What is this place?"

"We do most of the real work here," Swan said. "Just wanted to give you a look-round."

The air smelled better here, fresher. Daniel glanced up: vents lay above him between the lightbulbs.

"The uppers come here a different way; you'll doubtless accompany the Little Masters once or twice when they're older, if they need you." He opened a door to the left. "For now, let's see what you're made of."

The door opened onto a room about the size of his own bedroom. A few chairs cushioned in black. A large dresser. All this furniture was made of unfinished wood, with random stains in various shades of brown.

The floor was carpeted with a black mat, but it felt like concrete lay below it. The walls were concrete, in places chipped, and no portraits hung upon them.

Daniel's first reaction at seeing the room was terror.

But Mr. Julius Diamond stood leaning upon a desk as dark brown as himself, arms folded and ankles crossed. He seemed perfectly relaxed, giving them a pleasant smile. "Welcome." Mr. Julius wore a suit entirely of black, even his shirt. "Want a drink?" He gestured to a large silver tray sitting on the desk beside him, which held three beer bottles and two liquor bottles, along with three glasses.

Avoid all appearance of familiarity. "No, sir. Thank you, sir."

The man's demeanor turned icy. He set his feet flat on the floor, his hands on the edges of the desk on either side, and leaned forward. "You're too good to drink with me?"

Daniel froze, heart pounding. "Not at all, sir." What should he say? "I — I don't much like it. Sir."

Mr. Julius burst into laughter. "Gods preserve us. An honest man!" Then he crossed his arms and ankles once more. "And if I ordered you to drink it?"

Daniel knelt before him, bowing low. "I would, of course, sir, at once. I'm yours to command."

"Stand up, boy," Mr. Julius said, so Daniel did. "Listen up. I don't care what you like. But I want you to tell me you don't like it. Keep being honest. Understand?"

"Yes, sir."

"But then, no matter how you feel about it, you must do it, exactly as I tell you to. Do you swear? Look me in the eye."

Daniel looked into the man's dark eyes. "I will, sir."

At that, Mr. Julius relaxed. "Very good." He gestured at Swan.

Daniel now realized Swan wore entirely black as well.

Swan went to a door behind the desk which matched it. He knocked three times, and a man also wearing black opened it. This man was much older, perhaps sixty, and looked familiar.

Swan and the man left, and the door closed.

"You're a good worker," Mr. Julius said, "but until you've proven yourself, you'll never be part of the Family. You don't look it, you don't talk like it, and you don't act it. You understand? No one here trusts you."

This hurt. But Daniel nodded. There didn't seem to be much he might say.

"Besides, you're soft," Mr. Julius said. "I can see it in your eyes. We're gonna take care of that right now."

He twisted around to press a button on the desk behind him, and at the same time, a buzzing noise came from behind the door. The door opened, and a man came in.

The man was gagged, and bound with his wrists behind him. Swan and the man who'd opened the door for him held the bound man tightly. They brought him in and forced him to kneel.

His hair was wavy and dark. His skin was pale, and his eyes, dark brown.

He looked remarkably like Jacob.

Mr. Julius went to the dresser, opened the top drawer, and pulled out a revolver. He handed it to Daniel. "Now shoot him."

The bound man's eyes went wide, pleading, flashing back and forth between them. "No! No!" Even though the words went around his gag, they were clear.

Daniel stared at the man in horror, at the revolver in his hand, at Mr. Julius. "Why? What has he done?"

"That's not for you to know. All you need to know is that I told you to shoot him."

The man's eyes had tears in them. What could he have possibly done to deserve death? "I don't like this."

"Good. You're being honest. I like that. Put the gun right there between his eyes, at that notch above his nose."

Daniel didn't move. He coudn't think.

"Go on. It's okay. Do it."

You must obey them, whatever they ask. Trembling, Daniel moved closer. The man began screaming, bucking to get free.

Swan and the other man each took hold of the bound man's hair with one hand, the man's arm with the other, standing well back.

Daniel put the gun where Mr. Julius told him to, heart pounding. Daniel couldn't look in the man's eyes.

He pulled the trigger.

In the small space, the noise was so loud he couldn't hear. He found himself on the floor, watching the man's gagged face, his terrified eyes. Blood soaked the black carpet. He felt sick.

Mr. Julius hadn't moved. "You did well, son." His voice came out as a whisper. He gestured to Swan and the other man. "Get him up."

Daniel was pulled to his feet, ears ringing.

"Now," Mr. Julius said, "you're going to clean up your mess."

Daniel, Swan, and the other man (whose name was Zeenay) dragged the body to what looked like a laundry chute. "We dug a tunnel between the rivers," Swan explained. "Goes diagonal, like so," he held his hands up to show it. "River goes in, right past us here, then out. Saves us having to cart bodies around."

Daniel felt astonished. "That must have taken years!"

"Mr. Hector made us a machine for it. Diamonds don't fuck around, son. We get shit done."

Zeenay nodded.

"I remember you," Daniel said. "You drove us when I arrived."

Zeenay grinned. "So I did."

Swan chuckled. "We paid too much for you to trust your safety to just anyone."

They fetched a bucket and mop from a closet down the hall, and mopped blood from the hall floor. By the time they returned to the room to scrub the carpet, Mr. Julius was gone.

Swan seemed in a good mood. "My grandpa always said the best way to wash your hands was to use them to clean your mess."

Scrubbing the floor was easiest for Daniel, although it took much longer. But he could focus on cleaning, forget an instant at a time the terror in the man's eyes. Forget what he'd just done.

"Next time, you'll use ear-plugs," Swan said. "And you'll do it in a better room." He let out a short laugh. "Mr. Julius likes to have new ones experience the full effect."

Finally, the carpet was cleaned to Swan's liking. He turned on a switch as they left; the sound of a huge fan began. "It'll be dry in a bit," he said as he closed the door behind him. "Now for part two."

Daniel shrank back. "Part two?" What new terror did they have planned for him?

Swan and Zeenay grinned at each other. Swan patted Daniel's shoulder. "Come on, it'll be alright."

Daniel followed them to another dark gray door. Inside were Mr. Neuberg, Mr. Hook, and Mr. Bastra, sitting around a round table. The room was large and luxurious, paneled in silver-wood with comfortable-looking blue-gray sofas and thick plush carpeting in white. Food and drinks were on a side board, but no one had touched them.

Daniel felt alarmed. "Who's guarding the little Masters?"

"Concerned for their safety," Mr. Hook said. "Very good. Never fear, my boy, they're safe as can be."

Zeenay smiled at Daniel. "I'll be off, then. Have a good night." He closed the door as he left.

Mr. Neuberg stood. "Today we're here to celebrate your entry into the Diamond Family." He picked up a white pouch from the side board and brought it around to stand beside Daniel and Swan.

Daniel stood there, unsure what to do.

Mr. Neuberg took out a card from the pouch. One of the Holy Cards: the Ten of Diamonds.

Daniel gaped at it, making the sign of the Board. The actual Holy Card in front of him made his knees weak. "Where did you get this?"

Swan grinned. "We have our ways. Give me your hand."

Daniel extended his hand. Swan took a needle from the white pouch; Neuberg took out a clear glass ashtray.

Swan pricked Daniel's finger, drawing a drop of blood. "Now put the blood on your Card."

"Why?"

Mr. Neuberg said, "This binds you to your Card forever. You stand beside your Jack, ready to defend him with your life. If you are willing to shed your blood for him, take this vow."

Daniel touched the card. The drop of blood hung there, then began to slowly slide down, a millimeter at a time.

"Now you will burn the Card," Swan said. "Once you do that, you've sealed yourself to the Family. There is no turning back."

Burn a Holy Card?

Neuberg lit a match. "You must do it before your blood dries upon the Card. Or leave here now."

For an instant, he wanted to flee.

But then he came to his senses. They'd bought him. He had nowhere to go. Surely these men wouldn't let him just walk out of these tunnels now that he knew their secrets. Even if he made it to Nitivali, Baraja was bought too. The only way she and their daughter might escape was for him to stay, send her the money to buy her freedom.

Daniel took the card from Mr. Neuberg and put it on the match. The Card lit aflame.

Swan took the Card and put it into the ashtray.

Daniel watched it burn. *I'm doomed*, he thought. *I've burned my Card.* His vision blurred. "Am I dead?"

Of course, he didn't mean dead as in right then. But would his hand be given to another when he died? Or would the rest of his Cards be sent to the Fire for his crime?

"You're not dead, son," Mr. Neuberg said. "You're Diamond-sworn. You're part of the Family now."

Sworn

The group ate, drank and talked until well into the night. Daniel tried some sweet wine and found that it wasn't too bad. In fact, by the second glass it tasted pretty good.

"When we say you're part of the Family," Swan said, "we mean it. If anyone so much as looks at you cross," he glanced around to the other men, "we'll come to your aid. We're your brothers now. We're under obligation to you, and you to us. Your woman —"

Daniel froze, remembering the warning Swan himself had given never to speak of her.

"— and your daughter: if anything happens to you, we'll make sure they're taken care of."

The other men, evidently not knowing what Swan did, looked at Daniel with new respect. Daniel was just glad Swan wasn't calling Baraja a whore anymore.

"But it goes both ways. You see one of your brothers in trouble, you **must** aid them. That clear?"

Daniel nodded, overwhelmed at all he'd experienced.

Yet it hadn't ended. About an hour in, a man came in with a toolbox and sat on a padded stool beside the recliner.

Everyone cheered.

"Time for your mark," Swan said.

Alarmed, Daniel said, "What mark?"

Swan took off his jacket and unbuttoned his shirt, pulling it aside to show the deep brown skin under his left arm. Close to his coiled salt and pepper hair, a raised scar in the shape of the Holy Symbol of the Diamond Family lay there. He pulled his shirt closed. "You're pale enough that a tattoo'll work better. Come on, my boy, this won't hurt much."

It did hurt, but not as much as the noise of that gunshot did. Daniel's ears still hurt.

Mr. Bastra sat beside him. "I got the same when I was about your age. It's in your skin, so it'll last your entire life." He smiled warmly. "Anywhere you go, this marks you as Diamond-sworn. It's the proof."

Daniel blinked. "Couldn't someone fake this?"

Mr. Neuberg snorted. "They could, if they knew about it. A whole other matter. You must never reveal what happened this night, no matter what. Not to anyone. Not to those in the household, not even to your little Master."

Daniel felt confused. "Don't the boys already have one?"

"Heirs have their own mark. When they're ready," Mr. Hook said. "When they've proven themselves capable. They're still much too young for such things."

Swan said, "Sure, anyone could fake it, but not for long. We know your face, you see, and you know we were here. First thing they'd ask is who was at your marking. Then one of us would be called in to verify it." He glanced around. "Unlikely any traitor'd know to kill all of us."

The thought of someone killing these men, now dear to him, brought tears to Daniel's eyes. He looked up into each of their faces. They'd brought him in, trusted him with their young Heirs. Trusted him with these secrets of their Family. *They want me.* "I'll be your brother," he said, "come what may."

***

In the candlelight of his room that night, Daniel examined the Diamond outlined in black upon his inner arm, the redness around it. The man who put it there told him that the redness would subside with time.

Daniel felt as if he'd moved up in the world.

One day he'd be at the side of a Diamond Heir, one who valued him above all else.

If you play your cards right, you'll become his most trusted adviser.

Surely it wouldn't be wrong to advise Master Jack to travel?

Daniel's clothes were spattered with blood. He bathed, changed, and soaked his clothing overnight.

He never did get the stains entirely out of his shirt.

The next day at morning meeting, all the uppers attended, even the two younger Heirs and Gardena, who now wore a high-necked dress that went to her mid-calf. Mr. Neuberg called Daniel to stand. "Daniel is now Diamond-sworn," he said.

Gasps filled the room, then applause.

Jack looked astonished and proud.

"Daniel has proven himself with our little Masters, beyond any of our expectations. He's showed his worth and done the young Master's bidding. He has taken the vows. Daniel is one of us."

At that, Mr. Neuberg stared at the group who'd been suspicious of Daniel this whole time, who for some reason always sat together. "And let none of you forget it."

***

The next afternoon, Daniel was altering a pair of Jack's white trousers which had just arrived when Flannery knocked on the door. "Mr. Julius wants to see you."

Daniel followed Flannery to Julius Diamond's study. Mr. Julius sat behind his desk studying some papers, glancing up when Daniel entered. "Ah, very good." Mr. Julius gestured to a chair across the desk. "Have a seat."

Servants are never supposed to sit in the Master's presence. After a moment's hesitation, Daniel said, "As you command, sir," and sat.

"How's your ears doing?"

"My ears?" For a moment, Daniel felt confused. "I hear a buzzing still. But the pain is much improved."

"Good. I have a job for you."

Daniel didn't know what to say. "Is Swan well?"

"This isn't something Swan needs to know about."

Daniel gaped at Mr. Julius, completely astonished.

Mr. Julius snorted, a wry smile on his face. "This is delicate work, boy. The fewer people who know of it, the better. For now, that list is you and me."

"Sir, I feel unworthy of such honor. But I'll do my best."

Mr. Julius handed over a sepia-toned paper portrait. "I wanna know everything about her."

The girl was dirty, around five, thick curls framing a baby-fat face. She had stunning clear eyes shaped much like Miz Annabel's were, back at the Academy. A ragged dress hung loosely on her thin body. She stood in an alleyway, but the buildings nearby were broken, ruined.

Mr. Julius leaned forward, put his elbows upon his desk. "My father has tasked me to find this girl. But we gotta find her without drawing any attention. None whatsoever. She can't know when we find her, nor that we observe her. No one else must ever know. And she must never, ever, lay eyes upon you."

Daniel nodded. How might this be done so very discreetly? The first thing to learn was where the child was.

Mr. Julius sat watching him as if he should know. So maybe he could figure it out.

People thought he was a Spadros spy. Mr. Hector thought he looked the part, as did Mr. Neuberg. But he'd never seen such destruction anywhere but in the Diamond part of the Pot.

Daniel looked at Mr. Julius. "The Spadros Pot?"

He nodded. "You catch on quickly."

"Thank you, sir. And the child's name?"

"That's one of the things we want verified. Who is she? Who are her parents? What does she do there?"

"But how —?" Then it dawned on him. "I see. To ask for her by name would draw attention."

"Indeed it would. But I'll not leave you entirely at ends. This girl is just now eleven, and lives in the Cathedral."

Daniel had never been to the Cathedral, but he doubted he'd have trouble finding her, even this much later. There couldn't be two girls in all of Bridges with those eyes. "I'll find her."

Julius Diamond leaned back, with his hands behind his head. "What you'll do tomorrow after morning meeting is put on your shabbiest clothes. Go out of the side door and tell the gate-men I've sent you on an errand. Across the street and four blocks to your left, there's a taxi-stand. Go to one of those poorhouse sales places. One of the maids can tell you where to find one. Get an even shabbier set of clothing, then take a taxi-carriage to the Seamont. It's a tavern on the Spadros side of the river, west 5th and Promenade. When you're in the taxi, change into the clothes you just got and muss up your hair some. A bit of dirt on your face and hands wouldn't hurt either. Go inside and order raspberry wine and pork pie. Ask for an extra napkin. My man will come up with a cigarette and ask if you have a light. Tell him no, but you heard there was matches for sale next door."

"What's the man look like?"

"What do you think he looks like? Like you. Like he belongs with them. Invite him to join you. He can get you into the Pot without drawing attention."

Daniel nodded. "What about the boys?"

"They'll be kept occupied."

"How long will I have?"

"Be back in time to clean up and dress them for dinner. That'll give you a good four hours there in the Pot this time."

"This time?"

"You don't expect to learn everything tomorrow, do you? And have a reason for being there."

"Sir?"

"In the Pot." Mr. Julius gave an amused snort. "I'm sure you can figure something out. And try not to talk too much. You sound like an outsider."

***

Daniel went to Jack's closets and retrieved the trousers he'd been working on when Flannery had called him. He laid a towel upon his tea-table, spread the white trousers upon them, and returned to his work.

He didn't know enough of the Pot to fool anyone by claiming to be one of them. Yet according to Mr. Neuberg — and, well, everyone here — he looked like a Spadros man.

Why would a Spadros man be in the Pot?

To say he'd been sent there by the Spadros Family would be foolish. Surely they'd know the men sent there. And they wouldn't trust him until it'd been verified.

So the best bet would be not to approach anyone or say anything, unless he had to.

Not everyone in Diamond was a Diamond-sworn, or even one born. Perhaps it was the same in Spadros quadrant.

He recalled how Jonathan acted back when they'd pulled him out of the brothels. Maybe he was just a drunk outsider kid who'd stumbled into the Pot.

The thought made him laugh out loud. Spill a bit of wine on his trousers, and he'd even smell the part.

"There you are," Jack said from behind. "What's so funny?" He put his arms around Daniel's neck and kissed his cheek. "Where have you been?"

Daniel turned to face him. "Your father wanted to see me."

Jack's face turned alarmed. "Are you in trouble?"

"No, not at all." Then he thought about what Mr. Julius had said. "Do I sound like an outsider?"

"Sort of."

Daniel smiled to himself. "Have you ever been to another city?"

Jack blinked. "No, never." He pulled up a chair, sat. "You said you were in Nitivali for your Academy school."

Daniel, focused on his seam, nodded.

"And you grew up in Dickens?"

"I did."

Mr. Neuberg came to the door, giving Daniel a disapproving look. Then he said to Jack, "Tea is served, sir."

"Let's talk more later," Daniel said.

That night was spent talking about travel. Jack wanted to know everything about Daniel's adventures. And when the boy finally fell asleep, Daniel felt both relieved and happy.

Jack wanted to travel. Perhaps one day, Daniel really could see Baraja again.

***

The poorhouse shop, although bedraggled, had a warm, comforting feel, and the cheerful middle-aged woman behind the counter wasn't much darker of skin than he was. Besides clothes and shoes, Daniel also bought a satchel to put his clothes into.

At the taxi-stand, a sign said, "To Spadros quadrant." The line of people waiting daunted him: he'd never be able to change in the taxi as Mr. Julius suggested.

And ask as he might, none of the stores had toilet facilities. "What do you think this is," one shopkeeper said, "your home? Use the street urinals like everyone else."

So he went round back to the alley behind the shops. A wall of privet eight feet high stood there, and several gaps were large enough to afford privacy. Evidently, from the odor, others had used the area as well.

He changed clothing, putting the set of clothes and shoes he'd worn his first day — now much mended and patched after almost two years there — into his satchel.

He hadn't found a worse-looking shirt than the vaguely blood-stained one he'd worn during his initiation. The stains now looked more like dirt than anything else, so he kept that shirt on.

Twenty feet to his left, a red-haired woman and two small girls also exited the hedge, glancing his way. The woman blushed, hurrying her children in the other direction.

Daniel rode a taxi-carriage with several others going into Spadros quadrant. On the wooden bench seat across from him sat an enormously fat brown-skinned merchant with a maid of perhaps twelve.

The girl had the lightest skin he'd ever seen and two fuzzy white-blonde braids. She held a covered basket on her lap and hid her pale blue eyes from the sun.

Next to Daniel sat two young men a bit older than him. They teased each other and laughed, speaking rapidly in a language Daniel didn't understand.

Daniel gazed at the river outside. Far off in the distance lay the island of Market Center, and the shores of Spadros lay not so far ahead. Boats passed under the bridge they rode upon.

The young man next to Daniel jostled him.

"Whoa there," Daniel said, turning.

The young man drew back. "My pardons, sir."

"An accident, I'm sure." But Daniel did rub his side when the man wasn't looking.

Or at least he thought the man wasn't looking, because the motion caught both their attention. "We've caused distress," the second said.

"Not at all." Daniel began to feel concerned. He particularly did not want to attract attention. "Think nothing of it."

The carriage crossed onto Spadros quadrant, turned left on the first road, then stopped. A voice came from the speaking tube. "The Seamont."

Daniel opened the door.

"Now, we can't have you leaving on bad terms," the first said, giving his friend a meaningful glance.

The driver said, "You getting out or not?"

"Not at all," Daniel said to the young man beside him. "Now if you'll excuse me —"

The second man opened the door on his side. "Here's as good a place to get out as any."

Daniel hurried out and around to the street behind the back of the carriage, which was loaded with people as well. The gray cobblestone streets were crowded, as was the gray stone sidewalk.

Daniel hurried inside, hoping the others wouldn't follow. But to his dismay, they did.

The Seamont tavern was a cozy affair, with dark brown paneled walls, black tables, and black chairs. Lanterns fitted with electric bulbs hung from the rafters and sat on small shelves, making the place well-lit. The place was about a quarter full: any of these men could be the one he searched for.

"Let us get you a beer," the first man said.

"Sir," Daniel said, "whilst I appreciate the sentiment, I'm here on business."

The second frowned. "Too good to drink with us, are you?"

"Not at all," Daniel said, "but the man I meet with must leave shortly." He held out his hand. "Might we part friends?"

That seemed to disarm them. "Of course!" The first man stuck out a hand. "Billy Spadros." He held up his lapels, preening. "But you can call me Blitz."

His friend rolled his eyes, then shook hands with Daniel as well. "Alan Pearson."

Billy poked Alan in the side. Alan batted Billy's hand away in irritation.

The bartender called across the room. "You young gents wanna play, go outside."

Alan said, "We gotta go anyway. Nice meeting you." He grabbed Billy's arm and hustled him out.

Daniel took a table off to the side and peered at the menu. To his relief, both items he was supposed to order were there.

The bartender came up and Daniel ordered. When the man returned with Daniel's food, he said, "Anything else?"

"Might I get an extra napkin?"

The man seemed surprised. "Of course." He returned with it a few minutes later.

The pork pie was delicious. The raspberry wine was sweet and flavorful. Daniel liked it the best of all the alcohol he'd had so far. Yet he drank it cautiously, remembering how drink had affected Jonathan so.

He was over halfway through his pie when a short middle-aged man with straight black hair and a swarthy complexion wearing workman's clothes came over from one of the other tables. He held a cigarette. "Got a light?"

Daniel gaped at the man a moment, until he remembered what he was supposed to say. "Sorry, no. But I heard the store next door has matches for sale."

The man chuckled. "Mind if I join you?"

Daniel gestured to the chair across from him. "Please. I insist."

The man sat heavily. "Gods preserve us! They said you were new-minted, but —"

Daniel felt embarrassed. "Is it that obvious?"

The man winked. "Never fret: I'll sharpen you yet." He held out a hand. "Call me Zeus."

Daniel shook his hand. "Daniel. Pleasure to meet you."

Zeus sat back and folded his sun-roughened arms. "So what's that rascal got you doing?"

The fewer people who know of it, the better. "Nothing special."

"Good boy. I certainly don't need to know. Don't want to know. Better for all of us." He pointed at Daniel's pie. "Go on, finish up. We got time."

So Daniel ate his pork pie and drank most of his wine.

He was going to spill the last bit upon his trousers, but Zeus stopped him. "After you pay, take a bit there in your palm and run it through your hair when you get outside. Won't be noticed, and you won't stain your clothes that way."

"Good idea." So that's what he did as they stood outside a street vendor on the sidewalk. "Where to now?"

"First let's walk a bit."

As they walked along, Zeus began talking about words. "You sound like an outsider. Let's see if we can fix that."

Daniel nodded. "Yes, sir."

"You got no idea what I mean, do you? You just said 'saa' instead of 'sir.' Just one thing you folk from Dickens do."

"Sir," Daniel said, trying it out.

"That's better. Something's got an 'r' in it, you say it. And tighten up on it. You don't say 'sar' but 'sir.'"

"Yes, sir."

"Good!" They went on like this for some time as they walked along, turning this way and that. They waited at the Main Road, then hurried along at a gap in the traffic. "You learn pretty quick there," Zeus finally said. "Anyone asks, just tell them your ma was an outsider. That'll explain it." He grinned at Daniel. "If you gotta explain back home where you been today, tell them you were off taking lessons."

"Good idea."

"I-dee-ah, Daniel, not i-dee-err."

"Sorry, sir." He tried to say it like the man instructed.

Zeus clapped him on the shoulder. "You'll learn."

About a mile or so later, they stood in the middle of a broad boulevard, cracked and covered with weeds. Across from them was a tall yew hedge with an opening large enough to drive a carriage through. "Here we are."

He led Daniel across and through the opening, past a shattered building, weaving his way to the left. The narrow paths were empty of people. But sacks of trash, some fresh, spilled down alleyways, into empty lots, the smell thick in the hot humid air. Across the way, out of sight of the alley, a bit of remaining roof on a ruined structure left a patch of shade. "Let's sit."

On the ground? But Daniel sat as instructed.

"Now you can tell me true," Zeus said. "Where'd they want you to look?"

"The Cathedral."

Zeus nodded. "Tough assignment for a cub. But you do look the part." He took out a cigarette and lit it, leaning back against the rough wooden wall. "Just remember that any time you're in the Pot, you're being watched. You're not going to get anywhere near the Cathedral today without raising an alarm. They've never seen you before."

"You mean here, right now?"

Daniel started to look around, but Zeus stopped him. "Maybe right now, maybe not. But don't ever look: you may as well wear a sign. You hear a whistle, it means they think you don't belong." He took a drag on his cigarette, blew out smoke. "Your goal is to never hear one."

"What happens if they do? Whistle?"

Zeus shrugged. "You'll probably have to use whatever story you cooked up as to why you're here. What happens next depends on whether they think you're a threat."

"So what did you do just now? Why did they not whistle?"

"That's because I live here."

Daniel didn't want to ask too many questions, so he waited, arms resting on his knees, until Zeus finished his cigarette.

Then Zeus rose and offered Daniel his hand to hoist him up. "Come on, let's walk a bit."

The buildings next to the hedge were mostly rubble. They walked slowly, around buildings, through fields, like they weren't going anywhere special. They stopped at a bit of shade for Zeus to light another cigarette. Once he finished it a couple of blocks down, they played kick the can. The whole time, they moved away from the Cathedral along the enormous piles of trash rotting in the afternoon sun.

The trash flowed over the ruins, down the narrow alleys.

"Every morning before the sun," Zeus said, "men with ladders toss whole truckloads over the fence."

At first, Daniel felt horrified at the mess, the waste, what it said about the people on both sides. But then he really looked at it. "Doesn't seem like enough for this whole city."

Zeus lit a cigarette as he walked. "Well, the trash-men take the best stuff, you know, from the Manors and the mansions. Then there's people come here right early to grab the best of what's left, stuff they can sell come tonight. The street people come next, for food and such. Sometimes kids come looking for things they can make mischief with." He shrugged. "But most of it gets rifled through before the trash-men even pick it up."

This surprised Daniel. "Why?"

"Servants sometimes go through their master's trash for things they can sell, or give to their families, or use on the sly. Dangerous, that: it's a good way to earn a whipping. But some do it even so."

He took a drag from his cigarette. "Merchants send boys to collect expensive stuff like bottles. Then there's bits of information to sell to one Family or the other."

They walked another block or so as Daniel considered this. "I don't understand."

"What you toss tells a lot about you. A man who's supposed to be in good health throwing out an empty bottle of laudanum, for example. Or one with his can full of liquor empties. Or a tied-up pack of love letters." He grinned, tapping his temple. "Lots of information in that last one."

The satchel's strap irritated his neck. "Why does anyone care?"

Zeus kicked a rock, which went skittering down the street. "Round here, you never know when knowing something'll come in handy. If the guy with the can full of liquor empties every week is a man supposed to have your back, well ..."

Daniel nodded. Yet it disturbed him. "I'm not used to distrusting the people around me."

Zeus smiled to himself. "You'll learn." He shrugged. "Or else you'll die."

Daniel could find nothing to say to that.

"But our people send us messages this way, too. Let's see what's here today."

Zeus abruptly turned right, through the roofless ruin of an ancient building, and Daniel followed him past it and down a narrow street. Ten yards further, Zeus jiggled the handle of a weathered wooden door with peeling yellow paint. Inside, the air was fresh and cool, a sweet smell wafting from the other room.

Eight feet on a side, the room appeared to be a bar, but only a few bottles were on the shelf behind the counter. Two heavy-set men were at the bar, one leaning on it facing them, the other sitting on a stool to his right. A thin, dirty blond man sat dressed in rags at a table to Daniel's left, hunched over a half-full pint bottle.

This man seemed to ignore them, but the other two glanced over. The seated man said, "Zeus! How goes life?"

"Still kicking."

The man facing them chuckled. "Who's your buddy?"

Zeus turned to put a hand on Daniel's left shoulder. "A good friend of the family."

"Well, then." The man facing them sounded impressed. "Welcome." He held out his hand. "They call me Slim, and that guy there is Deuce."

"Daniel." He shook their hands, wanting to ask more but remembered the warnings he'd been given.

"So," Zeus said, "what's good today?"

Deuce lit a cigar.

Slim's eyes flickered to the blond man. "Ol' Liquor brought us a dropped earring off Scoop Street. Gems alone'd be worth it."

Zeus nodded sagely. "Let's see it."

They left Deuce sitting there. Slim lumbered into the other room past several thin men and women smoking from pipes and a man sitting on a stool, then into a short hallway. The sweet smell filled the air.

At the end of the hall sat a third room: a wooden table, a few chairs, some old cabinets. Slim shut the door and bolted it, then turned to face them. "He looks good. Smells of outsider, but we can fix that."

Zeus laughed. "Only had a few hours to work on him."

Heat rushed to Daniel's face.

Slim clapped him on the arm. "All in good fun, boy." Slim touched the front of Daniel's left shoulder. "You're one of us."

Daniel nodded. "So what do we do now?"

Zeus said, "We talk in here for a bit, then we go back. Slim tells people about his buddy Daniel. Next time you're here, he introduces you to a couple of his friends, guys he trusts. Maybe the time after that, they introduce you to their friends. People get to know you're okay."

Daniel felt dismayed. He didn't want to be here any more than he had to.

"This ain't a horse race," Slim said. "You wanna get what you came for, you gotta do it slow like. Specially if you don't wanna be noticed. Get to know the place before you start asking for things."

Zeus gestured to the table. "Let's go over what happened."

Daniel sat, but felt confused. "Happened?"

Zeus chuckled. "Lots happened out there. 'How goes life' means 'Zeus, you're with a guy I don't know, what's going on?'. If I said 'not bad' then I've been forced in there, or this guy's a threat, and shit's going down. But I said 'still kicking' which meant I'm okay and we got business."

Daniel gaped at Slim, who nodded.

Zeus continued, "So then Slim's question 'who's your buddy' is sure, you're okay, but who is he? If I said 'a guy I know' then he knows don't trust him. Or if he's a friend I could have just introduced him. Or if he's one of our Associates we might say 'a friend of ours'. But you're Diamond-sworn, so I say 'a good friend of the family'. Got it?"

"Yeah," Daniel said, starting to feel better about things. "What if he were a Diamond-born?"

"First of all, we know who they are. But if it was someone new to you, then we might say 'this here's my uncle' if they're older or 'my little cousin' if they're younger."

"Isn't that confusing? I mean, what if he really is your uncle?"

Zeus shrugged. "If they're a Diamond-born, that comes first. Otherwise you just introduce them by their name and explain the relationship later. Don't worry, you'll figure it out." He leaned back. "But you always put your hand on their left shoulder if you're gonna say any of the Family stuff. You tell us some guy's your uncle and don't put your hand there, we know you're being forced into it. Feds have tried this shit before to try and worm their way in."

Daniel frowned. "Feds?"

Slim's face twisted in disgust. "Bunch of bottom-dealing railbirds trying to take our city. Don't worry, you're not likely to come across one."

"All you gotta know," Zeus said, "is if you don't know who someone is for sure, don't trust them." He let out a short laugh. "Sometimes not even then."

Slim nodded. "So what about Deuce out there?"

Daniel thought back. "He's your friend, but not in the Family."

Slim smiled. "Exactly. Works for me."

Zeus said, "You see? It's not that bad, if you stop to think about it." He rose. "Time we be moving on."

Daniel and Slim got up. Daniel extended his hand. "Thanks for the help."

Slim shook it. "Here's to a long association."

Deuce still sat at the bar but the blond man was gone. "Had to kick him out: kept begging for another bottle." He turned to Slim. "They want the earring?"

As Zeus closed the door behind them, Slim said, "Don't worry about it."

Zeus lit another cigarette. They took a different way back, ambling along as if they had all the time in the world. The shadows lengthened. "From now on, you'll leave that satchel at Slim's when you go out. Attracts way too much attention."

Daniel nodded.

A curly-haired blonde girl of perhaps twelve dressed in rags poked her head sleepily out of a broken doorway. "Hey, Zeus."

"Hey, Stella." Zeus patted her cheek as they passed.

Daniel felt amazed. "So you pretty much know everyone here."

"Yep. Taken me years to do it. Didn't have anyone here when I started, now we got people all over this place."

Daniel felt impressed. "Why?"

"Why what?"

"Why do all this?"

Zeus draped his arm over Daniel's shoulders, stumbling as if drunk, and pulled him along an alleyway. They were close to where they'd come in. "Because, in case you didn't know," he whispered roughly, "we're in a war."

War

Daniel stared at Zeus, astonished and alarmed.

Zeus nodded. "And we're the ones gonna win."

"But how?"

"Information is everything, my boy." Zeus straightened, began to whistle. They moved past the gap in the Hedge, towards the Seamont. "I might sound like a Clubb, but it's true."

"Sounds like we have something in common."

Zeus snorted. "In that they want to take over the city, yeah. Arrogant sons of bitches. They stole the Aperture during the Coup, so they think they're better than us. But they started off servants just like you. Only they were bought to plow fields and dig carrots, not to dress boys and shine shoes."

Daniel nodded. Lady Luck had smiled on the Clubbs for certain. "So how are we going to win?"

Zeus chuckled. "That's not something to speak of here. You real curious, you ask Mr. Julius 'bout it. Now let me tell you how you're getting back into Diamond."

***

When they returned to the Seamont, Zeus introduced him to the bartender, a big man he called Bug. Then he brought Daniel to a back room to wipe himself down with a wet handkerchief and change into his clean clothes. Daniel couldn't get the wine smell from his hair, but at least he didn't smell so much like trash.

Once back over the bridge to Diamond quadrant, the carriage stopped at a guard station across from the taxi booth. A guard came over. "Everyone out. Over at the station one at a time, for entry into Diamond."

Daniel let the uppers to go first. Finally it was his turn.

"Reason for entry?"

He'd been warned not to say much, even to their own guards. You never knew who might be listening. "Just visiting friends."

"Address?"

He gave the address he'd been told to give, at the same time scratching the front of his left shoulder as Zeus had instructed.

The man gave him a sharp, surprised glance, then wrote the address down. "Very good, sir."

Daniel returned to Diamond Manor an hour after tea, with time to bathe before the boys came upstairs to dress for dinner.

As Daniel dressed Jack, the boy was full of news about his day: they'd visited some of their cousins, then they all went together past the city to a special school for several hours to learn to shoot. "Daddy — um, Father — says Jon's a natural. We can practice in the range now if we want. The doctor says it's okay for him."

Daniel recalled Flannery mentioning the range out past the gardens. Then Daniel remembered the face of the man he'd shot. "How did you do?"

"I did okay. I don't like the noise of it, but I can hit the target." He nodded, gaze turned inward. "We have to learn to defend ourselves." Then he looked at Daniel. "I can't rely on my men always being there to protect me."

Daniel nodded, but the thought of these boys being taught to kill someone, the way he had ... it pained him. "One day you may be alone, or your men hurt. These are your people, and they look to you for guidance." *You must teach them to be men of worth.* "You must stand for those who can't stand for themselves." The words just came from his mouth, but they felt right.

Jack's jaw dropped. "I never considered it that way."

Daniel slid Jack's coat over his shoulders and began brushing it. He needed to improve his ability in arms, if he were to protect these boys the way their grandfather wanted. "Would you like to practice together sometime?"

Jack's jaw dropped. "I didn't know you could shoot!"

Daniel smiled to himself. "I learned at the Academy."

Jack still stood there, mouth open. "Why ... that would be splendid!" He raced to his twin brother's room, returning a few minutes later. "Jon wants to shoot with us!"

"I'm glad," Daniel said, and meant it. He'd wanted to spend more time with Jonathan.

Jack turned his head to look at him. "Something's changed."

"In what way?"

"You seem different."

Daniel shrugged. "We all change. Look at you: I'm going to have to order a new set of trousers if you keep growing like this."

Jack blushed, beaming. It wasn't so much that he got red in the face, but the boy positively glowed. He rested his hand on Daniel's shoulder, gazed into his eyes. "I'll always protect you, Daniel. Diamonds always protect their own. You can count on that."

After Jack slept, Daniel fell into bed, exhausted by the excitement of the day. He wakened into dim-lit darkness: someone was shaking his shoulder. An oil lamp sat on the floor, turned low.

"Sorry," Mr. Neuberg said. "But you didn't wake at my knock, and I feared to disturb the young Master."

Daniel felt disoriented. "What's happened?"

"Mr. Julius wishes to see you."

Alarmed, Daniel hurried to dress and comb his hair.

After a few minutes, Mr. Neuberg picked up the lamp. "Come now, my boy, let's not keep him waiting."

Daniel followed Mr. Neuberg down to where Mr. Julius sat writing. He glanced up when they entered. "Very good." Mr. Julius gestured to a chair. "Come, sit, and tell me what you've learned."

Mr. Neuberg said, "Will there be anything else, sir?"

"I'll ring if needed."

Daniel moved forward, hesitant to sit.

Mr. Julius glanced up. "Come on, sit down. I'll not crane my neck in my own study."

Cheeks burning, Daniel rushed to sit. "Yes, sir. Thank you, sir."

"So what have you learned?"

Daniel told him everything, from the people in the Seamont to the condition of the Pot to what happened in Slim's bar to the talk he and Zeus had. "He said I should ask you about the war." Daniel had only a vague notion of war, and the idea frightened and confused him. "I don't understand what's going on."

Mr. Julius gave an amused smile. "You heard about the Coup?"

"Swan said it was well before he was born."

A small laugh burst forth from Mr. Julius. "Almost ninety years past. And since then, we've taken and held this quadrant for our own. **Our** own. Our people are safe here to walk the streets, to enjoy the peace the Inventor King meant for us. But this was done at great cost. And our most vicious enemy lies right over that river." He pointed towards it. "The Spadros Family despises us. They cheated us during the Coup. They're led by a madman who had his own father murdered to gain power. And they've made one attack after another on us." He shifted in his chair. "We have a cease-fire at present. But we've just made a plan which will one day give us half the city. We'll at last be in position to take the Spadros quadrant as well."

"That sounds good!" Daniel almost asked what the plan was.

Don't be inquisitive.

Inwardly thanking his teacher, he pressed his lips together.

Mr. Julius snorted to himself. "I've not survived this long by confiding in servants. But I'll let you know of anything which endangers my son, never fear."

Daniel quickly stood. "Will there be anything else?"

"No. You're doing well."

Daniel bowed low. "Thank you, sir."

As the weeks passed, whenever Mr. Julius took the boys on an outing, Daniel visited Zeus at the Seamont. Each time, Daniel met more people of the Pot.

Once Zeus said, "The quadrant-folk call them 'Pot rags,' but you must never say that, even if they do."

Daniel nodded, taken aback at the intensity with which Zeus spoke those words. And as time passed, Daniel learned why Zeus felt so passionate.

The man was Diamond-born: his father Diamond-born, his mother a whore in the Diamond Pot. After hiding young Julius Diamond from a gang of men who'd tried to kill him, Zeus earned the Family's favor.

"So Diamond-born aren't automatically in the Family?" There was family and there was Family. Daniel didn't completely understand all the differences, but he thought the latter was the same as what they called the Business.

"They gotta prove themselves like everyone else. And some just don't have the stomach for it. But they're still our people, and we gotta protect them. Sometimes if they're real smart ... like there's this little kid, one of the Jotepas. He's gonna be an Inventor for sure one day. Can't risk boys like that getting killed."

"Makes sense."

"For some time, I got information from Diamond Pot for the Family. But then Mr. Julius thought it'd be best to start a new game here. Remember the first day we were at Slim's shop, the guy boozing it up in the corner?"

Daniel nodded. "You called him 'old liquor'?"

Zeus chuckled. "Close enough. Name's Ely Kerr. That guy would sell his entire hand for a bottle of booze. Hell, he tried to sell us his kids once."

What kind of man would sell his own children?

"But anyways, he got me in. He'd been using the place Slim's in now as a hidey-hole, but it was all wrecked. We fixed it up, made it a paying establishment."

Daniel never knew what happened to his parents, and the thought that a child could end up in an orphanage in exchange for a bottle of alcohol disturbed him. "It looks good."

But Daniel later learned that selling kids in the Pot didn't mean sending them to the Home. Men came from all over Merca to visit the brothels of the Bridges Pot, and most of those outsiders looked for children.

Daniel and Zeus had been sitting in a patch of shade three blocks from the Cathedral. The day was bright, unseasonably warm for late winter, and the sun shone hot upon the Cathedral's steps. Through a huge gap in a broken building, they could see who came in and out.

"Don't never sit in the same place twice," Zeus said, "even a good place like this one."

They'd been sitting there a while, and Zeus gestured its way with his chin. "If you're looking for someone," Zeus said, "rather than for something, the Cathedral's the best place for them to be."

Now how did Zeus know he'd been sent to find a person? Daniel couldn't remember ever saying. "Why's that?"

"They don't force anyone to whore." He lit a cigarette, leaned back against the wall, then gestured with his chin, behind him and to the left. "Remember Stella?"

Daniel nodded: the little blonde girl.

"Her daddy's got a whole list of men who thinks she's their only one. Girl's a bit dim, but she's great with names. She don't like doing it, but he threatens her before they come by. Can hear him yelling at her all the way to Slim's."

"That's just wrong." Daniel started to get up. "We gotta do something —"

Zeus put his hand on Daniel's shoulder, pushing him back down. "No, we don't. This is the way it is here. You want to do your job for Mr. Julius, or you want to 'save' Stella?"

Daniel stared at the cobblestones, demoralized. *They bought you; you're obliged to obey.* "Do my job."

"What would you do with a dim-witted whore anyway?"

Daniel shrugged. "It's still wrong. She's just a little girl."

"But she ain't your little girl. You get one of them, you do what you want with her."

It's not right. The thought of his little Hermosa forced to be a whore tore at his heart. This whole place was wrong — men selling their children, boys taught to kill. He put his head in his hands, fighting back angry tears.

Zeus patted Daniel's shoulder. "Must be hard, being an outsider. Was it so much better back where you come from?"

Daniel shrugged. "I was an orphan. I lived my whole life in a few rooms and a garden." A bitter laugh burst from him. "I never even saw a dog until I came here."

When Zeus spoke next, Daniel could hear his smile. "Dogs are a good thing."

Daniel nodded. They were always happy to see you. "Sorry to be such a bother."

"You ain't a bother, boy. You're my brother. You got a whole lot of us around. You ever have something you need, something that pains you, you tell us. Those you feel you can trust." He scratched his arm. "This here thing with Stella, I know it pains you. I do wish we could help her. But we can't." Then he nudged Daniel on the arm, but down low, where it wouldn't be seen. "Look there."

Daniel wiped his nose on his sleeve and looked up. A group of thin little girls, maybe ten or twelve years old, came down the cracked marble steps. One looked his way, and those eyes —

It was her. Taller, still not even close to puberty, but the round face from the portrait had turned oval, her tightly-curled reddish-brown hair thick and well past her shoulders. Light brown skin, eyes a deep clear blue, but shaped just like Miz Annabel's.

One of the other girls said something, and the taller girl looked towards her. She'd never noticed them sitting there.

Zeus chuckled. "That's her, huh?"

"Thought you didn't want to know."

"I don't. But you've not learned to hide your interest. Guess it's another lesson." He grinned at Daniel. "I oughta charge Mr. Julius double, making me train a new-minted outsider like you."

Daniel looked at Zeus. "Not so new anymore."

Zeus snorted quietly. "Hate to think of what old Swan went through with you."

Daniel chuckled, remembering all the scrapes he'd been in that first year with the twins. He hadn't seen Swan much since the night of his ceremony, but he guessed the old man was as busy as usual. "He's a good one, that."

"He is."

They sat there as the sun dipped below the buildings. A woman's voice called out. The little girl and her friends went inside. "You want to know who she is?"

Daniel shrugged, turning his head away.

Zeus smiled. "Much better." He stretched out his legs. "Name's Jacqui. Her mother owns the Cathedral."

"Oh." Daniel felt impressed. "I didn't know anyone actually owned it."

Zeus nodded. "She's had it 'bout twelve years now. Around the time I came here. A guy used to own it before that. Older man." He leaned forward and drew his knees up, resting his arms on them. "Not sure what happened there; haven't seen him since." He flicked ashes off his cigarette. "Anyway, yeah, she owns it now. Place is doing real good business, I hear."

Why would Mr. Julius care about a little girl whose mother owned the Cathedral? "What else you know about her?"

"Wrong," Zeus said. "Don't never ask questions direct. You wanna know something, you say it sideways. Like 'pretty little thing.' Let them tell what they know." He yawned. "Best thing is to just stay quiet. Some guys hate quiet. They'll tell everything they know without you needing to ask."

Daniel nodded. "Sorry."

"Better to make the mistake with me than with someone ready to stab you for it. So Mr. Julius wants to know about Jacqui, huh?" He leaned back, hand at his chin. "She'd make a good informant, tell you the truth. Smart kid, but don't never let **no** one tell her what to do." He sat up, crossed his legs under him tailor-style, his face thoughtful. "We've never had anyone inside the Cathedral — other than as customers, that is." He let out a laugh. "But what they're really up to? No idea."

"Why do they have to be up to something?"

"Everyone here's up to something, boy."

Daniel was well of age, hardly a boy. But saying so wouldn't solve anything.

"There's too much we don't know about the Cathedral. Not even the Clubbs know what they're doing."

Everyone said the Clubbs knew everything about what went on. "You sure about that?"

Zeus shrugged. "Can't never be sure about what they know. But they're sure interested for people who know everything."

Daniel smiled. So the Clubbs weren't as good at being spies as people made them out to be. "And does Mr. Julius think the Cathedral can help us win this war?"

Zeus leaned back, his face thoughtful. "That I don't know."

Focus

The months passed, the days growing warmer. For Daniel's nineteenth birthday, Tolo and Siziba took him to The Twenty-Eight tavern on Market Center for luncheon.

Daniel showed the boys what he knew about shooting, and the boys took him along on one of their boating trips along the river.

He never saw their little sister, though. Gardena never appeared at morning meeting or even at prayers, and from what he heard from the boys, was kept constantly busy elsewhere.

Daniel liked going on a boat, gliding on top of water. *Jacob would've hated this.* Even the motion of a carriage had caused his friend to go white.

He wondered how Jacob was now. Had he found friends? Was he happy?

He hoped Jacob had found taking care of that little frightened Anthony an easier task than he'd had it with Jack.

Jack had been right about one thing: Jonathan was particularly good at shooting. After a bit of instruction, Jonathan soon became even better at it than Daniel was.

This seemed to greatly encourage the boy. Mr. Bastra told Daniel once that Jonathan spoke of building a cottage out past the range, so he might practice for as long as he liked, without having to return the quarter mile back to the house.

Impractical, of course, but Daniel thought it good that Jonathan had other things to focus on than his malady.

One of the servants must have mentioned their time at the range to the uppers, because one day Jack burst into his room. "Grandpa wants to take all of us to the Country House for our birthday!"

"Me, too?"

"Especially you! They said you should come watch over us." Jack preened. "It's going to be all men. Besides, we're much too old to be followed around by the likes of Miss Kaluki."

"That's unkind," said Daniel. "She's cared for you since you were born." He'd seen how she loved them. "She may be a servant, but she deserves your respect."

Jack hung his head. "I'm sorry."

"You need to think before you speak," Daniel said. "Think of how she would feel if she overheard that, or worse, if another servant heard it and told her."

Jack's face flushed, and he ran to the doors, peering out. "Thank the gods, no one heard."

Daniel smiled to himself. "Let this be a lesson to you."

"Do you want to come with us?"

"Of course I do. Do you want to wear white the entire time?"

Jack raised his chin, spoke boldly. "I do. Every minute."

"How long are we to be there?"

"A week. Neuberg probably knows more."

Daniel wondered why Mr. Neuberg hadn't told him about this already. "So how long do I have to prepare for this journey?"

"Oh. Um. We're leaving tomorrow."

Daniel almost laughed. "I suppose I best get to work then."

Apparently Mr. Hector had surprised Mr. Neuberg with the news as well, because the entire schedule wasn't planned yet. "Three days of shooting at least," Mr. Neuberg said. "At least one formal dinner —"

Daniel nodded, taking notes on a pad.

"— but mostly casual clothing for the house. They may want to play tennis, so some proper shoes for that." Mr. Neuberg shrugged. "I'd pack the young master's swimming suit as well. There's a lake nearby he used to enjoy."

The closest thing Daniel had found to an all-white suit was one with wide horizontal black and white stripes. Jack hadn't wanted him to purchase it until Daniel told him how long it'd taken to find.

But it would have to do.

Most everything was in order, but he had to have the trunks brought out of storage. Garrett refused to help him. Anton had just been awakened to help Mr. Lucas, and Oscar was trying to do everything at once. So Mr. Bastra found Daniel dragging Jack's trunks out of the storage room himself.

After Mr. Bastra complained to Mr. Julius about it, Garrett was reprimanded by Mr. Neuberg and forced to carry the trunks to Jack's room. When Mr. Neuberg left, Daniel grabbed Garrett's arm. "Why do you hate me? Is it something I've done?"

Garrett shook off Daniel's grasp. "Don't touch me. It's bad enough having to look at you." Then he stormed off, leaving Daniel as confused as he'd ever been.

There seemed nothing he could do. So he went back to work.

The trunks had to be dusted inside and wiped down outside. Then Daniel arranged the clothes for each day and packed them tightly into sets, so that nothing moved about during the journey. Cufflinks and collars, tie pins and suspenders, caps and dinner shoes. By the time the sun rose, Daniel felt exhausted. But when Garrett, Oscar, and Anton hoisted the trunks up to the back of the carriage, Daniel felt proud.

But then something strange happened: instead of trying to trip him, Garrett roughly grabbed his arm, jerking him aside. "I don't care what happens to me. But if you hurt her, I **will** kill you."

Daniel felt entirely confused. "Hurt who?"

"Come away from there," said Mr. Bastra. "It's time to go."

Daniel didn't understand what was going on. But he felt relieved to get into a carriage and away from Garrett for a while.

Daniel, Mr. Hook, Mr. Bastra, and Mr. Lucas (who was Mr. Hector's manservant) had their own carriage. The way to the Diamond Country House was quite a ride, and Daniel slept much of the way.

He woke to the sun low through the trees. Apple trees, by the look of it.

"Ah, you're awake," Mr. Hook said. "We're almost there."

"Just as well," Mr. Lucas said.

The way he said it made Daniel wonder. "What do you mean?"

Mr. Hook said, "We don't tell just anyone where this place is. For security." He chuckled. "What you don't know, you can't tell, not even on accident."

So they still didn't fully trust him.

"It's not that we don't trust you," Mr. Bastra said.

Daniel glanced at him, startled. Could the man read minds?

"But you're still very young." Mr. Bastra spoke gently. "And not raised as we are. You're not used to hiding things as yet." He gave Daniel a warm smile. "You should never give anyone something they're not yet able to handle. Just like the guns we'll be handling later on. The boys now know how to use them, and can be trusted." He leaned back, glancing outside. "Truth in the wrong hands can be more dangerous than a gun."

"Hear, hear," Mr. Hook said.

Daniel had never thought of the truth this way before. "Why?"

Mr. Lucas leaned forward. "If the wrong person learned where we're going, they'd send men to kill everyone inside." The man's eyes went distant for a moment, then he again focused upon him. "A gun only holds six shot. Dozens live at the Country House, innocent servants — just like you and me."

Daniel gasped, picturing a slaughter of people dead, just like the man he'd killed down with Mr. Julius.

Mr. Lucas nodded, leaning back.

We're in a war. For the first time since he'd arrived, he understood a little of what that meant.

Outing

The Diamond Country House was grand, with a roof that resembled the pointed base of a huge cut crystal, like those in the chandeliers at Diamond Manor.

The Country House staff were lined up in the huge circular drive to greet them. The boys rushed inside as the uppers went down the line, greeting a few older folk.

Meanwhile, Daniel followed the other servants to begin unloading the carriages.

Mr. Hook grabbed his arm. "That's for the footmen to do. Come now, Mr. Julius will want to introduce you."

Me? "Of course, sir, my apologies."

Mr. Hook chuckled. "You're just trying to help. Come along."

Mr. Julius stood beside a thin, kindly-looking, elderly white-haired man. "Mr. Bradford, may I introduce Daniel, Master Jack's manservant. Mr. Bradford is the butler here."

Daniel bowed low. "I'm honored, sir."

"Mr. Bradford will assist you with anything you might need," Mr. Julius said, then disappeared through the front door.

A wry smile came over Mr. Hook's face. "I don't suppose you have the schedule for this chaos?"

Mr. Bradford laughed. "Other than the note Mr. Neuberg sent? We have all the amusements. But the house will be well-full: the school has agreed to let the older boys join us tonight, then stay on for Saturday."

"Very good," Mr. Hook said. "With any luck, they'll all go out for the day. Leave us alone for once."

"Heh," said Mr. Bradford, a grin on his face. Then he turned to Daniel. "Let me show you to your rooms."

The other servants had followed Mr. Julius inside. What looked like a front antechamber led to a maze of open-air courtyards and narrow covered halls with equally narrow openings in them. Like windows, yet without glass.

"You're being given quite an honor," Mr. Hook whispered. "No one born outside the dome has been allowed inside those front doors since before the Coup."

"Oh," said Daniel, surprised.

"But you've made quite an impression upon the young Master. He all but begged for you to be allowed to attend him."

"I see."

Mr. Bradford led them to another door, this time to the house proper. Up a grand staircase much like back at Diamond Manor, then directed Mr. Hook to his rooms. He took Daniel then to the boys' rooms, and his own.

Daniel's room here was even larger, but done up in white like the rest. Jack's closet was smaller than the one at the Manor, but he hadn't brought nearly so much as all that with him.

"The young Masters will be having their dinner upon the veranda," said Mr. Bradford. "Informal dress. They should be up momentarily."

Daniel washed his hands and face, took off his jacket and hat, and got to work. Quickly finding Jack's all-white dinner clothing, checking each item for any wrinkles. He got everything laid out just as Jack bounded through the door.

The boy cast his jacket upon a chair. "Oh, to get out of these clothes! I feel I need a bath already."

"There isn't time," said Daniel. "Undress, and I'll bring a hot cloth if you wish."

Jack began shedding his clothing upon the floor, whilst Daniel went to his bathroom, soaking a cloth in hot water. That plus a bit of cologne and a dry toweling, and the boy was ready to be dressed for the evening.

After Jack left, Daniel spent some time unpacking and hanging Jack's clothing. A formal dinner was planned for the next evening, so he had to make sure Jack's white tuxedo was ready.

A knock at the door. Mr. Bastra came in from across the hall, where his and Jonathan's rooms were. "Might I assist you?"

"I'm finished here," said Daniel.

"Then let's go down to meet the others."

Daniel and Mr. Bastra went to the ground floor to confer with the housekeeper about what the boys liked to eat and didn't. Then they went downstairs. Daniel thought they went to see what they might do there.

The kitchens were in a flurry of activity, both for the night and for the next day. Although the Country House was huge, it had a relatively small staff for normal times, being mostly used as a seasonal resort. To Daniel's surprise, Cora, the kitchen maid Kindra, and one of the scullery girls had been brought there as well. Little Malena waved shyly when she saw him.

Mr. Bastra pulled at his arm. "Come, the first dish has gone up. We're eating in shifts, as it were, due to our late arrival."

Daniel's stomach growled. "Has the little girl eaten?"

Mr. Bastra chuckled. "They've been passing Malena bits of dinner all night. She's off scrubbing pots. We, on the other hand, are eating with the manservants tonight."

Platters holding mounds of chicken, sliced potatoes, cubes of spiced pumpkin, pickled cabbage, and cider had been set up along one wall of their staff hall. After filling their plates, the four sat with the manservants for the five older sons around a long table.

"Ah, this is good," Mr. Lucas said, leaning back to pat his stomach. "I'd forgotten what a splendid Cook we have here."

Cora came in. "Might I take your plates, sirs?"

Daniel smiled up at her, and she blushed. "Thank you."

As she left, Mr. Hook said, "She likes you."

Daniel shrugged.

"You could do worse," said Mr. Lucas. "She's a comely woman. The two of you would make some fine children."

Daniel went through a list of things he might say, then settled on, "I thank you for the advice, sir."

Mr. Hook chuckled.

Why did Mr. Hook go along with this? He knew about Baraja, as did Mr. Bastra.

But Swan had warned him not to say anything about her. Perhaps Mr. Lucas and the others didn't need to know.

***

After eating, Daniel wanted to go help with the kitchen, but Mr. Lucas only laughed, speaking to Mr. Hook and Mr. Bastra in a joking tone. "Have you never taught him his place, sirs? Daniel, my boy, we don't clean kitchens. We're manservants! Once your young Master is grown, you'll handle his finances, not wash his kitchen pots. Your place is upstairs. You wish to help, but there is plenty to do elsewhere." He leaned forward, spoke quietly. "Remain in your station and you'll prosper. Leave the others to their work."

Daniel nodded. "Yes, sir."

Mr. Bastra smiled, putting a hand on his shoulder. "I'm off to bed; we have much to do tomorrow."

The rest left, yet Daniel stayed there, nursing his glass of cider. His teacher had said much the same, but he never realized how it would play out in reality. It felt wrong to sit whilst others toiled, when he could be of service.

"Sir," Kindra said from the door, "it's time for the next group to eat, but I must clean the table first."

Daniel jumped to his feet. "Oh! Please excuse me." Embarrassed, he found his way upstairs. The laughs and banter of the uppers echoed through the well-lit halls: they were still at dinner.

"Did you need something?" Cora stood behind him, and her voice startled him.

"Not really." He shrugged. "The other manservants have retired. But I slept most of the way here." He wondered how they planned to dress their charges for bed whilst asleep, but perhaps things worked differently here.

175

"They have no further need of me in the kitchens," Cora said. "Would you care for a walk? They say the courtyards are lovely in the moonlight."

And so they were. Some had fountains with bits of darkly-colored stone round them making patterns. Others had full gardens, others were well-kept grass. The sounds of the uppers at dinner could be heard even here. "This place is amazing."

"It is."

He couldn't help but recall the things the other manservants had said to him. He stopped, faced her. "What can I do for you?"

Cora seemed taken aback. "I don't understand."

"Forgive me." Daniel felt confused. "I —"

"This was a mistake." And with that, Cora turned and ran.

"Wait." He followed her, only able to make it back to the house by glimpses of the edge of her skirts as she ran. But the door had locked behind them, and he had to ring to get back inside.

Mr. Bradford said, "Whatever are you doing out here?"

"Nothing." Daniel felt embarrassed. "Got lost, that's all."

"Good night to you, then."

Daniel went up to his rooms, laid out Jack's pajamas, and got into bed. Were the others trying to match him with her? Why?

All he ever wanted was to be with Baraja. He brought out the portrait of her and their little girl, gazing upon it in the candlelight. *You are my Beauty.*

Then he blew out the candle, falling asleep in the darkness.

***

Daniel had yet to meet Jack's older brothers. But the seven Heirs were all at morning prayer, far up at the front. From what he'd heard, the oldest one was a couple of years older than he was.

After prayers, Daniel went to Cora. "Forgive me for last night: I suppose I'm not used to your ways."

Tears filled her eyes, and she turned away to the corner.

Kindra stood nearby. "Go after her."

The boys were off to breakfast. So he did. "Wait, Cora. Please."

She stopped, head down.

"I'm sorry. Whatever I did wrong. I didn't mean to hurt you."

She nodded. "I thought maybe you liked me."

This surprised him so much he chuckled. "I do like you."

"More than that."

"Oh." He didn't know what to say. He glanced around: the room was almost empty. "There's something you should know." They sat there in front of the Blessed Dealer. "Swan said I should never tell anyone. But you deserve to know." So he told her about Baraja and their daughter. About his plan to earn enough to buy, if not Baraja's freedom, their daughter's. "I don't want Hermosa to grow up like that," he said. "I want her to be free."

Cora nodded.

And something in her beautiful green eyes, there in front of the Blessed Dealer, touched something inside him, made him want nothing more than to tell her all he could.

So he told her about Jack, and what they'd done, the life Daniel had been forced into. "So there's no hope for us, you and me, not any time soon. I couldn't do that to the little Master: it'd break the boy's heart. Swan and I want one day for him to love a woman, and forget any feelings for me." A touch of despair struck, and he pushed it aside. "But I feel honored at your regard."

That made her smile.

Mr. Bastra poked his head in. "They're leaving for the shoot soon. And the young Master's asking for you."

Daniel smiled to himself. He said to Cora, "I'd fancy a walk tonight, though."

She nodded, eyes haunted. "I would too."

Daniel hurried up to change into his casual clothing, rushing out to his carriage just as the uppers' carriages pulled away.

Again Daniel and the other Manor manservants rode together. Yet this trip felt different. Everything Cora had said and done meant different things to him now.

He'd never thought of Cora the way he had Baraja, yet ...

Now what Garrett had said made sense. He must have known of her feelings, and didn't want her hurt by a harsh refusal.

The footman who had taken Daniel's bags for him at the station almost three years back was now opening his door. "Careful now, sir, the ground is rocky."

And although he felt glad to see the man again, the circumstances of it angered him. Why should this man defer to him? Why did this place have some above and some below? He just wanted to live in peace.

But it wasn't this man's fault. And he took care not to let his anger show as he went along with the rest.

The footmen had set up tables with food and drink, and canopies to shade them, and chairs to lounge in. A smell of water hung in the air. Off in the distance within view of the canopies stood a firing range.

To his surprise, Cora and Kindra were with the footmen, setting out the already prepared platters, which had been kept safe inside boxes with little shelves inside. "You've done a splendid job," he blurted out.

Cora, Kindra, and the footmen stared at him, mouth open, then bowed or curtsied as was their wont.

Jack pulled at his arm. "Come, Daniel! I put you in the rotation."

Jack had put him in the rotation after himself, which put him before Jonathan. "Your brother should go before me," Daniel said.

He hadn't noticed anyone being tense before this, but everyone there instantly relaxed, nodding and smiling.

And so they began.

Everyone there was good at shooting. Or rather, all the uppers were, including the five older brothers. The other manservants didn't so much as attempt to join in, only standing to hold the master's cup or wine glass, or to hand the master a different gun.

Daniel felt quite conspicuous, but he did his duty for Jack, then fetched his own gun to shoot.

Either Jonathan or Mr. Hector won every round, and his older brothers scowled at him, particularly the eldest one. Mr. Hector said, "We're going to have to do this more often, Jon, so I can figure out how you're beating me."

Jonathan beamed at his grandfather, his stance that of a man feeling both happy and accomplished.

Daniel so wanted this boy to find a useful life that his eyes stung at the sight. He turned away.

"Come on, Daniel," Jack said. "We're going swimming now!"

So the entire set-up was moved a couple hundred yards down a path to a large lake. That is to say, the footmen and maids moved it: none of the manservants would allow Daniel to touch a thing.

Jack called out, "Hurry up, Daniel!"

So he trudged down the path ahead of the other manservants, who strolled along together, chatting as if on holiday themselves.

Bathing huts for each of the uppers had been set up there already, complete with bathing suit and towels. Once dressed, Jack flung himself into the water with the rest.

Jonathan stood in the water for a while, as if uncertain how much he might do, then did some gentle swimming out twenty yards and back. Then he got out, spoke to Mr. Bastra, and the two went to his bathing hut. When they emerged, Jonathan was dressed, and he sat in the shade with some lemonade.

Finally, Jack's travel trunk arrived, and Daniel could get Jack's discarded clothes shaken out and folded into a section separate from his clean clothes, for washing later.

The eldest brother, a man of one and twenty, came past wrapped in a towel. "Good to see you finally doing some work."

Daniel stared at him. "I beg your pardon?"

The man spat. "You should."

Mr. Hector had been sitting in the shade, yet his shout could have cut iron. "Cesare! This man is Diamond-sworn." He stood, pointing at Daniel. "You will apologize at once."

Everyone had stopped, including the boys still in the water, and were staring at them.

Cesare rolled his eyes. "Sorry."

Mr. Hector stormed over to stand beside his grandson. "And you have no reason or right to speak that way to another man's servant, whatever his station. Is that clear?"

For the first time, Cesare looked uncertain. "Yes, sir."

"Now you will stay on the shore for the rest of the day." He pointed at the shaded area. "Go."

Cesare looked to his father, but Mr. Julius only began to laugh.

So Cesare slunk to the seats and threw himself into one, scowling the remainder of the trip.

Mr. Hector turned to Daniel. "My apologies." He glanced at Mr. Julius, speaking loudly enough for all to hear. "It seems my grandsons aren't being taught nearly so well as I imagined."

Mr. Julius stopped laughing.

Daniel only bowed and returned to his work. He particularly did not want to be involved in whatever conflict there was between those two, which seemed to be of a long-standing nature.

When Jack came from the water, Daniel held the towel for him, as he'd seen the other manservants do. Jack said, "Why won't you come in the water?"

"It's not my place, sir."

"You shouldn't listen to Cesare," Jack said. "He's mean."

Daniel wrapped the towel around Jack to the shouts and splashes of the four still in the water. "Would you like to sit for a while? I'll get you a drink."

"Okay."

Mr. Bastra stood behind Jonathan. Once Daniel got Jack settled, Daniel stood behind Jack as well.

He'd never seen a lake before. It was beautiful still water, with lush trees around a gentle sandy shore. *Baraja would love this.*

In that dusty place she lived, he felt fairly certain she'd never seen one before either. One day, when he'd gotten Baraja and Hermosa free, he'd find a place for them beside a lake.

He glanced over to see Cora watching him, and he smiled at her, then looked away. She seemed like a good person; she'd always been kind to him and to the children.

Daniel sighed. Baraja was with another man even now. He wanted nothing more than to free her. But did that mean being alone forever? Would she even want that?

Jack looked up and behind at him. "What's wrong?"

Daniel smiled warmly at him. "Just thinking of how beautiful this place is."

Jack sounded surprised. "It is!"

***

Eventually, the group got dressed, returned to the house, had dinner. And after laying out Jack's pajamas, Daniel went out to the first courtyard.

Cora stood there; she held out her hand with a smile. "I have something to show you."

Her hand was soft, and she smelled of roses. Daniel became all too aware of how near she was as they walked.

"I want to tell you something, too," Cora said.

Daniel nodded, touched. She'd come to trust him. Perhaps she'd tell him more of what this was about.

They turned a corner right, then a few steps later, left. "There's a courtyard here with no windows, just open to the sky." She came to a door, opened it. "It's my favorite place to visit."

They stepped inside, and she closed the door behind them.

The courtyard was ringed with fragrant flowers, the floor covered in thick grass. The stars shone overhead, but he could barely see her in the dim light. She stood facing him, so close he could imagine her body against his. And he felt stirred.

"I know you're alone here in Bridges," she said. "This place is called the Courtyard of Love."

The Courtyard of Love? His heart pounded, his body taut, his mouth dry. "Oh, Cora ..."

She put her hands upon his hips, slowly, firmly, pulling him to her. "And I want to help you."

Oh, gods. He let out a groan as the pressure of her body upon his reached its peak: it felt so good!

He felt his resolve waver. He wanted her so badly! But could he do this to Baraja, to Jack?

"Your young master will never know."

And Baraja lay with other men.

Daniel kissed her with all his heart, pressing his body onto hers.

The grass was soft.

***

They returned to the house hand in hand. Daniel fell into his bed, exhausted, drained. He woke to darkness.

What did this mean? What did he want? Why did Cora do this, knowing that he loved another?

What should he do?

If you find yourself in a compromising situation with a woman, Master Écarté told them, *you must offer your hand in marriage. There is no excuse for any other course of action. And whatever her answer, you must never expose the truth, or leave her in disgrace.*

It was then he realized: *I don't want to marry Cora!*

Why had he done this?

He couldn't blame her, as he'd done Jack. He could have said no, asked her to leave, left the courtyard himself. This had been his decision, and no one else's.

But he couldn't avoid it: he had to go to Cora, make things right. If she became with child, she'd be dismissed. He might not love the woman, but he would never ruin her life. Not when she'd only tried to help.

They were leaving that day for the Manor. When might they talk? He had to get the trunks out, pack his things and Jack's. Then he must get Jack ready to travel after breakfast.

Could he speak with her after prayers?

But what would he say? What could he offer her?

How could he ever explain this to Jack?

This made him hesitate to do anything. Cora said Jack would never know. What did she mean?

Daniel sat on the side of his bed. He didn't know what to do.

He couldn't get the feel of Cora under him out of his mind, the way it felt to be inside her. Was it like it had been with Baraja?

It'd been so long he'd almost forgotten.

This thought made him feel miserable. *I never want to forget you, my Beauty!*

182

He felt like a traitor to her, to his daughter. How could he help them if he was married to Cora? Would she even countenance that?

Daniel felt trapped. What should he do?

As much as he tried, there never was a time during the rest of the week where he and Cora might speak together. Back at the Manor, Jack lounged about, tired from the active weekend, and went to bed early.

But when Daniel tried to go to the maid's area to ask for Cora, Mrs. Whist stopped him. "You go back up where you belong, sir. I'll have no maid of mine out with a man after dark."

Garrett wouldn't look him in the eye, but at least he stopped trying to trip him. And Daniel wondered how much Garrett knew.

Finally, Daniel wrote her a letter, asking to meet with him on a matter of great import, at her convenience.

An hour later, when the boys were downstairs taking tea on the veranda, a knock came at the door.

Cora stood there, the suction cleaner trailing behind her. "You called for this, sir?"

He smiled at her. "I did."

She pushed the thing to the center of the room and turned it on. Then she took his arm, pulling him to the bathroom, and shut the door. "What the hell are you doing?"

Daniel was so surprised that he stood there speechless.

"You're acting like ... I don't even know what. Some lovesick puppy. Do you **want** your master to find out?"

"I — I ... I need to marry you. Don't I?"

She blinked. "Why?"

"Because, um ... I thought that was how it was done here. After ... you know."

She took a deep breath, let it out, not looking at him. "You don't have to marry me, Daniel." Their eyes met. "And I wouldn't marry anyone out of obligation."

"But what if there's a child? I won't have you dismissed, or —"

She grabbed his face. "Don't you understand? They **want** a child from you. Us." She let go, walked away to rest her forehead upon the wall. "I like you, Daniel. I do."

"Then tell me the truth. What's going on?"

She sighed. "I was commanded to bed you before we returned here, or be punished."

Daniel didn't know what to say.

"It was the only way Mr. Hector would let us marry —"

"Wait," Daniel said. "You ..." Suddenly, it came to him. "You and Garrett. You're —"

"Yes." Cora sighed, turning to slump against the wall. "I'm Mr. Hector's bed maid, just like you're Master Jack's. Since before the Old Mistress turned in her cards. Garrett and I have wanted to marry since before they bought you. But when Swan told the Old Master about you, that became the bride-price: your child in my womb." She shook her head. "Then we'll be in a rush to marry, and seven or eight months later, no matter what the child looks like, I'll swear it's Garrett's."

Daniel couldn't believe what he was hearing. "But why would Mr. Hector do this? Why do they care so much about me?"

"Who knows why these people do what they do?"

No wonder Garrett hated him. Now everything he'd done and said made sense. "Thank you for telling me the truth."

Daniel stumbled past her and turned off the suction cleaner. He lay face down upon his bed, not hearing anything she said, until finally she went away.

***

Daniel returned to his work. He went to the Spadros Pot when Jack was away. But he felt as if in a fog.

Siziba tried to reach him. "What's going on with you, boy? You don't seem yourself these days."

Daniel would only shrug and go back to throwing the ball. Little Flannery was getting good at catching, and the dogs found it as much fun to chase the ball back and forth in the air as catching the ball themselves.

The children were the only thing that mattered anymore. He'd be Flannery's real friend, and pretend to be Jack's lover. He'd spy for Mr. Julius about that little girl. He'd stand guard for the boys at those interminable meetings.

He'd send money for Hermosa; he was her father.

But what else was there for him here?

What he and Cora had done in the courtyard must have worked, because there was a scandal and a hastily-arranged wedding, just as she'd said there would be.

He was never alone with her again.

Mr. Wheeler was promoted to Under-butler. And Garrett — now, Mr. Garrett — was given the title of First Footman. He didn't try to trip Daniel anymore.

That only made Daniel feel worse. When Zeus would drink, so would Daniel, and sometimes, the stumbling around would be real. "Don't drink so much," Zeus said one day, "not 'til you're out of the Pot. Then go to the Seamont and have all you want." He shook his head then. "If these folk think you're vulnerable, they'll leave you in an alley wearing nothing but your skin."

That scared Daniel for a while, made him think about what he really wanted out of all this. And back in his room, after Jack had used his hands to fall asleep, Daniel thought about it.

He used to just be happy to live. To survive. Once he had Baraja and Hermosa to think of, though, he wanted to get them free.

And now?

Daniel didn't blame Cora: she was just doing what they all were. The masters owned them — as servants, they had no say in what they were asked to do.

But to know that the old man used her and Garrett like that, forced her to whore, to deceive, just to get a child? And for what? It felt wrong.

Miz Annabel had told him these people were criminals. He hadn't listened.

Swan had said most of the job was making the uppers feel good about themselves. So some of them must have some doubts. Some of them must care. Yet was Swan truly helping them?

Then what Miz Albaletta told him back at the Home, all those long years ago, came to mind: *Your duty is to these children, just as mine is to you. They need you. We're tasked with bringing them up to be men of worth. If they see you falter, what will become of them?*

His duty was to these children. Maybe, just maybe, he could make one of them care.

***

The summer passed, as did the fall, and the days grew windy and chill. When Daniel and Jack met the carriage to go to the meeting that day, he felt astonished to see Gardena and Miss Kaluki standing there as well.

And he realized that the girl had grown: her coat blew aside to reveal a simple yet elegant gown, which showed off her young figure well. And he felt glad for Mr. Neuberg's warnings. She was but fourteen and beautiful already. What might have happened should she have fixated upon him as well?

Gardena caught him staring and blushed; Daniel wrenched his eyes away, heart pounding, the heat rushing to his cheeks. *She's a child*, he reminded himself. *And she's not for you.*

He felt grateful that Jonathan, Jack, and Gardena took their own carriage with Miss Kaluki, whilst Daniel rode in back with Oscar. He needed some air.

What Cora had done was fine. But he needed Baraja. Letters and photos weren't enough. He desperately needed her, in his arms.

But would he ever see her again?

The man they met with that day was called Mr. Hart: a big, capable-looking red-haired fellow with eyes like Miz Annabel's. He reminded Daniel of someone.

Mr. Hart brought his grand-daughter with him, a girl named Ferti. The child was seven, perhaps eight, and unattractive. After a few minutes of listening to her, it became clear that the child had some sort of impediment. The girl's nursemaid seemed to have given up on getting her to act with decorum: she rolled around on the floor with dolls like a much younger child would.

They all sat there. Daniel stood forcing his eyes upon the wall until the door opened and Mr. Julius came out, along with a man who resembled Mr. Hart, but with stiff-straight black hair.

"Daniel," Mr. Julius said, "come here with us. This man will stand guard."

Daniel felt relieved. "Yes, sir."

Mr. Julius led him to stand before them. "Now tell us everything you've learned whilst in the Spadros Pot."

So Daniel spoke of the conditions, the way people were treated there, the buildings around the Cathedral, and what he'd learned about the little girl, Jacqui.

Mr. Julius leaned back, smiling broadly. "Now you see the value we bring to the table. This is just one young man out of an entire network we have in that quadrant. And no one would ever remark upon any of them being there."

Mr. Hart had been peering at Daniel the entire time, but at this, he nodded. "And did you see the child?"

"Yes, sir. She appears healthy and well."

"Very good," Mr. Hart said, relaxing.

"So do we have a deal?"

The two men rose. Mr. Hart said, "We have a deal."

And as they shook hands, Daniel had a twinge of fright. Who really was this little girl, and why were they so interested in her?

"You can go now," Mr. Julius said. "We'll be out in a minute."

As he left, he couldn't help but thinking: had these men just sold this little girl, too?

Suspicion

On the day before Yuletide Center, the uppers went to spend the day with friends. When Daniel stopped by the Seamont, it was pretty clear Zeus had been drinking for some time.

After a while, Daniel said, "We gonna go?"

Zeus laughed, his words slurring. "You're good enough to be on your own now." He clapped his hand on Daniel's shoulder. "You're welcome by Slim's, or here for that matter, anytime you want. But if you get into trouble, don't lead them to us!"

It was then Daniel realized he was part of something much bigger going on. "You've got people in the other quadrants too."

Zeus smiled broadly. "Indeed we do. See, the Clubbs, they like everyone to think they know everything. We don't. We just go our way all gentlemanly-like, and don't no one learn nothing from or about us." He took a long drink of his ale. "Not to mention they think we all look like Mr. Julius, so someone like us never gets a second glance."

Daniel nodded.

"Well," Zeus said, "let's go see what Slim's got for us today."

They ambled along towards the Pot, past the Main Road, to the Gap. The bar was decorated in holly. There was a crowd, and they all cheered when Daniel and Zeus came in.

Slim gave them both a drink, then Daniel rose from the bar. He was finally on his own; he wanted to get this spying business over with. "I'll see you later," he said to Zeus.

Zeus nodded, and Slim grinned at Daniel as he left.

Daniel at first went left, away from the Cathedral, then ambled down a side street he'd been down dozens of times. After a few blocks, he turned right, weaving along. People knew him. He knew them. He passed by two men sitting along the wall across the narrow street.

"Hey, Daniel! Got anything good?"

Daniel shook his head and yawned. "Not today; just got around. Lemme see what I can find ya."

"Good man, that," the man who'd spoken said to his friend. The implication hung clear: *How'd a guy like that end up here?*

Those kind of questions were dangerous. Daniel let himself weave, stumble a bit, as if drunk already. He leaned one hand against a wall, stopping for a few moments, leaning his body on the wall as if dizzy.

A group of young toughs went past the other way, and Daniel nodded to them. They waved and went on past. Daniel crossed the street unsteadily and went on his way. He didn't know what they thought of him, but his long association with Zeus seemed to make him off-limits.

Turning left, Daniel staggered in a undulating line down along one side of the street, stopping every so often to pick up something he thought someone might want and stick it in his pocket. Everyone did that here.

He turned right, then continued on. As the day passed, he'd stop and talk with someone, offer something from his pockets or trade for something they had.

"Where's Zeus?" An older man, standing outside one of the many brothels.

Daniel would normally shrug, but this time, he said, "Last I saw him he kept moaning about his head."

The man laughed. "So the mighty Zeus finally got himself a hangover! That man can out-drink just about anyone."

Oops. "Guess he did."

"Just wait 'til I see him!"

He'd have to warn Zeus — hopefully he'd see the man before he had to return home.

Best keep your mouth shut.

Bit by bit, Daniel wound his way towards the Cathedral. Two blocks away, three blocks toward. One block away, two blocks toward. During mid-afternoon, he found the shadow of a ruined building a block off from the Cathedral, where a gap between buildings gave him a view of the wide front stair. He leaned back against a charred wooden upright, stretched out, feet up, and pulled his cap partially over his eyes, so as to appear to be asleep.

But he couldn't help thinking about the little girl, Jacqui. What if they **were** planning to sell this girl to someone?

Then he felt dismayed. What could he even do about it?

"What you doing here?"

"Huh?" Daniel turned his head towards the sound.

A boy, thirteen or so. Medium-brown skin, straight black hair which brushed his shoulders. Skinny and dressed in rags like the rest, but this boy's clothes were clean.

Daniel went through several options, then settled on, "What's it look like?"

The boy frowned. "I keep seeing you."

Daniel shrugged. "Good stuff round here."

This seemed to mollify the boy a bit. But then he said, "Are you a spy?"

For some reason, this made Daniel laugh. Was it that obvious?

It seemed to be the right thing, because the boy relaxed a little.

Daniel didn't move. Perhaps he might save this after all. "What's your name?"

"Benji." He still seemed suspicious. "What's yours?"

"Daniel."

Benji stood motionless, his dark eyes evaluating. "I don't like people watching us."

"Who's us?"

The boy gestured towards the Cathedral with his chin.

"Wait. You live **there**?"

Benji nodded.

Daniel shrugged. "Oh." He relaxed into the upright, waiting.

"Why you here?"

Daniel yawned, pulled his cap lower over his eyes. "Tired."

"Yeah, I'm tired too, but I don't come in from outside, walk all over, then sleep," he pointed through the gap, "right where ya can see the front stair."

So Benji had followed him. Daniel forced himself to yawn again. "Don't know whatcha mean."

This seemed to dismay the boy. "I seen ya."

Daniel snorted. He and Zeus had worked on this story for months, and it felt ironic that the first time going off on his own, he had to use it. "Yeah, I go out. I go around, get stuff for my friends." Daniel sat up then, leaning forward, and looked into the boy's eyes. "Something you want?"

Benji recoiled. "No." He straightened, spoke proudly. "We got what we need."

Daniel nodded slowly. A lot of pride at being in the Cathedral.

Benji frowned, leaning forward. "So where you from? What brothel birthed you? Why no one see you here 'til lately?"

This kid was smart. Not only that, a thinker. Deeply grateful for the instruction Zeus had given him, Daniel glanced away. Then he grimaced, head down. "Don't wanna talk 'bout that."

Benji's shoulders drooped. "Sorry."

Now the kid would believe some tragedy drove Daniel here. It was a common story amongst the people of the street, the ones not born in the brothels. Daniel shrugged, turned away.

But when he turned back, Benji still peered at him, eyes evaluating. "I know what you are."

Caught

Daniel felt so surprised that at first he didn't speak.

Benji ran straight for the front stair.

By the time Daniel recovered his wits, he'd have had to shout at the boy to get him to stop. If he'd mistaken what the boy meant, a shout would give away everything.

The boy ran inside.

No one came down the stairs. No whistle sounded.

Slowly, heart pounding in fear, Daniel got up, moved out of view of the Cathedral. What should he do? Where should he go?

Don't lead them to us.

By the sun, it was close to three. He had to get back to Diamond Manor soon. But if Benji had raised suspicion, the Gap would be watched. He'd be followed, and that would take them right back to Diamond Manor.

Daniel didn't want to try climbing the Hedge. Was there another way out?

"Hi, Daniel."

Stella stood behind him, smiling shyly.

"Hey, Stella."

Her cheeks reddened and her smile grew bigger. "Whatcha doing over here?"

Daniel shrugged.

Then he thought: *she can help me get out.* Feeling dishonest, uneasy, he said, "Have you ever been outside the Hedge?"

She gave him a sly smile. "Yeah."

He took her arm. "Let's get a treat from the Promenade."

Stella's eyes grew wide. "You have money?"

"I found a penny."

The girl beamed.

"But we can't go out the Gap. They watch it."

She nodded. "I know how we can go."

***

Daniel let Stella lead him to her house. Inside, it smelled of alcohol and cigarettes and dirt. A faint snore came from the other room.

"Pa sleeps the day," she said.

Daniel followed her to a back room full of junk. In the floorboards lay a door.

She pulled at the handle, and he helped her raise it. Underneath was a stair, going down.

Daniel felt wary. "Where does this lead?"

Stella pressed a button under the floorboards and a light came on. "Under the Hedge."

Down the stair, along a hallway. The walls and ceiling were paneled. Daniel looked at her, surprised.

"The men like it better if it's clean," she said.

The hall was lit at intervals by a fine glass lamp overhead. After a hundred yards or so, another set of stairs appeared.

"Help me push the door," Stella said.

On the other side was a surprisingly clean sitting room, without windows. Daniel turned to Stella. "Thank you."

She smiled. "They say you're a spy. But I like you."

He sighed. So they hadn't fooled anyone. "I like you too." He could never take her to the Promenade, dressed as she was. "But you must go home now."

Her face fell. "No treats?" Then her eyes filled with tears. "You **lied** to me! You scoundrel! You **are** a spy!" She grabbed the handle inside the door. "I hope never to see you again!" The door slammed shut.

His vision blurred. *I wanted to save you.*

Then he came to his senses. He had maybe ten minutes before she woke her father and he got men back up here looking for him. He had to get away.

Punished

Daniel found a side entry, which opened to an alley. A rain-barrel to wash in and a good shake of his clothes helped with the smell. He could appear passable by running his fingers through his wet hair and shining his shoes with a scrap of damp paper.

But he had to warn Zeus. That meant getting back to the Seaport without being caught.

Daniel peered around the corner of what had to be East 2nd Street. A couple of Constables, one light-skinned, one dark, ambled along, moving away.

Letting out a sigh, Daniel walked in the other direction towards the tavern, checking every few minutes to make sure no one followed him.

It took an hour to get to West Promenade. When he rounded the corner, the two men he'd met on the carriage stood there.

"Well, looky here!" The shorter one grinned. "Haven't seen you in a while. Whatcha doing along here, outsider?"

Daniel shrugged. "Going for a drink." Then he realized he'd left his satchel with his clean clothes and money behind at Slim's place.

"Then we'll join you!"

The other one looked hesitant. "They told us to stay out here."

One went to put an arm round Daniel's shoulders then backed off. "Phew! Ever hear of a bath?"

"I was robbed." Daniel pushed past them. "Just leave me alone."

The other one — Billy? He wasn't sure — backed off, hands up. "Meant no offense!" Then he dropped his hands. "Sorry to hear that. Go on, a drink'll do you good."

Daniel went inside, going to the bar. "Is Bug here?"

"Naw, it's his day off."

"I need to find him. He live round here?"

"Depends on what it's about."

What should he say? "You know a guy named Zeus? He was here about mid-morning."

The man shrugged.

"Never mind then. Just tell me where I can find Bug."

"You in some kind of trouble?"

Daniel snapped, "Forget it." He walked out and turned left, ignoring the calls of the bartender and the two guys outside.

He waited at the taxi, but they wouldn't let him on. "I'm not running a poorhouse, kid. You gimme the fare, you can go anywhere you want."

Daniel sagged onto the taxi-stand bench, head in his hands. How was he to get home?

One of the guys he'd run into stood beside him. "You okay?"

Daniel shook his head. "All my money's gone." He felt miserable. "I just want to go home!" Not back to Diamond Manor, but back to Nitivali. Back to the Rising Sun, safe in Baraja's arms. Back where things made sense.

The man dug a penny out of his pocket and handed it to him. "That get you far enough?"

Daniel nodded, too overcome to speak.

Then he remembered the man's name: Alan. "Thanks."

Alan clapped him on his shoulder. "If you're ever at the Casino, you can spend one for me." He walked across the street and towards the tavern.

The next taxi made Daniel ride in back, but he eventually made his way to Diamond Manor and his rooms.

To his horror, Jack stood there. "Where have you been? What are you wearing?" His nose wrinkled. "What's that **smell**?"

Daniel closed his eyes and took a deep breath, just trying to figure out what to say. Then he opened his eyes. "I went for a walk and was robbed. I woke up in an alley. They took my money; I had to walk home."

Jack's jaw dropped, eyes wide. "Good gods! I should tell my father at once —"

Daniel raised a hand. "I'll tell him. But I need a bath first."

"Yes, of course. I —"

Then he realized: it was nowhere near time for Jack to be here. "What's happened? Why did you return early? Why were you looking for me?"

"Father's upset. He sent me to look for you."

Oh, gods, Daniel thought. *He's heard.* "Go to him. Tell him only that I'm back, and will attend him once I'm dressed." He grabbed Jack's upper arms. "Only that, you hear? He'll want to know everything from me in any case. And tell nothing to anyone else — not one word."

"I want to know everything, too, Daniel —"

"Not now. I — I can't talk about it. Maybe another time."

Jack's face held a mix of fear, curiosity, and concern. "Okay."

Despite what he'd told everyone so far, Daniel hadn't been hurt, not physically. But he hadn't been prepared for the horrible turn things had taken that day.

As he scrubbed the grime from himself and shoved his old stinking clothes in the bottom of the trash can, he tried not to panic. Tried not to picture what would happen if they believed Stella's story, when they realized he was a spy. That Zeus had helped him.

He dressed and went down the back way to see Mr. Julius, trying to avoid Jack seeing him. When he stood outside those white doors, he hesitated a long while before knocking.

"Come in," Mr. Julius said.

Daniel opened the door.

Mr. Julius sat behind his desk. "Close the door there. Tell me what happened."

Daniel closed the door and approached the man's desk. "I did just what he asked. But one of the kids said he knew who I was. He went to the Cathedral." He thought he might faint. "Please, you have to warn Zeus. He —"

Mr. Julius raised a hand. "Already done. He told the girl to go to you if anyone from there approached you. When you went with her, his men sent word. They're all out of there."

Daniel's knees gave way, and he just barely held onto the edge of the desk so as not to fall. His vision blurred. "I'm so sorry." He felt shamed by the magnitude of what it all meant. "Years of work, ruined. I failed you. I've failed everyone."

"Nonsense," Mr. Julius said. "Sit down."

Once Daniel sat, Mr. Julius said, "You're a good kid. You didn't squeal, and you didn't run. You came to me not out trying to defend yourself but concerned for Zeus." He shrugged. "We got about all we could from there. If anything, I blame him for sending you out too soon." He stood beside Daniel, resting a hand on his shoulder. "You did what you could. Don't worry yourself over it."

Daniel felt overwhelmed. In all the time he'd been there, the man had never shown kindness to him before. "Thank you, sir."

"Now go up and rest. I told Jack not to pester you about this, so if he does you send him to me. Understand?"

"Yes, sir."

Mr. Julius snorted. "I'm the one who owes you the apology. You were right. You're an excellent manservant, but a terrible spy."

***

The next day was Yuletide Center; the servants were supposed to have the afternoon off. But Swan called every one of the servants down to the youngest out to an area past the stables, where a stout wooden post stood. It held a thick metal ring at the top, with chains and manacles dangling from it. When Daniel saw the manacles, he stopped in horror.

A commotion came from behind, and two men led Zeus to the post. Then Zeus removed his shirt as calmly as if this were an everyday matter. Scars crossed his tanned back. Once Zeus had removed his shirt, the men put the manacles on him.

Flannery Hook gripped his father's hand, eyes wide.

197

Daniel turned to Mr. Hook, confused, afraid. "What's going to happen to him?"

Mr. Hook snorted. "Just you watch."

Mr. Neuberg came forward then, a pistol at his side. "On order of Mr. Hector, this man is to receive ten lashes for incompetence, leading to the dissolution of work we'd spent ten years building."

Daniel lunged forward. "No!"

Everyone turned towards him, their jaws dropping. Mr. Neuberg frowned. "Do you defy our master's order?"

"**I** made the error! It should be **me** there, if anyone."

Mr. Neuberg drew his pistol. "So now you question the master's judgement as well?"

Everyone had drawn back from Daniel, staring at him in fear. The man he'd seen in the underground tunnels sitting upon a stool as they passed now stood beside Zeus with a horse-whip coiled in his hand. Zeus stood chained to the post, face now horrified, fearful for him, and when their eyes met, Zeus shook his head.

They own you. You must do whatever they ask of you.

Daniel hung his head. "No, sir."

Mr. Neuberg turned to the crowd. "Mr. Julius has ordered that Daniel not be harmed. If not for that, I would give him two lashes for insubordination."

Flannery gasped. "No! Don't whip Daniel! He's my friend!"

Mr. Hook's eyes widened, and he pulled his son close, voice stern. "Hush, child. Keep quiet."

Mr. Neuberg ignored them both. "Since the masters have nothing scheduled for you, Daniel, instead of our Yuletide feasting you're to be confined to your quarters for a week on bread and water." He turned to the man with the whip. "You may begin."

Zeus grunted with each blow as the whip tore through his skin, as the blood flowed.

This is wrong, Daniel thought. *Zeus is Diamond-born!*

Flannery's eyes were full of tears.

They used the little boy as a servant. They took a whip to their own family!

If not for Mr. Julius, Daniel realized, *they'd take a whip to me.*

As the men led Zeus stumbling away, head down and bleeding, the group that had hated Daniel now looked upon him with scorn. Mr. Vukay passed close by. "If he were looking like us, you'd not be a-crying there."

That entirely surprised him. "What?"

The man spat on him. "Spadros spy."

Mr. Neuberg snapped, "You dare spit upon a Diamond-sworn?" He gestured to some of the other men. "Take him."

As they dragged him off, Mr. Vukay shouted, "He's a spy! A friend of mine said he saw him take money from a Spadros Family man just yesterday!"

The rest looked at each other.

Someone saw Alan give him the penny? Daniel started forward. "You don't understand! I'm not a —"

Mr. Hook put his hand upon Daniel's shoulder. "Hold now, son. Don't let them rile you. Low-cards, they are, not worthy of your attention."

"Do **you** think I'm a Spadros spy?"

Mr. Hook chuckled. "Of course not. With all the carrying-on those ones do, I'd not be surprised if it was one of them." He tapped his temple and spoke loud enough for everyone to hear. "Send a pale-faced outsider like you in to spy on us? Even the Spadros Family has more wit than that."

Daniel wasn't sure whether to be relieved or offended.

"Daniel." Mr. Neuberg's voice came forth sharp as the whip. "You must return to your rooms. Now."

"Yes, sir." He turned to Mr. Hook. "Thanks for your counsel."

Mr. Hook looked amused. "Any time, my boy. Any time."

***

The fact that none of the uppers attended the whipping hadn't escaped Daniel's notice. *Your first job is to protect your master.* So he told Jack nothing of what had happened.

"Want to go riding? We have time before dinner."

Daniel took one of Jack's clean, dry shirts from the laundry basket, placing it upon the ironing board. "Not today; I have too much to do here."

"Very well." Jack stood silently musing for some time, evidently unused to having his fun diverted. "Why are you so quiet?"

"I'm more tired than anything else," Daniel said, straightening the shirt upon the board. Caring for an all-white wardrobe was ever so much more work. "But if you're to have anything to wear, I need to get cracking."

Jack rubbed Daniel's back. "I'm sorry to be such a bother."

"You're not a bother." Daniel forced himself to smile at him. "It's my duty and honor to have you look your best."

Jack chuckled at that.

"You go on. Have a good time."

"I don't want to go without you," Jack said.

Daniel sighed internally. "Why don't you get a chair? You can read to **me** this time."

Jack's eyes went wide. "A splendid idea!" He rushed out, returning with a chair from his tea-table and one of his books.

When he began to read, Daniel realized it was the book Baraja had read to him. He forced himself to focus on the ironing, not think about how he missed her, how much he wanted to see his little daughter.

Jack read, "The poet is the sayer, the namer, and represents beauty. He is a king, and stands in the center. For the world is not painted, or clothed, but is from the beginning beautiful; and the gods have not made some beautiful things, but Beauty is the creator of the universe."

Daniel remembered the day Baraja read that to him, and he thought his heart would seize up within him.

"You are my Beauty."

"As you are mine."

Jack continued to read, never noticing anything until Daniel put the iron aside. Then he looked up. "What's wrong?"

Daniel moved past him, hoping Jack wouldn't see his face. "I don't feel well." He went into his room and shut the door. He moved across to the hall and locked the door, then heard the door to Jack's closets opening. He rushed to take up the covers as the door opened behind him.

"This won't do," Jack said. "Take off your shoes."

Daniel quickly did so, his face turned away, then got into bed facing the wall.

He felt the covers go over him, felt Jack kiss his cheek. "There," Jack said. "Just rest. I'll have the doctor check on you."

When the door closed behind him, tears wet Daniel's pillow. He covered his mouth to keep anyone from hearing his sobs.

Grief

Flannery knocked on the door with tea, but Daniel said nothing. He heard the lock rattle, then the tray set upon the floor. The boy's steps retreated.

Daniel curled upon his side, feeling as if in a nightmare. He kept hearing the sound of the whip hitting Zeus, the way he cried out at the end. Kept seeing the blood soaking his trousers as it streamed down his back.

And he thought: *how can I live here any longer?*

But where would he go? Even if he might escape, he didn't know how to get to the zeppelin. Even if he did, he had no money to get there, much less go to Baraja. And what might he do there? The Academy wouldn't take him back. The fact that he'd fled his duty would only shame his teacher.

And he knew nothing about how servants fared in Nitivali. He might find himself in a worse situation than the one he faced here.

A few hours later, the lock rattled again. Then a key opened it. The heavy tread of several men came in.

"Daniel," Swan said. "Get up. This here's the doctor."

Daniel wiped his face on the sheets, then turned round and sat up. Swan, Jack, Mr. Neuberg, and a finely-dressed man Daniel presumed to be the doctor stood there.

Jack burst out, "What's wrong? Why have you been crying?" His voice broke. "Are you in pain?"

Standing behind Jack, Swan's face turned amused.

Daniel shrugged, hanging his head.

Swan said, "Alright, young Master, you go on your way. The doctor will tend to this."

"But —"

Mr. Neuberg said sharply, "**Now**, sir. The doctor can't do his work with a crowd standing by."

Embarrassment came over Jack's face. "Yes, Neuberg."

Mr. Neuberg gave Jack a fond smile and put a hand upon his shoulder. "Come, sir, let's get you some warm milk and cookies."

Jack went, giving a backwards glance as they left.

Swan shut the door behind them, then turned to face him. "What's got into you?"

Then Daniel realized that no one, not even Swan, knew about what he'd been doing with Zeus. His blurting out that he would take the punishment for what Zeus did must have confused everyone. "I've never seen anything like that before."

The doctor turned to Swan, a question in his eyes.

"A servant was punished, that's all. The boy's not from here." A hint of disappointment touched his voice. "It seems he doesn't know his place nor our ways, even after all this time."

That hurt, and Daniel stared at the rug, saying nothing more unless asked as the doctor listened and poked and prodded.

Then the doctor stood. "The boy's got a mild case of melancholy. Nothing to worry about; quite common after a shock. Give him a day of rest, and he should be good as new."

"Thanks, doc," Swan said. "The Masters will be pleased to hear it." The two left without even so much as saying goodbye.

Daniel lay upon his bed, staring at the underside of the cabinets above his bed. He'd seen Zeus, a man he'd come to see as a friend, brutalized in front of him for a mistake **he'd** made.

Why did I go to the Cathedral? Why did I try and rush things? Why didn't I talk to more people, find out that they already thought me a spy?

The devastation in little Stella's eyes rose before him, and his vision blurred.

*I **do** have melancholy.*

The thought horrified him. Daniel recalled another boy with the ailment, and just like Jacob, one morning they'd found him hanging out in the garden shed.

No one had been there to save him. And that made him consider what Jacob would do if he heard Daniel had fallen to the same end.

He rose, pacing about his room as night fell. He couldn't let Jacob down: Jacob was his brother, and he'd promised to be there for him if needed. He couldn't help Jacob if he was dead.

Daniel resolved to fight this melancholy before it took hold.

Give him a day of rest, and he should be good as new.

He sat upon the floor, his back to the cabinets below his bed, and put his knees up, resting his arms upon them. The curtains were open; the moon was up, staring back at him.

Perhaps rest was all he needed.

He felt so tired: tired of miles of clothing, of endless work, of playing bed maid, of being used, of pretending to be besotted with a spoiled boy.

Tired of everyone's suspicion, just for how he looked.

This left Daniel dismayed, angry. He muttered, "I didn't ask for any of it."

You didn't ask to be an orphan, nor to be sent to the orphanage, nor to be chosen and sold. Yet these are the cards the Shuffler sent, the ones the Blessed Dealer has placed in your care. Mourn your cards if you must, but it's your duty to play them.

Master Écarté's words came to him as if the elderly teacher stood before him.

If only he'd known what it meant then. He felt as if he'd become a completely different person from the boy Master Écarté spoke to.

A knock on the door to the hall.

"Come in."

Mr. Bastra stood there, holding a tray. "You must eat, son. Don't let this ruin you."

Daniel took a deep breath, let it out, then got off of the floor to sit at the tea-table across from the old man.

Then he laughed: upon the tray was a plate holding two slices of bread and a glass of water.

"It's nice to hear you laugh," Mr. Bastra said. "I've not heard you laugh in some time."

"They didn't even give me butter," Daniel grumbled.

Mr. Bastra chuckled. "Wouldn't be much of a punishment if you had butter with it."

"True," Daniel said. He shoved the bread into his mouth, washing it down with water. He set the glass down. "There. You satisfied?"

"What's wrong, son? Tell me what troubles you."

"Do you think of me as your son? Or am I just some pale Spadros spy?"

Mr. Bastra shook his head, lips pursed. "I'm sorry they said that. But really — do you seriously think the Masters would let you swear if they thought so?"

Now Daniel felt foolish. "No."

"No one with any sense thinks so. And you're a man with sense. What's really bothering you?"

Daniel swallowed, unsure what to reveal. "The man who was whipped. I know him. I'm the reason he got into trouble."

Mr. Bastra nodded. "I gathered as much. But surely they wouldn't whip a man without cause. Would they?"

Daniel shook his head.

"When a man is put in charge, whether to guide or to train, the responsibility always goes to the one in charge. He receives the praise for the results, as well as the punishment should things go awry. The two go hand in hand."

Daniel sighed: this made sense. "It still seems unfair."

"Would you rather have been whipped?"

"No."

Mr. Bastra chuckled. "Then be glad it wasn't you."

Daniel felt startled by the way Mr. Bastra said this. "Were you ever whipped?"

He snorted, a wry grin on his face. "A few times. Back when I was a footman. My master didn't abide with the horse-whip, though; we servants just got the belt."

Daniel felt appalled.

"It's the way of things in Bridges. Stay out of trouble, and you'll never feel the blows." He glanced outside, then back. "That can't be all." He leaned forward. "Come on, now. Tell me everything. I want to help."

Should he say? "I don't know who I am anymore."

"What do you mean?"

"I murdered a man who'd done nothing to me." He felt distressed, angry, and he spoke louder than he meant to. "I have to lie **all** the time."

Mr. Bastra nodded, his face saying he understood why. He leaned back, looking ouf the window once more. Then he took a deep breath and spoke quietly. "Yet you've become a capable manservant. You're a father, a Diamond-sworn." He peered at Daniel. "Yes, your life has become a challenge. But you don't have to let that change who you are inside."

Daniel put his head in his hands, unsure if that felt true. But he felt better, now that he'd told someone. He raised his head. "Thank you for coming to see me."

Mr. Bastra grinned. "Us manservants have to stick together."

***

The next day saw three meals of bread and water. Yet no visitors came, and not even Jack knocked on his door. *Your life has become a challenge. But you don't have to let that change who you are inside.*

How could it not? He felt as if his life was spinning apart, and he didn't know what to do to stop it.

Daniel wrote to Baraja, sending a lock of his hair. *I love you. I wish for you and our Hermosa to never forget me, no matter what happens,* he wrote. *Even if I should die. Tell her each day of her life that her father loves her.*

He thought a lot about Jacob that day, wishing there was some way to learn how he was he doing, if he was safe and well.

When he woke, Jack sat in Daniel's room, at his tea-table.

Daniel got up on one elbow. "What are you doing in here?"

"Why do you feel you have to lie all the time?"

A spike of dread. "You were listening at the door the other day?" What had they discussed? Daniel took a deep breath. "I'm a Diamond-sworn. There are things going on I can't tell you."

"Do you lie about us, too?"

"You know I can't tell anyone about it. What do you think?"

"No, I mean me. Did you lie when you said you loved me?"

The words just came out. "Don't be ridiculous. Would I give you that ring? Stand guard for you, on top of all the other things I must do?"

Jack hesitated, twisting the ring on his left small finger. "No."

Daniel sat up and rubbed his face. "Why can't you just be happy? You have everything in the world. Your brother and sister have no one, yet here you are continually doubting."

"I'm sorry," Jack said. "I don't know why. It's just ... sometimes I don't know if this really is true."

Hope flared. "Why? Is there someone else you love?"

Jack stared at him, mouth open. "No. Never!"

Daniel smiled to himself at Jack's reaction, swinging his feet over the side of the bed. "Go back to bed, you dolt."

"Hmph," Jack said, his face pleased. "What will you do?"

"I have to get my bath before I can draw yours. Or would you prefer me disheveled, in my pajamas, stinking up your rooms?"

Jack laughed. "Very well; I could use a bit of sleep in any case."

After Jack left, Daniel sat on the side of his bed feeling shaky.

I lie and lie and lie. I've become a liar.

He just wished Jack would fixate upon someone else. All Daniel wanted was to do his work and be left alone.

Discovery

The rest of the week was spent in dodging Jack's questions.

"Why can't you go riding?"

"Why won't you go down to Yuletide feast with everyone?"

"Aren't you going to come out back and shoot with us?"

Daniel was just sitting down to a very late "tea," after finishing a particularly troublesome seam, when Jack burst in. He stared at the bread, the plate and the glass. "What's all this?"

"Do you never knock?"

"Where's your tea? Why do you only have bread here?"

Daniel sighed. It was only a matter of time before Jack learned of this. "I got into trouble with Mr. Neuberg. This is my punishment."

"But you need more than that. I —"

"I'll probably get something worse should you go to him."

Jack stopped, hesitation on his face. "Oh."

Daniel turned to face him. "In this place, Swan and Mr. Neuberg are like your father and grandfather to me. I must obey them; if I don't, I get punished."

Jack's eyebrows raised. "Oh."

"I ask that you knock before coming in. And stop listening at my door. You're a man now, not a child."

Jack seemed crestfallen. "Okay."

Daniel chuckled. "Now what was it you wanted?"

"We're going to a meeting upon Market Center tonight. It's important. Father said I should tell you."

"At night?"

"Yeah, it's for dinner."

Daniel nodded, but his mind was on Jack's outfit. Did he have something ready that was suitable for dinner with an upper?

"Did you hear me?"

"I did. Go on, now — I have to make sure I have something for you to wear."

***

Daniel had laid out Jack's white suit, shirt, cravat, cap, and shoes upon the boy's bed, when he heard a soft knock at his door to the hall. He went through Jack's closets and to his room, curious as to who this might be.

Mr. Bastra stood there.

"Well, hello," Daniel said. "Please come in."

The old man took a step into the room, closing the door behind him. "Ready for your night out?"

"I am." Something felt odd. "Won't you sit down?"

"That might be wise."

As he sat, Daniel wondered what might be wrong. He'd never seen Mr. Bastra so reticent before. "Has something happened?"

Mr. Bastra let out a breath. "It has." He hesitated. "I hate to tell you now, during Yuletide, when you're on your way out. But I didn't want you to hear this from anyone else."

Cold fingers crept up Daniel's gut. "Just tell me and get it out of the way."

"Siziba is dead."

Daniel stared at him, not knowing if this were a bad dream. "You're joking, of course."

Mr. Bastra leaned on one elbow. "I wish I were. It's why the others suspected you of being a Spadros spy."

Daniel frowned at him. "I don't understand."

"When they brought Mr. Vukay to be punished for his offense against you, he told them how you'd spent so much time with the groundsman. The others — who hated you for your appearance, I suppose — had looked into the man. Apparently, they found enough proof to have Siziba's quarters searched. He had notes hidden under the floorboards, listing everything you spoke of."

Daniel couldn't think. It made no sense. "But ... you mean, the man **used** me?"

Mr. Bastra shrugged. "It seems so. We've learned of his contacts, his informants, who he passed the information to." Then he sighed. "Mr. Julius had a man over in the lower South Side he wanted to bring into the Family." He glanced away. "I'm sure you recall your swearing-in."

Daniel looked at Mr. Bastra with horror. "The man I killed."

He nodded.

The face of the man he'd killed swam before him, the terror, the way his eyes stared after he lay dead. Then he pictured Siziba lying there and Daniel thought he might be sick. "Who was he?"

"The man you killed?" Mr. Bastra shrugged. "A spy, perhaps, or some merchant who didn't pay. Or maybe someone who'd offended Mr. Julius once too many times. Who knows?"

Terror gripped him. "What's going to happen to Tolo?"

Mr. Bastra snorted. "Tolo's a garrulous fool. He'll be punished, of course, for speaking of things he should not. But no real harm'll come to him."

Daniel went to the cabinets above his bed and leaned his forehead upon them, picturing Tolo's back being opened by a horsewhip. Was that what they'd threatened Garrett and Cora with as well? "Thank you for telling me."

He had to go with Mr. Julius tonight, guard his sons, stand as representative, when the man had just killed one of his few friends.

"Daniel, I'm —"

"Go," Daniel snapped. "I want to be alone."

"Of course," Mr. Bastra said, and after a moment, the door clicked softly shut.

Or had Siziba actually been his friend at all?

Plot

The night was bitter cold and the moon was high. As usual, Daniel and his wards were kept in the anteroom whilst Mr. Julius and Mr. Hart talked. Daniel stood off to one side, Miss Kaluki to the other. Jack read a book. Jonathan lay sprawled on his back upon a sofa, staring at the ceiling.

Ferti's nursemaid had excused herself to the Ladies' Room. Gardena, now in a high-necked gown reaching to just above her boots, played on the floor with little Ferti. They rolled a ball between them. "I don't know why we're even here," Gardena said. "This is utter boredom."

As pretty as Gardena was, unlike the last time he'd seen her, Daniel had no thoughts at all about the girl. His mind was fixed upon his plan.

"Nothing they do is without reason," Jonathan said. He gestured at Ferti. "We're to become friends." He got a somewhat furtive look to him. "Although I can't imagine why."

Daniel began nodding, then caught himself. Jonathan had seen the deception, the calculated plotting. But as a servant, Daniel had to make himself invisible, even to these children.

"Friends," Ferti said, a huge smile on her round face.

Gardena sighed, rolling the ball back to the girl. "Yes, dear, friends." She got up, began to wander around the room.

Ferti held the ball up in her chubby hand. "Ball?"

"Yes, it's a ball," Gardena said brightly. "You want your dolly?"

Ferti beamed. "Dolly."

Gardena went to Ferti's bag, fetched out the doll.

Ferti tossed the ball over to the big double doors, where it gently rolled to a stop. "Ball!"

Gardena snorted, then handed the doll to Ferti. "So now I'm playing fetch, am I?"

Ferti hugged the doll to her chest, beaming, twisting side to side. "Dolly." She flopped backwards onto the carpeted floor, holding the doll high in front of her, her dress flying up past her knees.

Jack looked away.

Gardena pulled the girl's dress over her stockinged legs with a sigh. "Good luck marrying this one off."

Jonathan turned his face towards them, as if just realizing they were in the room. "I'd never considered such a thing. What'll happen to her?"

Gardena slumped into a chair across the room. "She'll be a spinster, I suppose. Unless someone takes a fancy to her."

Jack frowned to himself, shook his head. "Doesn't seem right. She's like a child. I mean, she **is** a child. But she's eight and it's like she's two. She can't work like this. She certainly couldn't run a household. What if she never gets better?"

Gardena shrugged. "She's as rich as we are; I suppose she'll have maids and waiters, just like we do." She stopped, evidently pondering the matter. "It doesn't really seem right to me either."

A lot of things didn't seem right, but that was the way of it.

The answer to his sorrows had come to Daniel on the way there. These people owned him. He had to do what they said, whether it was use him to kill, or for their pleasures, or to guard their lives. That was his duty, his curse for being an orphan. But as everyone said, they were his cards, and he had to play them.

But he didn't have to like it. And one day, when he'd saved enough to travel, he'd take Baraja and their daughter and run somewhere no one would ever find them.

Ferti let her right hand drop to the carpeting, and still clutching the doll, gazed after the ball. "Ball?"

"Oh, very well." Gardena chuckled. "I'll get your ball, silly."

Jack resumed reading. Jonathan stared at the floor.

Gardena went to the double doors and retrieved the ball. Suddenly, she straightened, a puzzled expression on her face.

"Miss Gardena," Daniel said sternly, "come away; it's bad manners to listen at doors."

"Yes, but —"

Daniel went to the doors, took her arm gently. "Come away now, Miss." She smelled of roses, and for an instant, he was reminded of Cora.

The girl moved back to the others.

"It's done," Mr. Hart said from behind the door. "Ten o'clock tonight, Shill and Snow. He'll kill him then."

Shill and Snow was just down the street from Slim's place.

Julius Diamond said, "We can't be seen to have anything to do with killing Roy Spadros —"

Daniel froze, mind racing. Ten tonight.

Roy Spadros — killed?

"— and we won't be part of any war —"

What would happen to Jacob?

Decision

"Never you mind that," Mr. Hart said. "I'm just telling you this as a courtesy."

The clock chimed nine.

"That's all well and good for you," Mr. Julius said, "but they'll immediately look at **us** if anything happens. Are you gonna back us up when they attack?"

"Daniel," Jack said from across the room. "What's wrong?"

He was here to protect the young Masters. That was his duty.

But Jacob was his brother.

He had to warn Roy Spadros. If he did nothing and Roy died, then Jacob could fall under suspicion. Jacob could be killed!

Maybe Mr. Spadros had been lying about that part, been just trying to scare him, to get him to spy.

But Mr. Spadros had threatened to have Jacob killed if anything happened to him. He could have given orders to do so, as a precaution. If there were the slightest chance of harm coming to Jacob, he couldn't stand by and allow that.

*You see one of your brothers in trouble, you **must** aid them.*

Jacob was his brother.

Yet Daniel had sworn obedience to Diamond.

But I never swore an oath to Mr. Hart. He said, "Wait here."

Daniel ran towards the door, through the halls, to the front entrance. The freezing air hit him like a blow, and for an instant he considered going back for his coat.

But there was no time. And if he went back in, they'd try to stop him for certain.

The coach stood bathed in moonlight; Daniel started unhitching one of its snow-white horses.

Tolo came around the carriage. "What's that you're doing?"

"I need a horse at once," Daniel gasped. He had the urge to strike the man, knock him out, take the horse.

Then he hesitated, panting. Tolo had never done him wrong. This was his brother. "I must get a message out."

Tolo's eyes widened. "Well, then let me help you!"

Shouts echoed in the hallway. The horse came free.

"You sure you don't want a saddle?"

He had to get out of there before the others came outside to stop him. "No time."

Tolo held out his hands, clasped at the level of the horse's belly. "Up you go then."

Daniel galloped off, shivering. He'd never ridden bareback before, and he clutched the horse's mane, desperately trying to stay on as shouts receded in the distance.

It didn't matter if they tried to follow. Only the two men inside the meeting-room might guess where he was headed, and it'd be some time before anyone put the pieces together.

He had a good start. Now if only he might reach the Spadros Pot before the foul deed was done.

He couldn't let them kill Roy Spadros. He couldn't let Jacob die.

You're betraying your Family, he kept thinking.

No. They were on Market Center. Miss Kaluki and little Ferti's nursemaid were with the children, and Tolo stood outside. Jack and Jonathan were safe enough.

But Jacob was not.

He pictured Jacob's face the night he'd almost killed himself, pictured him lying dead on the floor with a bullet in his forehead.

He couldn't let that happen. Jacob was his brother. He was younger. Daniel had obligation to protect him. If there were even the smallest chance Jacob might be blamed ... might be hurt ...!

Let the chips fall where they may. He didn't care what Mr. Julius did to him anymore.

Daniel clattered through miles of darkened streets on Market Center. He didn't remember the way to the bridge, and made a few wrong turns until he found it. Then, gathering his courage, he charged past the Market Center guards and across the bridge to Spadros, ignoring their shouts, urging the horse on.

The guards at the Spadros side tried to stop him, standing in a row hand in hand to block his way. The draft horse seemed to sense Daniel's urgency, though, and to his surprise, leaped right over their hands the instant before they scattered.

"Good boy!" He felt moved. These creatures wanted to help, just like dogs did!

Daniel went past the long stretch of Hedge, then left. He had to slow his horse to get through the Gap, but they galloped the way back through winding streets, drunken crowds, and shouting vendors, to stop a block from the intersection.

No one was there. Daniel got off the horse, his body aching, particularly his inner thighs. He could barely walk, stumbling through snow as he went.

But he remembered the way. The debris here was too thick to pass on horseback, so he climbed over.

The clocks in the distance chimed ten. Two men stood in the distance, in the intersection.

One of them was Roy Spadros.

Relief flooded over him. He was alive. He might still save the man. It wasn't too late.

Dream

Daniel yelled, "Stop! Look out!" He ran as fast as he could over the icy ground towards the two men.

Mr. Spadros simply looked back at him without any expression in those cold blue eyes.

The other man — filthy, ragged — seemed surprised, fearful.

And in the ragged man's eyes, Daniel saw the decision.

The man's thin, grimy hand reached behind his back, producing a gun.

A sharp punch in the chest, taking Daniel's breath away. He stared at the two men in shock. The ragged man had to have been the assassin Mr. Hart sent after Mr. Spadros.

*Why would the man shoot **me** instead?*

The world went a bit gray. Daniel felt himself falling. But as if in a dream, his landing didn't hurt at all. He stared at Roy Spadros, feeling suddenly very tired.

Roy Spadros seemed, if anything, amused.

Daniel felt bitter. *He thinks it's funny.*

I should have let the man kill him.

Time seemed to slow, become foggy. A horse's hooves on cobblestones approached from behind and to his right.

Whoever followed him must have found a faster way in.

The hooves trotted closer, right up to him.

Daniel felt himself being raised up, held. Then Jack said, "Daniel? Oh, gods, Daniel!"

A spike of surprised alarm. Why was Jack here?

Then the reality of the horrible decision he'd made fell upon him. For a brief moment, Daniel felt despair. What had he done?

Jack howled in anguish.

Daniel's cheek pressed against Jack's chest as he rocked to the sound of Jack's sobbing cries. He felt himself slipping away, and it scared him.

I'm going to die.

What would happen to Jacob?

Master Écarté's voice, his words came to him: *I pass the charge to you to remain true.*

Had he done enough? Had he fulfilled the vow he'd made towards his teacher? Would Jack Diamond become a good man? Would he know enough to help others too?

He didn't know.

Had he failed his teacher?

Had he failed everyone?

But then he remembered that angry, frightened little boy he met when he'd arrived, and relief flooded through him.

He'd helped Jonathan. Maybe that was good enough.

However long Master Jonathan lived, at least he had a chance to really live, to grow up. To become a good man.

And Jonathan had helped little Gardena. Daniel realized then how frightened she'd been. She was so smart, so beautiful. She really seemed happy.

Perhaps Master Jonathan would help others before he died.

But he'd never see Baraja again. He'd never see his little daughter. Never hold her.

Daniel had guessed all along that he'd never see them, that his dream was only that. But now he knew for sure, and remorse surged within him. *Oh, Baraja, I'm so sorry. I've been such a fool.*

The sound of Jack's weeping faded. It never occurred to Daniel to speak to the boy, even if he could have.

Baraja whispered, *"You are my Beauty."*

Hearing her voice made him feel better. They were in her warm, dark room, the place he'd always wanted to be.

Comfortable and free and safe, in their bed together. Where there was no duty, no fear, no obligation ... only love.

"You are my Beauty."
And there came an echo: *As you are mine.*

Free

The next day, a letter arrived:

Daniel —

Hermosa is still too young to understand, but I tell her of your love every day. I am grateful you are safe and well.

By now you must realize that the Rising Sun lied. We were never Companions, only whores.

But with your help, I collected enough money to take the entry test for Companion training.

I would never have dared to risk this play without you. And I feared to tell you of this test in case I should fail.

But I passed. The Board of Companions has paid my indenture and given me a full scholarship.

Hermosa and I are free.

Thank you for all you have done.

Baraja

Brothers is a prequel to the **Red Dog Conspiracy**
steampunk noir crime fiction series,
which starts with Part 1: *The Jacq of Spades*.

The night Daniel died, 12-year-old Jacqui was sold to the Spadros crime family. Her best friend Air also died that night while trying to stop her sale.

Ten years later, Jacqui has secretly become a private investigator so she might earn enough to escape. When Air's little brother vanishes, she begins her own investigation.

Learn more at JacqOfSpades.com

The Players

Dickens

The Home

Miz Lizbet
Miz Albaletta

Nitvali

House-Servants Academy

Master Wápái Écarté: the teacher
Annabel Lee: a helper
Gia: her daughter, a girl of eight
The other students:
Righly Hanafuda
Feint Barkis
Reuben James
Kier Connor
Elias Gin
Hudson Thomas
Adam Card
Helix Coil
Yen Tobias
Dakota Bledsoe

The Rising Sun

Baraja: a woman
Hermosa: a baby

Bridges

Diamond Manor

The Family

Mr. Hector (the Old Master): Patriarch of the Diamond Family

Mr. Julius (the Young Master): his son

Miz Rachel (the Young Mistress): wife to Mr. Julius

Master Jack: their son

Master Jonathan: his twin

Gardena: their younger sister

The retainers upstairs

Swan: an old man

Mr. Neuberg: Diamond Manor's butler

Mrs. Whist: the housekeeper

Mr. Lucas: a manservant

Mr. Brelan Hook: a manservant

Mrs. Hook: his wife, a lady's maid

Flannery Hook: his son, the house boy

Mr. Escoba Bastra: a manservant

Master Toran - Jack's tutor

Mr. Clay - Jonathan's tutor

Miss Kaluki - their nurse

Cora, Pippa, Eliza, and Penny: house maids

Mr. Wheeler: First Footman

Garrett, Oscar, and Anton: footmen

The retainers downstairs

Miz Johnson: the Cook

Kindra, Laura, and Ellie-Mae: kitchen maids

Malena, Nancy, and Lilah: scullery maids

The retainers outside

Siziba: the Stable-Master

Mr. Vukay: the groundsman

Tolo and Zeenay: drivers

Bridges (cont.)

Market Center

The Twenty-Eight: a tavern
Lance: a boy
Roy Spadros: a man
Anthony: his son
Ferti: a girl
Mr. Hart: a man

Spadros quadrant

The Seamont: a tavern
Bug: its bartender
Billy Spadros: a young man
Alan Pearson: a young man
Zeus: a Diamond spy
Deuce: a bartender
Slim: a Diamond spy
Ely Kerr: a drunkard
Stella: a little girl

Diamond Country House

Mr. Bradford: a butler
Cesare: the Diamond Heir

About the Author

Patricia Loofbourrow, MD is a NY Times and USA Today best-selling science fiction writer, PC gamer, ornamental food gardener, fiber artist, and wildcrafter who loves power tools, dancing, genetics and anything to do with outer space. She was born in southern California and currently lives in Oklahoma with her husband and three grown children.

Acknowledgments

Thanks to Julian White and Dawn Wilke for beta reading this book, and to my street team, The Commission, for helping to get it into your hands.

Special thanks to my Patrons: without your monthly financial donations, this series would not have been possible.

Julian White

Melissa Williams

Laura Prime

Jennifer Eades

Michaelene Alston

Cristina

Eirlys Evans

Jane Kamvar

Aramanth Dawe

Rachel Heslin

Phoebe Darqueling

Toni Mcconnell

James Mallison

Follow the Red Dog Conspiracy on Patreon
patreon.com/red_dog_conspiracy

News, clues, backstory, and more at JacqOfSpades.com